THE DELTA SEX-LIFE LETTERS

It was most embarrassing night of my life when my parents caught me having sex with my boyfriend on the living-room carpet. I was ordered up to my room and Steve was practically thrown out of the house. A few weeks later, I went round to his place and was about to knock on the window when I saw him in a passionate snog with a woman – my mother!

I watched in amazement as they stood by the bed and stripped off their clothes. Steve helped her, unclipping her bra and cupping her heavy white tits in his hands, then falling to his knees to pull down her knickers.

They went at it like hammer and tongs and she did things to him that left me flabbergasted. Fancy her calling me a slut! The way she was eating up my boyfriend I think dad must have been neglecting her . . .

Pippa, Newcastle

Also available from Headline:

NAKED AMBITION
CREMORNE GARDENS
EROTICON DREAMS
WHAT KATY DUNN DID
THE WIFE-WATCHER LETTERS
THE LUSTS OF THE BORGIAS
DANGEROUS DESIRES
AMOROUS APPETITES
A MAN WITH THREE MAIDS
SAUCY HABITS
EMPIRE OF LUST

The Delta
Sex-Life Letters

Edited and compiled by

Lesley Asquith

Delta

First published in 1994
by HEADLINE BOOK PUBLISHING

A HEADLINE DELTA paperback

10 9 8 7 6 5 4 3

ISBN 0 7472 4268 2

Typeset by Avon Dataset Ltd., Bidford-on-Avon

Printed and bound in Great Britain by
Mackays of Chatham plc, Chatham, Kent

HEADLINE BOOK PUBLISHING
A division of the Hodder Headline Group
338 Euston Road,
London NW1 3BH
www.headline.co.uk
www.hodderheadline.com

The Delta
Sex-Life Letters

INTRODUCTION

'Author compiling book of letters detailing sexual activities requests correspondence.'

The replies to this advertisement, which I inserted in several suitable adult magazines, could have filled two books such as this. My thanks are due to all who wrote of their adventurous amours, marital and extra-marital matings, lesbian loving and, always, copious copulating. Apologies to those whose missives have had to be omitted through lack of space. They have been filed for any future edition that may appear.

Lesley Asquith, London, 1994

1. AS YOU LIKE IT

Old Friends
Show Us Yours
Happy New Year!
Under the Doctor
Uncoupling
A Model Wife
The Biter Bit
In the Swim
I.O.U.
Sister Mine
Pillow Talk
X Certificate
It Pays to Advertise
Dick on the Dole
Lady Boss
Some Other Man's Wife

Old Friends

I'm the manager of a shop-fitting business which transforms empty shops quickly according to the requirements of the new owners. Most of our jobs are in towns over a wide area. I get the contract, go over the plans, and send in my team of skilled workmen. One job I did some time ago was to alter a large shop into a massage parlour. The proprietor was so pleased with the finished effect – the tiling, cubicles, showers, carpeting and so on — that he invited me to lunch and then gave me a free visit to his rub-down joint.

I enjoyed it. A pretty topless girl massaged me and then gave me 'hand relief' which I relished as I lay back naked and oily on the padded table, being expertly wanked off. After the treatment I left determined to visit again when in that town, even if I had to pay. In time I was attended to by several different masseuses. I was wanked while I played with a big pair of tits bobbing over me; I was sucked off by a girl who specialised in fellatio; and I had a damn good fuck with the oldest attendant – a big-titted woman in middle-age – who made me fancy a bit of mature for a change. This woman was there for customers who liked to be spanked and was kept very busy. I turned down her offer to birch my bum. Her own broad buxom arse was of more interest to me, so she cocked it up while on all fours for me to shaft her doggy-fashion.

The boss and I were pretty chummy by this time and on my arrival one afternoon he greeted me by saying there was a new girl who was a real beauty and I should try her. 'She does the lot,' he added, 'and she really enjoys her work!'

I was shown to a cubicle door. I knocked and entered, and then both the girl and I did a double-take. We stared at each other in shock. Standing there, cute and curvy in the tight white overall that the girls wore – so often discarded on request — was the wife of one of the men that I employed. Brenda blushed bright red and I stood stock still. Not only did Mike, her husband, work for me but she knew my wife well and had been at our wedding.

Mind you, I'd always fancied Brenda. She was a shapely lass with beautiful big tits – but then she wouldn't have been there otherwise as the boss auditioned all his girls and insisted on above-average breasts.

'You!' we both said at the same time, and then gave nervous little laughs.

'I won't tell your wife if you don't tell my husband,' she said. 'I need this job, what with no overtime for Mike and our mortgage so heavy each month.'

I nodded my agreement, knowing that in the recession empty shops were remaining that way and our work was slack. She added that Mike knew nothing about her job, thinking she was employed in a bakery. Life a crafty wife, she bought bread and cakes every night to take home, saying she got them free as perks.

'I'll ask for another girl if you prefer,' I offered even as I ogled her lovely tits bulging against the buttons of her skin-tight overall.

'That wouldn't go down well with the boss, would it?' Brenda said. 'I mean, he told me there was a good friend of his coming today. I don't mind if you don't, Bill.'

Mind? Even at my wedding reception I had longed to throw a fuck in her direction.

'Treat me like any other customer,' I said. 'To tell the

4

truth, Brenda, I've always fancied you rotten. Give me the whole treatment and I'll tell your boss you are the greatest and deserve a rise in salary.'

She directed me to undress and hang up my clothes, giving a little giggle when my Y-fronts came off, revealing an already erect dong rearing up my belly.

'I thought you were a horny bloke,' she teased me. 'I've seen you looking at my boobs and bum. I suppose we'd better do this as if you were just an ordinary client.' She went into her regular sales pitch as I got up on the massage table. 'Do you want the normal massage and shower, sir, or the special? It costs extra, but we recommend it—'

'By all means the special,' I said, grinning up at her.

'Yes, sir. Would that be topless or naked?' At my eager nod, she unbuttoned the nylon overall and two magnificently rounded breasts burst free, the rosy nipples pointed and thick. 'Do you require hand relief, with my mouth, or full intercourse? There are set charges for each if you are interested—'

'To hell with the expense,' I said, glancing sideways at a temptingly plump cunt mound forested with a lush triangle of pubic hair. She bent to pour some oil on my chest and I reached for her swinging tits, feeling their warmth, the solidness of rounded flesh, pulling them to me. My hungry mouth opened as I drew in a nipple to suck.

'This isn't the normal, sir,' she said, her voice shaky, 'but then you are a special friend of my boss. Oh, Gawd, that's nice – suck the other one too, please. Touch my cunt, Bill. Ooh, you have such a big stiff one—'

That big stiff one she had in her clasp, rubbing it. With a little moan she bent sideways and covered it with her hot mouth, sucking sweetly. She climbed up on the table facing my feet, presenting a lily-white bottom to me. I clasped the cheeks and parted them to see the goodies between –

5

the puckered ring of her arsehole and the wispy hairs surrounding the crack of her rounded cunt bulge. I delved in with my tongue extended, lapping and licking both orifices. Ambrosia!

She squealed and bucked, then crawled forward on the narrow table, grasping my upright cock while directing it to her hot little minge. It slid up and she jogged on the balls of her feet, my view of this being the curve of her back where it swept out to her shapely arse cheeks. Parted as they were, I plainly saw my shaft shunting in and out of her gripping cunt lips as she rode me. Delightful as the sight was, I wanted to see her bouncing tits, catching glimpses of them bobbing under her arms as she ground down over me. I gripped her hips, pulling her around in a twisting movement. Without uncunting she turned to face me and resumed her bouncing motions, tits flying up to her face.

I returned every week after that, putting the massage table to good use and screwing her in every possible position. Soon we had begun an affair that was pure lust between us – fucking in both our houses when our respective spouses were out and in my car on dates. I made sure her husband was given jobs that kept him away overnight, sometimes for whole weekends. It was rotten of me, I know, but he was very appreciative that I found so much work for him.

William, West Midlands

6

Show Us Yours

My husband, Joe, is a member of a football club and one night he went to a stag night where some strippers were performing. The thought of him going annoyed and upset me. He was football mad and no longer seemed to care about anything else, especially giving me regular sex. We were both in our early forties and he had remained a bachelor until we married. I was a widow and my previous husband was a randy chap who couldn't get me fucked often enough and who liked to see me naked about the house all the time. With Joe I hardly got any affection, so why did he want to see other women strip off? I would happily have given him a private show to get him worked up.

That night I had a bath and watched the telly. It was a woeful evening of lashing rain and sleet. Then my husband phoned to ask my permission to bring home a few friends. Evidently the night had been a wash-out and the money collected for drink meant there had been a share-out of booze. He knew I enjoyed a drink so they were bringing some with them to finish off at our house. I was glad that some company was arriving. I dressed myself up a little, tidied my hair and made some sandwiches. Joe arrived with three young men, all of them bearing a carrier bag full of whisky, gin and cans of beer. I had a good fire going so we sat in the cosy living room and saw off a good quantity of the excess drink.

As we did so, tongues loosened. A few lewd jokes were told, and when my reaction was to simply laugh along with them, the party got more ribald. The young visitors were in their twenties – Martin, Gus and Steve. They eyed my breasts with lust in their faces. No doubt they had been worked up by the strip show. I didn't care. I even winked back at one I caught ogling my neckline which revealed my deep cleavage.

While my husband refilled the glasses, I sat back and enjoyed being the centre of attraction for once. When I went to the kitchen to cut more sandwiches, the boy called Martin followed me with the empty plates. He came close as I stood at the table, brushing against my bottom.

In a very naughty mood, I said, 'Hey, I'll give you ten minutes to stop that,' and waggled my bum back into him.

He put his arms around me, breathing into my neck, pressing his crotch into my rear. 'I didn't know Joe had such a cuddly missis,' he whispered, then the hands slid up to cup my tits, as if testing their firmness and weight. I felt his hardness press into the crease of my buttocks and relished the way he fondled my bosom. I turned my face and he kissed me hard.

'I'm too old for you, Martin,' I said as our mouths parted. 'You wouldn't know what to do with me.' He gave a low growl as if to say 'Give me the chance', then his friend Steve came into the kitchen and we broke off our embrace.

'You'd better see to Joe,' he said, well aware, I'm sure, he'd interrupted us. 'Your old man's collapsed in an armchair spark out. He's been knocking it back all evening at the club.'

I must add that my husband wasn't a drinker, and all attempts to wake him proved useless. With the help of my guests I got him up to the bedroom. I took off his shoes and jacket, loosened his collar and tie and covered him with the duvet before returning to the living room. There the boys stood expectantly. One handed me my refilled glass. From the very atmosphere of sexuality in the hot room I was aware they were horny – for me!

'So where were we when we were interrupted?' I said. 'I was making more sandwiches, I think—'

'You were snogging with Martin.' Steve came right out with. 'Lucky sod, I saw him at you. Does this mean you like a bit of fun? We're all game—'

'Down, boys,' I said as they closed around me. 'Wasn't seeing that strip show enough for you?'

This brought mutters of disgust. 'Some strip show,' said Gus. 'The girls wouldn't travel because of the storm. They were on fifty quid each to perform—'

'Fifty pounds, eh? I would have turned up and stripped for that,' I joked.

To my great amusement the boys immediately dug into their pockets and produced some notes. These were laid out on the coffee table and I was informed it amounted to fifty pounds.

'You think I wouldn't?' I challenged them, feeling a strong desire to let them see me naked. 'Sit down, boys, and I'll make up for your earlier disappointment. Are you sitting comfortably?'

They were, two on the couch and one in the armchair as I posed before them on the fireside rug. I could have put a record of smoochy music on the turntable but didn't want to break the spell. They were eager and I was eager so, in a silence broken only by the occasional whoop of appreciation from my captive audience, I stripped off.

Soon, with my dress cast aside, tights discarded and shoes off, I was left in just my overflowing bra and tiny knickers. I reached behind my back slowly to unclip my bra, enjoying the open mouths and wide eyes before me. If

9

this was exhibitionism, I loved it!

I tossed the bra aside and shook my shoulders brazenly, making both tits shimmy and wobble. As an added touch I grasped one and held the pointed nipple within an inch of Gus's mouth, stepping back just as he made to suck it.

I know I've got big tits, full solid mounds, and they stared transfixed as I stood thrusting out my chest.

'You want more, boys?' I said, then turned my back and lowered my panties just below the inrolling curves of my bum cheeks. I gave them a wiggle and then stepped out of them, turning with arms raised and legs planted apart to show off my hairy bulge and cunt lips. I stood for a long time flaunting my naked body and feeling great to be ogled so intensely.

'There, you've seen all there's to see,' I announced, beginning to pick up my discarded clothes, for even in my tipsy and excited state I thought things had gone far enough.

'No!' was the unanimous cry from the boys. Martin took my arm and led me to an armchair and sat me down. He fell on his knees before me, lifting my legs high and hooking them over his shoulders. I knew he was looking directly at my cunt and squirmed at the thought – though I couldn't deny I was terribly turned-on.

Then his mouth clamped over my cunt, sucking in my outer lips and pushing a stiffly pointed tongue into me. He slid his tongue up my slit to titillate my clitoris. I was gone, muttering how *good* it was, grasping his head and tilting my pussy to his mouth. Gus and Steve, on either side of the chair, grasped a breast each and began sucking my nipples hungrily. I bucked and cried out, having the quickest come in my experience.

Thereafter I was laid along the couch by all three men in turn, who had followed my example by getting out of their clothes. In the orgy that followed I gave no thought to Joe, who was dead to the world in a drunken sleep while three young men shared his wife. Being as young and randy as you'd expect single lads to be, I was really given the treatment and used to fulfil their lewdest fantasies. I was screwed on my back, on hands and knees and mounted on top of them. They were insatiable, pushing cocks into my mouth to be sucked even as I was being fucked. For me, as for many women, I'm sure, it was the fulfilment of a dream.

By dawn we presented some sight. I was stretched out naked and full of come on the couch, the boys were shagged useless and in a heap before the fireplace.

I kissed all of them goodbye when they trooped out. Then I got into bed beside the still slumbering Joe, feeling marvellously aglow after all the attention that had been showered on me.

Joe is still soccer mad but it's funny how those boys don't seem so keen to support the team, especially on away trips. When Joe is out all day, Martin, Gus and Steve enjoy my hospitality. They've found a game they like much better, I suppose.

Zoe, Sheffield

Happy New Year!

When I first met Laura I thought, that is the girl for me – lovely face, friendly smile, plus smashing big tits and a curvy arse. I courted her and eventually we got engaged. She proved to be a randy piece, the only kind for me. Many an evening was spent in my flat, both of us naked on my bed, doing the lewd things we both enjoyed. She entered into all my suggested sex games eagerly, sometimes saying I was a dirty beast, a depraved young man to ask to do *that* to her. But she was always willing to go along. I'd never met such a girl for achieving orgasms, coming violently if I played with her tits and nipples, let alone licked or fucked her. We were two of a kind, horny youngsters, mad for sex.

She told me once, when I teased her about the climaxes she had so easily, that it ran in the family. She said she could hear her mum and dad going at it at night through the bedroom wall. Her mother would cry out loud, gasping as she came, so Laura claimed she took after her.

The family lived in a small village a mile or two out of town and one day I was invited home to meet them. There was just the one street, so I parked behind a baker's van with a woman standing behind it buying bread and cakes. I was immediately attracted to her. She was, I reckoned, in her forties but the curve of her back sweeping out to firm broad buttocks and the shapely legs below, aroused my lecherous nature.

I wanted to see if the front view was as good as the rear,

12

so I walked up and asked if she knew where Laura's family lived. She was full breasted, her big firm tits bulging her dress like footballs and I thought what a magnificent fuck she would make and fancied that fine body naked in bed beside me.

'You must be David,' she said when I spoke. 'I'm her mother. We're just outside our house.'

I thought, if your daughter turns out like you, missis, I won't complain. If I hadn't already decided to marry her, the sight of her mother settled it.

A year or so went by. I married Laura and we were thinking of starting a family, when her mother came to visit over the New Year. Always a big occasion in Scotland, the Hogmanay gathering in my home was large and boozy. Laura, not used to strong drink, overdid it and I carted her off to bed soon after midnight. The guests departed in time, leaving the house looking as if a bomb had struck it – half-eaten meals on plates, glasses, bottles and cans everywhere. Laura's mum, Isa, tore into clearing up, saying we couldn't leave it for the morning. Together we washed up and tidied the place, and it was almost four in the morning before we were back to normal.

I poured two stiff whiskies and gave one to my mother-in-law, thanking her for helping out. She liked a dram, so we sat in the quiet night having several, growing chummier.

'Here,' she said at last, 'you haven't wished me a happy new year yet.' We clinked glasses and then kissed, as is the custom. The thing was, with her lush warm body in my arms and both of us feeling the effect of strong drink, the kiss lingered. It was my fault to start with, for her lips were so soft and yielding, her tits so comfortable against my chest, that I forgot myself. I pulled her closer and the plump bulge of her cunt nestled against my cock which was instantly erect. I pressed it against her. My tongue slipped

13

into her mouth and she responded, then she pulled away breathing heavily.

'Oh, no, this is wrong,' she said, sounding strange and somehow reluctant to put a stop to it. We looked in on my wife, who was spark out, breathing regularly, obviously in a deep sleep until morning. I still had a terrific hard-on thinking about the deep kiss Isa and I had shared and was sure she was aroused by it as well, although nothing was said. She went to her room and I bolted the front door, going along the passageway back to join my wife. Isa stood by her bedroom door watching me.

As I came up to her we fell into each other's arms quite automatically. We kissed passionately, my stiff prick once more pressing against her ample cunt mound.

'Oh, we shouldn't, shouldn't,' she moaned between kisses but not stopping me leading her into the bedroom.

'I've always wanted you,' I said fiercely. 'We can't stop now.'

Beside the bed we quickly pulled off each other's clothes. Then she was naked before me, her white body pale in the glow of the bedside lamp, heavy tits lolling and a mass of hair between her strapping thighs. I pushed her down across the bed, kissing madly at her mouth, her breasts and nipples, my hand down between her legs, my fingers in a soft wet cunt. Just as I did with her daughter, I pressed my mouth to it, tonguing her as she moaned and arched her back to lift her cunt to me. She bucked and squirmed her arse, gripped my head and grunted, 'It's too much, too much – I shall come!' Then she pulled me up over her body and cradled me between her thighs.

My prick went in her without help from either of us, finding its target and going up her receptive cunt to the balls at first thrust. 'Oh, it's so *good*!' she cried. 'It feels so big and hard there! Oh, what are we doing – you're *having*

14

me! Oh my God, not with you—' But the urge was too strongly on her as my prick shunted in-out, up-down, making her claw me to her closer, bucking her hips wildly.

It was pure heaven, all that comfortable soft flesh below me, her big tits like cushions as I fucked her, feeling the come boiling up from my balls. To my relief she cried out that she was finished! 'I'm coming!' she shouted and, as if to prove it, she went into a series of wild orgasmic spasms, grunting as I shot wad after wad of my spunk into her.

'Get off me, you beast,' she said then. 'That should never have happened – and never will again.' There's gratitude for you!

It never did happen again, but I keep a warm memory of making that amazon of a woman come so strongly on my cock. Our relationship cooled for a while, she keeping me at a safe distance and never staying in a room alone with me on future visits to see her new grandchild. But I'm quite happy to think I've had those glorious moments with her and I wonder if she doesn't also look back on it with pleasure – especially when New Year comes around!

David, Paisley

Under the Doctor

I was invited to a fancy dress party and mentioned to my doctor brother that I had no idea what I'd go as. He suggested that I go as a medical man. We are both single and live in the house which we inherited from our parents, so he went to his room and brought out a short white jacket that buttoned to the neck, a stethoscope and a short strap that fastened around my forehead with a magnifying mirror attached to it. So, duly dressed up as a doctor, I went to the party.

This is absolutely true, which shows some of the funny desires that people have. A man at the party, whom I knew slightly, told me his wife's favourite fantasy was to be examined thoroughly by a lecherous doctor who would give her tits and cunt a good fondling and then fuck her. We were at a rather well-off friend's house and the drink was flowing, hence his loosened tongue. I knew from talking to my brother that many female patients got the hots for their doctor – and, of course, many GPs ended up screwing an attractive patient who had let it be known that she fancied him. Often they got struck off.

This chap, Brian, made a joke of his wife's little letch when she joined us, saying, 'Here's a doctor I'm sure would be happy to fulfil your ambition, Shirley.'

Looking at her I decided I wouldn't mind at all. She was a good-looking woman of forty with large breasts, a good deal of them showing in the deep-cut neck of her medieval style dress. She was dolled up as Anne Boleyn to her husband's Henry VIII – as a fat hearty type with a beard he looked the part.

I gave her a dance, enjoying her soft body pressing into mine, her tits hugging my chest. 'What was my husband saying about me having a thing about doctors?' she asked. In a moment of daring, thinking of those big tits, I said I'd gladly examine her any time – it would be my pleasure.

Many a hopeful hint is made in a jest, no doubt. The thing was we stayed in a threesome for the rest of the evening, getting steadily tanked up – you know, not sick or drunk but merry. Few of us had brought our cars, knowing we'd be drinking, and so I shared a taxi with Shirley and her husband. Reaching their house, I was invited in for a nightcap. Shirley put on slow music and asked me to dance with her and so we shuffled around the furniture in their lounge, clinging together closely. I was sure she pushed those magnificent mammaries of hers into me deliberately. With her old man at the sideboard continuing to drink and seeming quite happy, his wife and I danced close, almost standing still and rubbing crotches with my now-engorged chopper pressing into her ample cunt. I kissed her cheek. She turned her mouth and kissed me back with open lips, so I pushed in my tongue and we smooched openly.

Brian came across and said, 'Here's your chance, Shirl. Let a doctor give you that examination you've always gone on about.' I thought, 'What a good idea.' I was still in my medical garb and the last one to say I wasn't a real doc.

'Would you?' said Shirley, obviously taken with the idea too.

The upshot was that she went upstairs to divest herself of the Anne Boleyn costume, returning in a dressing gown.

'Let's have a look at you then,' I said in my most

authoritative voice. 'Off with that dressing gown so that I can examine you properly.'

She took it off and placed it over a chair and stood before me. She was a comely vision in a black bra that overflowed with creamy tits and a matching pair of briefs, her hips and thighs sumptuously rounded and at her crotch a tempting bulge with wisps of hair curling out of her panties.

'Yes,' I said, 'you look the picture of health, but I'll need to see more. Take off those undergarments, please.'

She simpered as if she were shy. 'Should I, doctor? I mean, do you really need to see all of me?'

'Oh definitely,' I said, 'if a full examination is to be conducted.'

I was eager to see her naked, with those big breasts thrusting and more of that well-forested cunt.

'Better do as the doctor orders, my dear,' said her husband.

It was clear then that we were all enjoying the game. Shirley took off her bra, demonstrating that her tits were full and beautifully self-supporting. When she slipped off her briefs I could have uttered a lustful 'Cor!' at the splendid split bulge at the fork of her thighs, so thick with lush hair. She stood obediently while I hefted her tits, as if to test their weight. I cupped and squeezed them, pinched and pulled out the nipples.

'All seems well,' I intoned, wanting to add they were bloody marvellous tits. I told her to lie on the couch and fingered her quim as if making an internal inspection, all the time enjoying the feel of a juicy cunt channel. I touched up her clitoris and made her writhe her cushiony arse about on the couch.

'Oh, doctor,' Shirley moaned. 'Is this right? What you are doing is making me feel so – so – uneasy. I shall get aroused, I know. I won't be able to help it—'

18

'Behave,' I told her sternly, my prick bulging my pants. 'This is strictly between a doctor and patient. Turn over, please, on your hands and knees so that I may inspect your behind.' Actually I was eager to see her with her magnificent arse upward. She gave me a look as if to say that this was more than she had bargained for, seeing her from that rude angle, but nevertheless she rolled over, breasts dangling, got on her elbows and knees on the settee and stuck her large buttocks up in the air. My hands immediately parted both cheeks and gazed at the puckered-up ring of her anus and the lovely split of her cunt, festooned with hair.

'It's not nice,' she whined, 'seeing all of me this way.' Her body shivered. 'I can't bear to think what you are seeing in there.' My hand explored, feeling her bottom hole, probing with a fingertip, making her jump and gasp.

'Stay still!' I snapped. 'I need to make a thorough inspection.' Then I tickled her cunt again, finding it almost running with juices and twitching under my finger. I went right in with three fingers and she squirmed and moaned and complained that she was sure no examination should be so intimate.

'Oh, I can't help myself,' she ground out through clenched teeth. 'I shall come, you will make me come, doctor! Oh God, what are you doing to me? I shall report you – you are arousing me, you beast!'

Before us her arse was gyrating madly – her back dipped so that it was tilted and ideal for my fingering – jerking quite helplessly in her throes.

'For God's sake, fuck the woman,' said her husband. 'Put her out of her misery, give her the meat injection she's so desperate for. If you don't, doctor, I bloody well will.'

Shirley turned her face, nodding as if in full agreement.

'Go on, fuck her,' roared her hubby, eager to see her shafted, I had no doubt.

19

It was but a moment's work to kick off my trousers and pants and I slid into the open gorge of her arse with a rearing prick pointed at her cunt. It entered slickly, bathed in her juice, touching way back, and I began thrusting without pause while she humped her bum back to meet my heaves.

'He's fucking me, Brian!' she screamed. 'The doctor is fucking your wife. My God, you are letting him! Oh, oh, he is so far up me – it feels so big and hard! Oh Lord, keep fucking me then, do what you like. I can't help it, I'm going to come – come! Ohhhh—' Just in time too, for I was bucking into her pliant bottom, shooting off jets of jism into her with wild abandon. When my limp dick slipped from her, my place was immediately taken by her husband and she restarted her undulations energetically, on the way to more climaxes. In fact, the lady kept us busy all night.

Needless to say I borrow my brother's medical garb and stethoscope quite regularly now and make house calls on Shirley, getting to know every nook and cranny of her lovely body. I fill those same orifices for her most willingly. All of them!

M.O., Warwicks

Uncoupling

When my wife and I go on holiday we try and pick up a young couple, aiming to swap partners. Our routine never varies much. We've found holiday camps a happy hunting ground. Couples on holiday are relaxed and eager to let themselves go whereas normally they wouldn't be uninhibited enough to get involved in a sexual situation. Given the opportunity, you'd be surprised how many ordinary young couples feel tempted – it's in all our natures.

Spain is ideal ground. Young Brits, and that includes married ones, engaged couples and boys with their girlfriends, all seem to think it obligatory to let it all hang out. Sara and I maintain a villa there – having made a pile in property development, we retired early.

One night in a crowded bar we shared a table with a young married couple, Frank and Jean. They were impressed by my wife's mature beauty, the swept-back dark hair, the low dress showing full cleavage, her jewellery. They told us it was their first proper holiday since their honeymoon and their two small children were at home with granny, Jean's mother. I ordered champagne and got them relaxed, even happily tipsy.

We were at least twenty years older than this nice young man and his pretty wife. They were very impressed when Sara told them we owned a villa overlooking the sea with a private swimming pool. When the pair got up to dance, my wife said to me, 'I fancy that boy Frank. I shall seduce him tonight with you and his little wife watching us. If she lets you fuck her as well, we'll make a night of it.'

The very idea made my prick harden. I took Sara's hand and placed it on my engorged stalk. 'Randy already?' she said, giving it a squeeze.

It was no problem, when they returned to our table, to get them to agree to come and visit our home. 'We can continue drinking there,' I said. 'We have guest rooms – if you wish, you can stay the night.' We had already learned they were in a cheap hotel.

At the villa my wife announced she was for a midnight swim in the pool. It was a very warm night and our young guests said they loved swimming but their costumes were at the hotel.

'It's a private pool,' Sara said. 'No one can see us and my husband and I always swim nude.' She stood beside the edge and drew off her dress, kicked off her shoes, and was left in an overflowing lacy bra and briefs. She took these off while Frank and his wife stood goggle-eyed.

'Come on,' she urged, going up to them with tits wobbling, her hairy crotch on view. 'We're all adults here.'

I started to undress, too, and Sara turned and dived in, giving us a glimpse of her fine broad arse as she parted the water. She bobbed up, calling to our guests. 'Come in, the water's lovely.' I dived in to let them make up their minds.

Thankfully they exchanged glances and began to undress, the young wife carefully folding her clothes over a chair. I saw Frank standing with a semi-erect dick of proportions that I knew Sara would enjoy. The slim young man had more than his share, it looked like eight inches even half-hard. He leapt in the pool immediately to cover his mortification, but not before Sara was floating behind me, rubbing her tits in my back, whispering, 'I shall have that,' and pressing her cunt mound against my arse. 'I want that big prick up my cunt and I don't mind if his little mouse of a wife sees it all—'

She swam off to join Frank, pressing against him in the water. I saw Jean taking off the last of her underwear. 'It's really great in here,' I called to her as she stood shy and naked. She was small but choice, I decided, as I took in her pretty pointed tits and wispy-haired cunt.

She stepped into the pool and I joined her at once, knowing pretty certainly that by now Sara would have hold of Frank's prick under the water. I chatted to her to keep her busy, then she noticed at the other end of the pool that Sara and Frank were climbing out.

'Where are they off to?' Jean asked me anxiously.

'Only to dry themselves in the house, no doubt,' I assured her. 'Let's go and join them.'

She was eager to leave the pool, certain by now that Sara was a manhunter, so I ushered her into our main bedroom. There her husband had a towel around his waist, no doubt hiding a big erection.

Sara had just stepped away from him and I suspected they'd been kissing. There was no doubt the bedroom was set for a seduction scene with its wall lighting and king-sized bed. My wife handed me a large towel.

'You dry Jean, let's all dry each other. But brandies all around to warm us first, Derek,' ordered the sly bitch.

She began to towel Frank briskly and I did the same to Jean once I'd made her knock back a large brandy. She allowed me to dry her tits and rub between her legs.

'Frank is the only man who has seen me naked before,' she said suddenly.

Meanwhile her husband was rubbing a towel over Sara's tits. 'She wouldn't even go topless on the beach,' he called, getting in the right spirit. The towel around him had slipped

23

and he stood with his huge erection on view as if proud of it.

'I bet she'll go topless after tonight,' Sara said. 'You could go to the nudist beach along the coast. Jean, you should be proud to show off your lovely slim body – those sweet pear-shaped tits and your darling little cunt. I'm sure Frank would be proud to let all the men admire you—'

'Frank has nothing to be ashamed of either,' I said in admiration. 'What a magnificent prick he has.'

This made Frank stick out his chest as he basked in my praise. 'It's not a bad one, is it, love?' he boasted to his wife. 'You've quite enjoyed it, haven't you?'

At least we knew we had him primed. Now we had to work harder on his wife.

Jean was given another stiff brandy by Sara. The two women standing naked side by side made a glorious picture.

'Only *quite* enjoyed it, Frank?' Sara teased him. 'You are too modest. It really is a magnificent penis, so proud and erect.' She turned to Jean, saying, 'I'm sure you love taking all that up you, Jean. I know I would, any woman would. Oh, I would just love it, if you'd let me—'

Sara was taking a chance, I knew, in case Jean suddenly decided enough was enough. She said nothing, so my wife walked across and took Frank's prick in her hand, stroking it gently. He loved it, standing grinning like an ape with a beautiful older woman praising his prick and gently rubbing it up for him.

'I want a good fuck,' Sara announced. 'Please, Jean, let your husband take me. I do so want this gorgeous prick I'm holding to pierce me. You have him always – let me have him just this once—'

Poor bewildered Jean didn't have a chance to say yes or no, for both my wife and her husband were so deep in a clinch you couldn't have parted their naked bodies. Her

24

arms were locked around Frank's neck and his big bricklayer's hands were splayed across both her wide bum cheeks, cupping the tasty orbs of rounded flesh and pulling her lower belly hard against his upstanding prick. It was with a low moan of pure lust that Sara drew him down to the bed and draped herself over him. She held up both her tits to his mouth and he raised his head to the tilted nipples, sucking avidly while his hand sought between her legs to finger her cunt. A few moments of this, with Sara writhing and moaning, was enough. She rolled over, clawing at the young guy, opening her thighs for his entry.

His wife and I watched in fascination as her hand directed the red plum-like knob of his prick to the outer lips of her quim, rubbing it against them sensually. Frank gave a loud groan and heaved his flanks at her. Inch after inch of his rigid stalk disappeared up her, plainly seen by Jean and I. We were standing at their feet and looking directly between their heaving arses – his on top, hers below – with Frank's balls buffeting her grand canyon as his prick pistoned in and out.

So erotic was the sight that my own prick was painfully engorged but I spared a moment to gauge how Jean was taking it and found her watching with evident delight. She stood with eyes wide and rooted to the spot for it was the most erotic and thrilling scene.

Frank's bare arse was going like a steam hammer as he shafted away at Sara while she uttered wild cries and lifted her pelvis to him. She was out of control, jerking madly as she tried to get more of the monster to plumb her depths. Of course I loved the experience of seeing my marriage partner getting beautifully screwed.

To my delight it was having the same salacious effect on Jean. She was all eyes, her face flushed with excitement and made lewd by the scene. She moved closer to the bed, seemingly unaware of her own nakedness and bent to look directly between the bouncing bottoms. There, in close-up, she watched her husband's balls pummelling Sara's plump bum as inch after long inch of his stout girth pistoned to and fro, stretching her cunt lips into a perfect circle.

My wife had worked her legs over Frank's shoulders, making sounds like the whinnying of a wild mustang in her frenzy. 'Keep it up, keep it in, fuck me harder – but don't you dare come – don't come!' she screamed.

I moved behind Jean as she bent over and my searching hand felt the warm crease of her tight arse. I touched up the slit of her cunt, probed a finger and found moist folds of flesh. Venturing further, I flicked at the tight little bud of her clitty, getting a shiver and a wiggle of her bottom against my moving wrist. With my wife and Frank fucking like dog and bitch before us – for now Sara had rolled over and offered her bum to him on her elbows and knees – and fondling the hot juicy innards of Jean's cunt, my prick demanded relief.

As if with a mind of its own, my engorged stander nudged between Jean's bum cheeks, then forced an entry past her outer lips and deep into her cunt channel. I heard the girl mutter, 'Yes, do that, Derek, I want that—' and she steadied herself by placing her hands on the bed between her husband's feet. A nice little bum tilted up for me as I rose on my toes and gripped her tits under her body – all the better to fuck her with. Her arse gyrated madly back into my belly as she grunted and urged me on like a real horny hussy. The quiet little Jean obviously had hidden depths once put to the cock, and I was doing my best to plumb those depths.

It was a glorious fuck, Jean's cries mingling with Sara's as both women were shafted urgently by their riders. Hoarse yells and coarse shouts foretold that we were coming off and the smell of fucked cunt was pungent in the room.

We orgied in every combination for the rest of their holiday – Sara even initiating Jean into female sex and giving exhibitions that delighted us two men. Frank and Jean were very different people when we drove them to the airport. They joined us on the nudist beach, going naked and unashamed. In all our activities, which included Sara and Jean rubbing cunts together and licking each other, I took Polaroid photographs as mementos of an erotic interlude spent by the four of us. They took some home with them.

Jean and Frank are but two of at least a dozen couples we have entertained. Wife-watching is one of my favourite sexual pleasures. Sara loves fucking for my particular obsession, especially with younger men. Approaching her fifties, she looks like a slinky beauty of much younger years. Why do we prefer married couples instead of single studs to fulfil our fantasies? We feel there is less chance of trouble than if we invited the wrong type of unattached man into our sex life. We've found enough willing husband and wife teams happy to let their normal inhibitions take a holiday and join in the romps with us over the past years. They're out there if you look for them!

Derek and Sara, Malaga

A Model Wife

When I was made redundant and took a job with much less pay, our lifestyle suffered. We had a big mortgage and had been used to going out a lot, taking foreign holidays. My wife Ailie didn't complain, in fact she took a part-time job in a shop. Then she said she'd seen an advert in the local rag for a nude model at the local art college. She certainly had the figure for it, curvy in hip and thigh, with large shapely tits and a rounded bottom. She got the job and the first night she went I sat at home, feeling unbelievably randy and imagining other men and women seeing her big bushy mass of cunt hair and pouting tits.

When she returned I wanted to fuck her right away and I kissed and fondled her and took her on the couch. It was a marvellous ride for both of us – our usual after eight years of marriage being confined to the bedroom. 'Thinking of me posing naked makes you horny,' she teased me. As she'd had a really strong climax, crying out and bucking against me, I pointed out that posing nude had turned her on too.

As winter went on she said the sessions were too long and bloody cold. I was still turned on to think she was showing off all her charms to a roomful of people. She told me the students were practically all men, that she was well aware they ogled her big tits and liked to have her cunt in full view. Then she mentioned that one of the men had offered a tidy sum of money if she'd pose privately for him

28

and allow him to take photos of her – 'art studies' he called them. He was offering several sessions at the same fee, which came to a respectable amount of dough.

'What do you say?' Ailie asked me. 'It would be turning down good money.' I pretended to agree reluctantly, but I was more excited than ever. The bloke, a keen amateur photographer, had said the art studies were for his private collection.

When Ailie told Martin she would pose for him, it turned out that he had a wife at home who would definitely not approve so, to my great delight, his sessions would have to be at our house. He turned up with adjustable lights and several cameras. I put him down as a dirty old man but found him quite likeable. We talked and drank from the large bottle of whisky he'd thoughtfully brought with him. Ailie went upstairs to undress, leaving us on our own. He actually offered me the money – £50. I refused it, saying it was Ailie's as she did the posing.

'I admire you both,' he said. 'My wife is a bloody prude, not that it's worth seeing her undressed these days. You don't mind Ailie posing nude, obviously. She's a delightful woman, quite beautiful with a splendid figure to match.'

I agreed, warmed as I was with several large whiskies. 'You mean she's got lovely big firm tits and a fine sticking-out hairy quim on her,' I laughed, slapping his back in good fellowship.

For a moment he stared at me, then grinned and nodded. 'Too true,' he agreed, man-to-man. 'I've often wondered who the lucky bastard was who was married to her. She's gorgeous.'

The gorgeous one appeared that moment in a kimono. Martin took her picture in a variety of poses – arms behind her head, kneeling, draped along the couch – none of which were truly pornographic. They were quite arty, in fact. It was certainly erotic and arousing to see Ailie naked in that room for an hour or so with another man present. He left her with her money in her hand and, as she'd had a drink or two, she let me screw her on the couch still clutching her earnings.

A few days later I answered a call from Martin when she was out visiting her mother. 'Are you free?' he said. 'Can you join me for a drink at your local? There's something I'd like to talk over.'

I joined him soon after, taking a corner table for privacy. 'All right for next Wednesday night?' he wanted to know. I knew Ailie had thought the money easy and was keen to get more, and I also had a strong suspicion that the private posing turned her on. I said that it would be OK. He then leaned towards me. 'If you two are agreeable, I'd like stronger pictures of her. Do you know what I mean? I'd pay very well, double the fee. If either of you would object, forget I mentioned it, Roy.'

'I don't see why not,' I said, the very thought making my cock rise and twitch. 'You mean open-crotch shots, cunt in close-up and such? I'd have to talk to her. Come along on Wednesday and we'll see.'

He reached over to shake my hand. 'If you want to be in the pics as well,' he added, 'that would be fine by me. It's all for a rather special private collection I'm putting together.'

Ailie turned out to be agreeable, permitting lewd shots of her lolling back with arse raised and thighs parted, even pretending to play with herself. I posed with her and she sucked my cock, getting on her hands and knees to take my prick, and all the time Martin snapped away busily. Ailie was sitting up on the couch with thighs parted while I nuzzled at her cunt when she whispered saucily to me, 'I can see Martin has a big bulge in his trousers.'

I sat up and turned to him. 'This must be hell for you, Martin,' I said. 'Get your clothes off and join in if you like. There's enough to go around.'

Ailie called me a cheeky sod, but was giggling when she said it. When Martin undressed eagerly I was rather sorry I'd made the offer, his erect tool being bigger and thicker than mine. My wife looked at it and raised her eyes. I knew she was eager to try it.

Martin fondled Ailie's tits and flicked the erect nipples, his first ever touch of her. He asked me if I would take the photos and I snapped away as the pair of them kissed and fondled each other's privates. Then he went down to kiss my wife's cunt.

'Do it if you want, Martin,' I heard her say. 'Fuck me, then Roy can do it. There'll be pictures of you both having me.'

Moments later I saw Martin get across her and Ailie fold her arms and legs around his back. I was almost crouching on the floor and could see his girth embedded up her cunt, the lips gripping his shaft. His prick was huge compared to mine. She moaned with pleasure as she wriggled on his cock.

'It's good, oh so *good*!' I heard her exclaim, thrusting her hips wildly, loving the big prick up her cunt. At first I forgot to continue taking the pictures of it all. Martin, even in the midst of screwing my wife, lifted his face from her tits to shout, 'I hope you're getting this on film, Roy!'

From their strenuous fucking after that, it was evident that all their concentration was on the job in hand. Ailie shook in long spasms but continued to meet his thrusts, coming several times in succession and screaming like an animal in her delight. Martin's arse shunted like a piston as he climaxed with a hoarse cry. Then they were lolling apart and I got a good shot of them, lying back gasping,

31

with Ailie's cunt pouting and Martin's dick limp and lifeless.

Weekly sessions that turned into regular mini-orgies took place all that winter, in fact until we had several photograph albums filled with our sexual romps. Ailie's bank balance increased too, along with her love of having two men to satisfy her. Martin retired to a villa in Spain with his wife the next summer but he always pays us a visit when he comes back to see to his business interests. I think Ailie looks forward to that more than I do.

Roy, Durham

The Biter Bit

I know that the correct way to deal with obscene phone calls is to slam the receiver down. However, my Harry was working late *again*, and I was bored and lonely when the phone rang.

'Hello,' I said, and the male voice at the other end of the line said, 'Oh good, a woman. What are you wearing, may I ask, madam?'

Feeling fed-up and in a wicked mood, I replied, 'Actually I'm in the nude, lying on the couch. Does that turn you on?'

There was a pause at the other end and I guessed I'd foxed him by my answer. Then he came back. 'Why are you naked?' he asked. I fancied I heard an excited tremble in his voice. 'Are you playing with yourself?'

I had to chuckle. 'Not quite,' I answered. 'I'm waiting for my husband to come home and when he sees me naked on the couch I know he'll fuck me—'

There was an audible gulp at the other end. 'You sound like a horny cow,' he said. 'What do you like your husband to do to you?'

'He sucks my nipples – I like that.' I hear an intake of breath.

'Have you got big tits?' he asked. 'Big tits with long nipples?'

Actually, my breasts are about average, but I thought a lie was in order. 'Huge,' I said. 'Great big ones that I like to

33

play with. My nipples get very long and stiff when they are sucked.'

I heard heavy breathing. The voice came back, quite hoarse with excitement. 'So big?' he said. 'I'll bet they are just right for a tit-ride. Does your husband fuck your tits?'

I assured him that my husband did that all the time. 'What about you?' I asked. 'Are you playing with yourself now? I'll bet you're wanking like mad. Let me know when you're coming. I want to hear it down the phone.'

'Horny cow,' the man called me again. 'What size is your husband's prick. Does it go right up your cunt?'

'It's a good ten inches,' I said, 'but even then I'd like more.'

There was quiet for a moment, as if my unknown caller was digesting that fact. 'You sound the sort that loves a big prick,' he said. 'I bet you suck it for him too, don't you?'

I said I loved doing that, especially when he came in my mouth.

'You *are* a filthy bitch,' he said. 'Is there nothing you won't do? Do you like to be fucked from the rear, doggy-fashion? What about sitting on his prick, riding it with your big tits bouncing? Do you do that?'

'What woman doesn't?' I laughed. But my own talk had made my hand glide down between my legs. 'I'm playing with myself now,' I said truthfully. 'Are you?'

'Wanking away listening to you,' said a strained voice. 'I shall come soon. Talk dirty to me more – tell me what it is like with your fingers up your cunt – oh, oh – that's it, I'm shooting my lot. Dirty bitch, you've made a mess over my trousers—'

In the throes myself, I listened to his final gasps then replaced the receiver, concentrating on bringing myself off.

My husband came in soon after. 'I've just had one of those anonymous dirty phone calls,' I told him.

He looked concerned. 'I hope you put the phone down on the sick bastard,' he said.

'Of course,' I said. Well, so I had, finally.

Sue, Leytonstone

In the Swim

The spring and summer days of the early 80s were carefree days for my wife and I. Our son had left for university and Betty and myself were free to get more pleasure and excitement in our lives. We took up naturism and enjoyed many sunny days at a nudist beach on the nearby coast. I enjoyed seeing younger men eyeing her big breasts and shapely bottom. As that winter came on, we decided to visit the swimming-pool complex in town, whose facilities included a sun-bed and sauna. So, every Sunday morning, Betty and I would drive there for a swim and sun-bed session, followed by a meal and a drink in a nearby pub.

The small private room with a super sun-bed was hardly used. It was alongside the pool and it was most exciting to fuck Betty on the sun-bed with male and female swimmers just a few feet away. We would hire the room for a whole hour, sharing the bed, both of us naked. I would rub lotion all over her curvy body and then she'd stretch out on the bed and purr like a cat in the warmth. I would sit at the foot of the bed admiring the view: a mouth-watering mound with dark curly pubic hair vainly trying to cover a pouting cunt which opened like a flower's petals to the moist heat. Then the twin peaks, full tits still upright in her reclining position, such was their firmness and fullness, with droplets of perspiration trickling down those lovely slopes. There was no doubt our nudity and the heat made it impossible to avoid sex-play and fucking before we cooled off with a swim.

On one visit we decided to try the sauna. A young man sat there wrapped in a large towel like us. He moved along the slatted seating to make room for us. He told us he was a sergeant in the Parachute Regiment, presently employed in the recruiting office in town. He had an excellent build and looked extremely fit. Betty and I sweated it out for fifteen minutes before showering and taking a swim. 'What a nice young man,' Betty said to me. 'What a good figure. We should try the sauna again, he said he goes every week.' I felt she was more than taken with him.

We found him there the following Sunday and we introduced ourselves. He said he was John, twenty eight years old with a wife in Germany and hoping to get stationed there again. Betty is fifty, but looks thirty and, as the heat increased, she stood up and announced she was for taking off the one-piece bathing costume she was wearing.

'You're supposed to be naked in a sauna,' she said. 'You can both join me if you want to.'

Both John and I watched in fascination as she drew down the shoulder straps and two lovely tits swung proudly into view. She went on to kick the costume from her feet, revealing her plump mound and a lush triangle of cunt hair. I discarded my shorts to show willing. John was slower, still taking in Betty's charms as she sat between us, then he unwrapped the towel from his waist, saying he would not be the odd one out.

I saw Betty look down, noting that his uncircumcised prick was above average size and in keeping with his athletic frame and tall height. It gave little jerks as if starting to erect.

'Don't mind us,' Betty said to him. 'We bathe nude in

37

the summer and we're members of a nudist club. Don't you like my all-over tan?'

She stood up and turned around to give us a front and rear view. She loved exhibiting herself to John, I knew. God, how her tits thrust out, the cleavage parting as she held wide her arms to show her tan. Her legs were apart too, the muff between her thighs on full display. I saw John swallow hard.

'Do you mind me looking at your wife in the nude?' he asked. 'She certainly has a lovely figure—'

Pleased that he had praised her, my wife suggested he join us in the sun-bed room. There we insisted he use it first. We were all naked.

'There's only one chair in here,' Betty said. 'I'll need to sit on my husband's lap. I'm sure he won't mind—'

The electric contact of her bare bum on my prick proved too much and a glorious stiff erection soon pushed its crest up the cleft of her bottom cheeks. She jumped up and laughed at me sitting there with a brute of a cockstand rearing like a flagpole.

'What a rude husband I've got,' she said to John. 'Do you think I should do something about it?' Our new friend, aware by now he was with an unusual couple, an exhibitionist woman and an amenable husband, nodded agreement, his face lighting up.

Betty faced me, legs astride, lowering herself as she guided my prick to her cunt.

Then I was up her and Betty rose and fell over me, working the cock into her.

Flushed with excitement, she turned to the young man on the sun-bed. 'We fuck in here every Sunday,' she explained. 'I can see you approve, John,' she added wickedly, the poor guy's prick being vertical too. Quite unabashed, Betty reached out and rubbed him while riding me. What a woman!

38

She was now lost to all thought but sexual gratification. As soon as I had come she suggested we change places. I got on the sun-bed while John sat in the chair and she impaled herself on his prick, riding him slowly and sensuously, his pelvis lifting and hers moving in snake-like motions over him.

'It's so good! Make it last, John,' I heard her tell him.

'Never mind about Ed, he's always wanted to see other men fuck me. He would have me doing this every day. I love doing it too. I can feel your big hard prick right up inside me—'

From my reclining position I could plainly see her arse gripping his stem and swallowing it up, rising then falling to engulf its whole length.

'I want to do it on the sun-bed,' she announced throatily. 'I want John to have me there. Leave us alone, Ed, go and swim in the pool.'

I rose at once, reluctant to leave them but finding it highly arousing. I swam for a good half-hour before Betty joined me, looking like the cat that had got the cream.

Her first words were, 'I can feel both your comes leaking out of me. That was really marvellous. Poor John is still laid out on the sun-bed.' No wonder, for she told me how he'd ended up hard again after she fucked him and she'd bent over the chair for him to have her again, doggy-fashion.

The following Thursday we gave him a lift in our car. Betty joined him in the back seat and within moments they were kissing madly. By the time we reached our house he had felt up her tits and cunt and she had his prick out. I told them I'd pour the drinks, but Betty said, bold as brass, 'No, I want him to fuck me first. I'm all worked up!'

We adjourned upstairs to the bedroom and I stood beside the bed while John fucked my wife heartily, she groaning and clutching at him in her throes.

'You fuck me now,' the wicked creature said when John had rolled off her. 'I bet my pervert of a husband is all randy seeing his wife getting screwed—'

John watched, cock in hand, rubbing it for another erection until Betty reached out to do it for him, sucking his cock even as I fucked her. Depositing a load up her with cries of 'Take that, you horny slut,' I got up leaving her stretched out on her back and holding her arms out for John.

I moved aside, saying to our guest, 'You're on your own now, forget I'm here, but I'd love to see you fuck Betty dog-style like she said you did at the pool.'

Hearing me, she rolled over, displaying her magnificent arse. John eased his prick between the splayed cheeks and I watched spellbound as he shafted her. She rolled her bum back at him, taking his all with sighs of pleasure.

Later, unable to get enough of each other, they demonstrated the sixty-nine position by licking and sucking each other. I watched closely, as she tongued the cleft of his knob and closed her lips over it as if she wanted to suck his balls into her mouth.

'After this I'll always want two men to service me – or even three or four!' she exclaimed while we relaxed on the bed. I made a trip below for drinks, returning to find them cuddling.

'Come on, John, fuck me again,' she encouraged him. 'Imagine it's your wife, if you like, but stick it up me.' She was drunk on sex, pulling him between her thighs and stuffing his erection into her cunt. Thus settled, she crossed her legs behind his back, urging him on while he manfully thrust back.

'It's getting harder, it's lovely!' she called out to me, tilting her cunt forward to get more depth from him. I stood by, enjoying seeing her heave her pelvis in time to his rapid thrusting. 'Yes, yes, it's touching the spot!' she squealed. 'Make it last, make it last, John! Oh, give it to me, make me come again and again—'

John settled into a slower rhythm, shafting deeply and withdrawing before plunging up her cunt to the balls, making her shout with ecstasy and jerk and writhe. I was just as thrilled to see my lovely wife being really well fucked. Her eyes opened glassily and she focused them on me while I stood, cock in hand, revelling in the exhibition. 'Yes, Ed, wank off while John fucks your horny wife! You come too!' she urged me. 'We're really dirty things, aren't we? Talk to me, Edward—'

Every shred of modesty and inhibition had been thrown to the winds by now. I said to her, 'Just what are you doing there, Betty?

Her voice was gruff in reply. 'Fucking,' she said. 'I'm loving it lying here fucking with John and he'd better not stop! I want his prick up me all night—'

To have such a woman under him mouthing obscenities proved too much. John let out a loud groan and worked his flanks faster, shooting off his load even as I wobbled at the knees and came off.

Betty lay back red in the face with effort, tits lolling and cunt pouting, regarding us males and our limp dicks with a look of disgust. 'They're no use to me,' she complained. 'I wanted to keep coming, damn you!'

'Finish yourself off, dear, and give us a treat,' I suggested hopefully. John and I stood over her as her hand went to her glistening cunt mouth, fingering away expertly as her hips swivelled and pelvis rose to rock against her wrist movements. All the time her eyes were on us as if to say, 'I don't have to depend on you for a good come.' Then she was issuing soft whimpers and sighs as if in torment, her bottom bouncing on the bed as she brought herself off.

That night was the first of many before John was posted to rejoin his regiment. He certainly had happy memories of my wife during his visits to us. One night, in turn, the two of us fucked her solidly for five hours – one on the nest and the other resting. She was insatiable for two pricks at the same time, stripping off at the drop of a hat for our threesomes and eagerly anticipating John's visits, which were frequent. He said she was the best fuck he had known out of dozens of women, including his German wife.

On his last night with us I let them sleep together as a farewell present, standing outside the bedroom and listening to the sounds of sucking and fucking.

Some time later we got a letter from him thanking us for our hospitality. Is that what they call it!

E, Sussex

IOU

I'd always felt overshadowed by my brother Tony. He had a better career, more money, and a positively gorgeous wife in Tina. I drooled over her in secret. One day in a bar at lunchtime, when he was busy in his office, I spotted her in a corner alcove holding hands with a guy, sitting close, and indulging in a long passionate kiss. As her mouth broke away from his, she looked aside and saw me. The usually cool Tina turned bright pink. I hurried from the bar to give her privacy, rather tickled that my successful brother was being two-timed. Then I realised I should have hung about and assured her I had no intention of telling Tony. I was sure she was worried about that.

I was invited to their flat for dinner soon after. She was bright and cheerful, making a fuss of me, never leaving my brother and I for long in case I spilled the beans, I guess. We had a fair amount to drink and I was really horny and jealous when they went off to bed. I was sleeping in the guest bedroom as I'd had too much drink to drive home. Lucky bastard, I thought, thinking of her proud tits, a good deal of which had been temptingly displayed in her low-cut dress. I'd bet she had a lovely cunt too – tight and sweet. I wondered if the guy I'd seen her with had fucked it.

From next door I soon heard the unmistakable sounds of a lusty bout of sex. Without a shadow of doubt, Tina was getting Tony's stiff prick up her cunt and responding with loud cries and groans of pleasure. I listened jealously,

43

my cock in my hand, wanking into my handkerchief and coming off as I heard her scream out she was too.

I dozed off, thinking my wank was a poor thing compared to what my brother had to play with, the full-bodied horny Tina. I slept awhile, only to awake to the sound of giggling next door, then more furious fucking from the horny couple.

When I woke up it was late. But then I'd been awake for hours tortured by the sounds from the next bedroom. There was a little knock on my door and Tina came in with a cup of tea, wearing a shortie nightie that barely covered her thighs. It was diaphanous too, so sheer you could see right through it, revealing the dark rounds of her nipples and a lush growth of cunt hair at her crotch. She put down the tea on the bedside table.

'Would you like me to pop into bed?' she asked.

Cor, would I?

'Where's Tony?' I asked, my throat dry with excitement.

'You know what he's like,' she smiled 'Gone to his office even though it's Saturday. I'm all yours if you want me, Philip.'

I could only mutter 'Yes', and she peeled off the nightie, standing resplendent with her boobs thrust out before my face.

'I think you've always fancied me,' she teased. 'Do you like me like this?' she held up her magnificent tits. 'Like these?'

I reached up to pull her into bed but she stepped back. 'Let's see if I've had any effect on you,' she said, peeling back the duvet. I'd slept in the nude so my dong was sticking up like a flagpole. To my great joy she sank down beside the bed and took it into her mouth, sucking hard. I let her continue until I felt the first urges of a come. Most of all I wanted to fuck her.

'Get into bed,' I begged.

'Did you hear us last night?' she said, coming into my arms. 'I thought of you in here, wishing I had both brothers fucking me.'

I certainly gave her the works, shafting her until she was squealing that she was coming. My spunk soon joined that of my brother's and my next erection came after sucking her tits and getting sucked in return. Then she piled up the pillows so that her lovely plump arse stuck up for me to ram it in from the rear position. What a sopping cunt she had!

Later she said, 'That was for not telling Tony you saw me with another man. How many times will you fuck me again before my secret is safe?' There was an offer, if you like – and she's still paying off her debt!

Philip, Chelsea

45

Sister Mine

My wife Sarah and her sister Chloe had always been close. They even look alike, both being well-built and attractive. Chloe's husband died early in a drowning accident, so she was widowed quite young. At the time I write of, we were all in our late thirties and she had come to stay with us for a holiday. Now, Sarah and I had always enjoyed fucking. I had an uninhibited wife who liked her nonsense, as she called it. As I left for work in the mornings, popping back into the bedroom to say cheerio, she'd peel back the covers to reveal her hairy pussy. 'Don't I get a goodbye kiss?' she'd say, so I'd plant a smacker on her quim. Some mornings I'd be late for work, the kiss turning into a good tonguing once I got the taste of it. Once tempted, I'd eat it out, the bitch giggling and urging me on.

So, you see, she was no prude and enjoyed sexy fun, including every position, even rear entry. On her sister's arrival we went out for a meal and returned home in high spirits. The talk got a bit steamy and Chloe said that what she missed most as a widow was having a man to satisfy her.

'He's OK,' my wife said, referring to me. 'If you want him tonight, Chloe, have him. He's often said he'd like to fuck you.'

The very idea had my cock twitching. Chloe giggled and said she wouldn't say no, it had been too long.

'Then what are you two waiting for?' said Sarah. 'Off to

bed with you and make the most of it.'

I escorted Chloe through to the guest room, meaning business, wanting to do right by her as well as for myself. First I told her it was true, I'd often said I'd love to get into her bed. Then I seized her cuddly form and kissed her deeply.

'Let me see you,' I begged, so we both undressed. Chloe was all creamy white skin with the big tits of a mature woman. She sighed gratefully as I cupped them and flicked the prominent nipples with my thumbs. I lowered her across the bed, admiring the strapping thighs, the black bushy hair and the crinkled cunt lips peeping out of the dense growth. I sucked her pussy greedily before being hauled up over her, her hand directing my engorged chopper to her crack.

'Put it in, Fred,' she begged. 'Put it right up me. It's been over a year—'

As she'd been a widow far longer than that, I wondered who the lucky one had been. As it was, I found myself cradled in her warm soft flesh, her hands clasping my arse as I began shafting her. She was so on heat, so wet with juice, that I could plainly hear the sliding of my cock in her cunt. I drew it back to the knob, making her cry out, before giving her the full length. It was then that I noticed my wife standing naked beside the bed.

'Go at it, you two,' she urged. 'I couldn't keep away thinking about what you mucky devils were up to.' Her sister moaned and said it was so good, so nice to have a real prick up her cunt again. 'Beats a vibrator any time, doesn't it, Chloe?' laughed Sarah, who must have been let in on her sister's secret habits.

I don't want to boast but refraining from coming off until my partner has been satisfied is something that I have trained myself to do. With the wife I had, it was a necessity, as she never settled for less than several climaxes when we screwed. Now I had Chloe rearing her arse up, clawing at me, and positively gurgling out her happiness as my prick pounded her cunt.

'Save some of that for me,' Sarah said. 'Seeing you two going at it has got me all worked up. Make her come, Fred, and then do the same for me. I'm standing here diddling myself—'

Chloe did come, bucking like a wild creature, squealing out that she was there! She was there! I rolled off her and drew Sarah down beside us, thrusting into her moist flesh and continuing my shafting uninterrupted. Sarah moaned that it was all in – 'Fuck me like you did her' – and I was only too keen to oblige.

Chloe sat up then, watching us at it, obviously thrilled. Suddenly she got up on her knees over my wife's head and presented her cunt to me. I grabbed her hips, pulled her close and buried my face in her crotch even while fucking Sarah below me. She agreed entirely with the formation. 'Yes, suck her, Fred,' she ordered. 'Clean her out, the horny cow – just don't stop fucking me!'

A man can only stand so much. With Chloe's fragrant cunt at my lips and Sarah jerking her body below me like a fish, I shot my bolt and collapsed flat on my back, panting like a dog.

'Poor Fred,' I heard Chloe say to her sister, the horny creatures giggling at my exhausted state. 'We've been too much for him. I hope he's not finished for the night – I was just getting started!'

'Don't worry, Chloe,' my missis assured her, 'he knows better than to cop out. I've trained him too well for that.'

For once, even with two naked women ready and willing, I had to beg for a rest. But that was some fortnight while Chloe stayed with us, me sleeping between them every night and expected to do my duty.

Later that summer we took Chloe with us for our Spanish holiday. I was the envy of every other man on the beach with two big-titted topless females fussing over me. I was pleased when we made friends with a large German tourist and he helped me keep two insatiable women happy. I didn't even mind when he was fucking Sarah – after all I was up her sister at the time!

Fred, Maidstone

Pillow Talk

Though I am getting on a bit the urge to fuck is still as strong as ever, even if rising to the occasion is not so easy. For a while, with a still active wife wanting her regular supply, I just couldn't get it up. Not surprising for a man in his senior-citizen years, perhaps, but that didn't suit Annie. She's not the complaining kind, yet in time her frustration brought out a few cutting remarks about my inability to fuck her. This was after she had done things to get me erect enough to give her the penetration she desired, things like cradling my prick between her ample tits and then sucking it. In the end I'd finger her off or use my tongue to bring on a climax. But I knew that what she liked most was the feel of a good stiff prick up her quim.

It was one Sunday morning, a time when we'd always enjoyed a lazy screw, that she lay back in our bed, tits lolling and legs parted and played with her cunt after giving up on me. I sat feeling miserably inadequate, my tool limp and a fine woman's body sprawled before me.

'She's always loved a prick up her cunt,' I thought, sad that she was missing out because of me. I had been blessed with a randy wife, an extremely highly-sexed woman. I used to wonder when the vicar and his wife came to tea, what the respectable ladies who were her friends would think if they knew that in bed she went bonkers for bonking. Well, I say you can be a good person and still love fucking your arse off.

On that particular Sunday morning, as she lay touching herself up for want of a stiff prick, she became nostalgic. Her glazed eyes were fixed on me as she muttered, 'I've had some lovely fucks with you, Harry. And with other men, too. You've never known how I've loved taking so many pricks. I just couldn't help it, it's in my nature—'

That made me sit up, my good wife Annie, mum to our devoted children and a much-loved grandmother, admitting that she'd fucked with other men! Curiously, it had the effect of arousing me. My impotent dick gave a twitch, a definite throb.

'Tell me about how you've been fucked, love,' I said in a strangled voice. 'Who was the first? Tell me who took your virginity and what it was like for you. Did he make you come? How old were you?' I said all this believing that I'd taken her cherry on our honeymoon, which shows how young husbands can be fooled. Right then I didn't care, I only wanted my excitement to continue, to get a hard-on as quick as possible.

'It was my piano teacher,' Annie grunted in the throes of working herself up. 'I went to his house Wednesday evenings and his wife was always out then. He was forever touching me, leaning against me as we sat at the piano, his hand brushing my breast as he turned the sheet music. I liked it, it made me blush and got me excited. I was only sixteen and my parents never allowed me to go with boys. I knew it was what I liked, what I wanted. He knew it too—'

The confession, her talk, aroused her as much as it did me, her hand working faster at her crotch, her hips jerking helplessly.

'One day he kissed me, long and hard with his tongue in my mouth,' she croaked out. 'He led me through to his bedroom and then undressed me – sucked my tits and licked me, then fucked me, fucked me – oh, he FUCKED ME!'

51

This last was screamed out as she went into violent convulsions, having the strongest possible climax. Looking down, I saw my once-reluctant prick rearing like a stallion, fully engorged and rampant for cunt.

'Then I'll fuck you,' I spat out, 'fuck you like you need, you horny bitch. Fuck you like your piano man and all the others who've been up your cunt – your greedy cunt!'

Anne stared at me, saw my upstanding tool and spread her legs. In a moment I was buried up her pouting slit to the balls, a hot juicy passage still palpitating from fingering herself off.

For all that, she was desperate for more, circling her arms and legs around me to draw me close, lifting her hips to thrust against me.

'Oh, God, yes! Fuck me, Harry. Shove it all up! Fuck me harder!' she yelled. 'Give me all that lovely hard prick—'

I certainly did, screwing her like a young stud, my buttocks clenching as I rammed up her, delighted to hear her scream out that she, was coming again – and again. 'Oh, you beast, you are killing me,' she cried. Our bellies smacked like handclaps as we went out of control, my jism shooting up her in long spurts as she clung to me and then begged for more. It was indeed the fuck of a lifetime.

Regaining my breath, I felt her hand fondle my now-limp cock. 'I knew there was life in it yet, dear,' she whispered saucily. 'You hearing about me getting fucked by other men turned you on, didn't it?'

On my asking if it were true, she nodded in the affirmative. 'It did the trick, didn't it? Wasn't it worth it?' After the great fuck we'd just enjoyed, who was I to complain?

Our so-called 'pillow talk' has continued and it does the trick each time. I love hearing her tell of all her infidelities in the most down-to-earth terms, especially when I'm fucking her myself. Even now I'm surprised what a busy little slut she's been over the years of our marriage – as ever, the husband is the last to know.

It emerged that she was regularly fucked by a near-neighbour whom I thought was a close friend. A young chap I once employed as a gardener used to shag her too. Evidently they had got chummy over morning coffee and the temptation had been too great – she'd bent across the kitchen table for him a few times. I know it's an old story, but the handsome milkman we'd had in a previous house collected more than his weekly milk bill when he called. There are plenty of others I don't know about. Annie could not resist fucking with men who gave her the eye – and plenty did. It makes me feel better about the few affairs I've had and it certainly comes in handy when the spirit is willing but the flesh is weak.

Harold, Wimbledon

X-Certificate

I want to write this because I must tell someone how my whole life has changed. My name is Susan and I'm a thirty-two year old housewife who loves sex! Fucking, sucking, watching, exhibitionism and swapping are a vital part of my life now – I honestly can't get enough. It all started when my husband John brought home one of those videos that demonstrate how to improve your sexual skills. After seven years of marriage our sex life was *very* routine – two fucks a week, sometimes a climax for me, then sleep.

I was surprised how explicit the video was. There were episodes called 'The Male Body', 'The Female Body', 'Sexual Positions', 'Masturbation', 'Foreplay' and 'Oral Sex'. I was prepared to be bored, but as I looked at well-endowed males with lovely erections and girls bringing themselves off, I sat up and took notice, my cunt pulsating and juicy. Four or five attractive couples took part and it was 'no holds barred' as they sucked and fucked. I looked across at John as he stared at a girl with large breasts holding them up for her taut nipples to be sucked. He was all eyes, all the more so as she bent down to kiss and suck a long and stiff prick, caressing her partner's balls as she did so.

My own tits felt swollen and my nipples tight. But for my normal reticence I would have asked him to suck my nipples while he watched the video. I *really* wanted him to. On screen, one of the men knelt between a girl's thighs, parted her outer cunt lips and the camera shot closed in to show him tickling her glistening red clitty with the tip of his tongue.

By now it had got us both terribly horny and John came over to me on the couch, kissing me deeply and fondling my titties. We fucked wildly and I came twice – our first time in the living room of that house.

The next morning, when I should have been doing the housework, I watched it again with my knickers discarded and three fingers up my cunt. Later I asked my husband if he knew of more such films and he said a workmate of his had several illegal ones – outright porn videos. He loaned one to John and we watched it together – a film with the most sexy sucking and fucking I could imagine, with lovely big-breasted girls and hugely endowed men, doing everything including anal intercourse. Of course John and I ended up naked before the television, copying what the actors were doing and with myself eager to try everything.

A few nights later John's pal, Brian, visited unexpectedly, clutching half-a-dozen video cassettes. I wondered if John had told him how aroused such films made me. John served drinks and suggested we should watch one of the tapes. I felt embarrassed but when the scene opened, with four couples fucking side by side on a bed, I felt the usual twitching in my cunt. The men had been chosen for their outsized cocks, as had the girls for their enormous tits. I felt smug, knowing my boobs were just as big but that John and Brian could hardly have such big dicks. We saw deep-throat sucking, 'sixty-nine' and even a daisy-chain screw.

Suddenly the scene changed. A naked couple were fucking on a bed when a fully dressed mature woman walked into the apartment. From the dialogue it was obvious that this was the girl's mother. The naked boy arose from her daughter and pleaded with her, making her relent somewhat as he began to kiss her and fondle her tits through her dress. Then he led her to the bed where he and her daughter undressed her and the boy licked her out and fucked her. It was all so erotic and salacious that in the semi-dark my hand was at my crotch, rubbing and stroking my clit through my dress. Unable to resist, John came over and pulled off my panties, pushing me back on the couch to delve his face between my thighs. I didn't care that Brian was present and told John to lick me out and make me come!

Glancing across as John tongued me, I saw that Brian was watching us instead of the screen, his erect prick in his hand. I know I wanted it and reached out to grasp his hardness, drawing it to my mouth even as a girl on-screen was busy sucking off her partner.

'Let's get down to it like they are,' John said from between my legs. In the film, the girl, her mother and boyfriend had been joined by the others and pricks of magnificent girth were being poked into every female orifice. As for us, we threw off our clothes in haste until I stood naked between two very rampant men, a prick in each hand.

'What fantastic tits,' said Brian, cupping and stroking them. 'I'd love to fuck them.' I giggled at the thought, his prick thick and throbbing in my hand.

'Fuck me first,' I told him. 'My cunt is burning – just bursting for a good stiff prick up it.'

He lowered me to the carpet and placed a cushion under my bottom to raise my cunt to the angle he desired. I was already wet and I held out my arms for him.

'Yes,' I heard John say. 'Fuck her, Brian. Give her that big prick of yours till she begs for mercy—'

Brian's prick was certainly bigger and thicker than John's and it filled my cunt channel, making me gasp.

'What a wonderful cunt,' Brian groaned as he shafted me. 'I'm up to the balls and she's stretching up to get more.

You got a right horny wife here, John, you lucky bastard. Christ, she's trying to get me in balls and all!'

It was true, in my excitement I was clawing him nearer, urging him on with the lewdest words. The fact that I was performing in front of my husband made it all the more exciting. He was kneeling by my face, putting his prick to my mouth. I licked the red helmet as if it were a lollipop, then covered it with my lips. When I climaxed it was with two loads of thick sperm spurting into my cunt and throat and I flopped about like a landed fish.

The video had ended but we three went up to the bedroom to continue our sex games in comfort. John seemed content to watch as much as take part and I realised how much I enjoyed performing for him. I got on my knees on the bed and offered myself doggy-fashion. Brian licked at my outthrust rear, then stood behind me and fucked me once again. John watched with a huge erection and I said 'Darling, I want you too. Both of you fuck me.'

How delightful it was to know that, while taking one prick, another awaited its turn. Before long the pair of them were laid out on the bed, quite shagged out. Had another male been present I would have welcomed his prick too.

Susan, Newport

It Pays to Advertise

I enjoy sexy letters in adult magazines – though I don't believe every word. Some turn me on so much I have to toss off, so who cares if they aren't all true? I like reading the classified sex ads as well. I've replied to a few in my time and had lots of fun. The most memorable was with a couple who wanted me to watch them make love.

Steve, the husband, phoned me and said he was impressed with the letter I'd sent, adding that some of the scrawls he'd received must have been written by illiterate sex maniacs. I told him that what I'd said in mine was all true: I was a self-employed painter and decorator of forty-eight, divorced and fancy free, and the photo I'd enclosed was recent. It had been taken on holiday in Spain as I emerged from the sea in tiny swimming trunks. Though I say it myself it showed off my broad athletic figure a treat, leaving little to the imagination.

Weeks passed and I forgot about Steve. Then came a call inviting me to his house on the following Saturday night. Fortunately, it was only a twenty-minute drive and I found myself travelling down a leafy drive with large houses set well back off the road. Obviously they're not short of a bob, I thought, wondering what kind of people would want a complete stranger to watch them bonking.

I was led into the house by a handsome young chap of about thirty. Linda, his wife, was a pretty enough woman of the same age. She looked, I thought, a shade apprehensive. As I shook her hand, I wondered if Steve had talked her into the whole business and she was only going along with it for his sake.

Of course I eyeballed the wife. She looked most attractive in a white blouse and skirt that showed off her full tits and nicely rounded arse. I'd like to see *that* out of clothes, I thought. We had a drink and chatted about normal things while I wondered if they really did want to fuck before an audience. As we seemed to be getting nowhere fast, I brought up the subject of their advertisement and asked if it were their first time.

'My wife and I did it once with a friend watching us,' I said, lying through my teeth to get them at ease with me. 'We found it gave a boost to our sex life, which had been getting a bit stale—'

I noticed the pair of them perked up at that. The young husband said, 'Well, we've never done it in front of a stranger before. We did it with a good friend of ours watching. He was an elderly neighbour but he went to live with his daughter last year—'

'Lucky old him,' I couldn't help saying, seeing the wife blush. 'You're an attractive couple, I'm sure he must have loved it as much as you did. Please don't have any qualms about me, do as you wish. I won't tell anyone.'

They looked at each other, quite flushed with excitement. You could say the air was charged with sexual promise, so much so that I felt my cock stiffen. They both began to undress and were soon stark naked. I enjoyed seeing her firm young tits jiggling and noted the curved bulge of her hairy cunt. He was fully erect, with a good six-inch stander. She glanced quickly at me to make sure I was watching, then took his prick in her hand and began to rub it up and down. Then she bent over to give the stalk some lovely slurpy sucks, before falling back onto the couch.

59

The lady doth show promise, I thought as she lolled before her husband with tits jutting and thighs splayed to reveal her delightful muff and cunt lips. She grasped her breasts and squeezed them, flicking her nipples, then she began to finger her quim, parting the hair to show off the pink gash of her pussy. Husband Steve stood over her, slowly wanking as if about to shoot over her lovely white tits.

'Let Edward play with himself too, if he wants,' said his wife, breathlessly, rolling her round arse about on the couch. 'Let's all play with ourselves, Steven. Oh, isn't it nice—?'

'Can I undress?' I asked. 'I'd like to wank off watching you at it.'

'If you like,' Steve agreed, 'but that's all. You can't fuck my wife, you know. I don't want Linda with another man—'

As I revealed a rearing cockstand that was thicker and longer than Steve's and seeing Linda eyeing it as she finger-fucked herself, I wondered if she might think differently. As if to dispel that thought, her husband began to fondle her tits, sucking on her nipples, then sliding down to fasten his mouth over her cunt. He sucked and tongued while she thrashed about on the couch.

'Fuck me, darling, fuck me now,' she pleaded. 'I do so want your cock. Fuck it up my cunt—' On cue he got between her thighs, stroking the knob of his tool up and down the outer lips of her eager quim, teasing her. 'In, in!' she groaned. 'Give it to me, shove it up to your balls!'

'Go on, fuck her,' I joined in, keen to see her shafted. 'Give her the lot, screw her rigid.'

'He wants to see you fuck me,' the wanton Linda cried, dragging her husband inside her to the hilt. As if for my benefit, he fucked her slowly, in to his balls and then withdrawing to the knob while she curled her legs around

60

his waist and clawed at his arse cheeks, muttering and mumbling deliriously all the while.

I had to still my hand, not wishing to come off before they did. Getting on my knees to see better, I had a close-up view of his stem shunting in and out of her cunt while his swinging balls pounded in the cleft of her cheeky bum. That Linda had climaxed several times was evidenced by her spasms and cries. Then Steve let fly, thrusting and bucking into her.

When he stood up, his dick limp and wet, Linda remained as she was, her legs parted, her cunt steaming. 'Congratulations on giving her a magnificent fuck,' I said enviously. 'What a lovely ride your wife must be. Thank you for inviting me along.'

'She's good, isn't she?' Steve said proudly. 'Look at her lying there. Wouldn't you like to feel her tits?'

She smiled up at me as my hands cupped both beauties, savouring their silky smoothness. 'You didn't come,' she teased me, noting my rampant cock. 'Wasn't it exciting enough, Edward? Didn't you enjoy seeing us at it?'

'I loved it,' I said. 'And I'm hoping for seconds. I'll come in good time.'

'Feel her cunt and her bum,' Steve invited. 'Get on your knees, Linda, let him see all of you.' His wife obliged, giggling at her naughtiness and presenting to me an obscene rear view. I felt up both orifices eagerly, her cunt wet and warm to my touch. I parted her cheeks, getting no objection from her husband, then dared to kiss her fig, my nose buried between her cheeks. My tongue probed and entered her soft folds, the tip reaching a hard little clitty. The horny bitch gave a soft sigh, pushing back her arse and tilting her cunt to give me better access.

'Oh, he's licking me – his tongue's in my cunt,' she said in a strained croak to her husband. As her juices flowed

61

into my mouth, I lapped her thoroughly, feeling her arse give little jerks as her excitement grew beyond control. 'Oh, Steve, what is he doing? Is he going to fuck me, darling?'

'Would you like him to?' said Steve, sounding as excited as his wife. My hopes rose, for they obviously *wanted* more. He wanted to see his wife fucking another man and she was eager to take me. To help them decide, I rose up, big hard prick in hand and directed it to the underslung cunt poised before me. It slid up beautifully first time into a well-lubricated and pulsating cunt channel. 'Oh yes!' murmured Linda. 'You dirty beast, you aren't supposed to do that. Oh Steve, look, his prick's up your wife—'

And didn't she love it as I thrust, her comfortable bum nestling against my belly, rolling back to me as my cock penetrated to the depths of her. I gripped her tits hard and rose on tip-toe to gain the extra inch, then I shagged her masterfully. In seconds, it seemed, she was moaning and screaming in orgasm and I was shooting jets of my cream up her lovely cunt. Then she pulled away and rolled over on her back, chest heaving, fucked out.

We had drinks after that, Linda still nude on the couch and her husband and I sitting near enough to fondle her. 'That was a first,' Steve admitted. 'I suppose it was bound to happen, bringing in another man. Actually, it was a real turn-on seeing Linda like that with you—'

'No regrets then?' I asked but it was clear they had none. That night the insatiable Linda slept between the two of us and we kept going until dawn. We sucked and fucked until exhausted, only to continue where we left off when we woke. I still visit them, although I have since married again. In time I hope my wife will agree to make up a foursome . . .

Edward M., Somerset

Dick on the Dole

I've been shagging myself stupid with a married woman who lives down our street. I'm unemployed so I've got time on my hands. Fucking her is a great way of spending a few hours every day. Don't blame me, and don't blame her. It's her nutty husband's fault for not giving her what she wants. He works every hour there is so that he can go bird-watching all over the country. It's his whole life, so his Isabel turned to me for some light relief. He may be keen on birds but I reckon I'm the one who gets the real eyeful. Every day, in fact, for his wife loves showing me all she's got. With her two kids off to school for the day, she half-lowers an upstairs blind as a signal that she's ready, willing and available. That's when I saunter casually down the lane behind our house and she lets me in through the garage. After that, anything goes.

I mean, she's keen, and her old man is missing out. No one's going to tell me watching our feathered friends beats that. We are throwing off our clothes even as we mount the stairs. She's in her early thirties and ripe: big tits, plump arse and a hairy cunt that sucks you in and drains you dry. Isabel can give me ten years but is all the better for that, me having a letch for older girls, especially married ones.

She lets me do anything and will do anything for me. Once in the bedroom we shift the dressing table with its large mirror so that we can watch each other sucking and fucking. In our romps she's not beyond slipping off the bed as I'm about to mount her, darting round the room as I grab at her. I know what she wants, it's for me to haul her across my knees and give her cheeky arse several good smacks.

I've screwed her with her wrists and ankles tied to the corners of the bed, so she likes a bit of dom. As my name is Dominic, that's very apt. We have fucked for hours at a time. The horny thing has even said she'd like my baby, though I know she's on the pill and doesn't want any more kids.

How did I get so lucky? Well, we've known each other since she came to live in the street and I was still at school. I lusted for her then, a big-titted young woman with a gorgeous arse on her, newly married and obviously a great fuck. I went to sea with the Merchant Navy until I got paid off. One day I passed her gate and she was there.

'No work yet, Dom?' she asked and we chatted, my eyes on the big bulge of her breasts filling out her summer dress. 'You're staring at my boobs,' she teased me.

I was taken aback but had the nerve to say something like 'No wonder, Anne, they stick out like melons – what a lovely pair—'

'They're too big,' she laughed. 'You should have them wobbling about on your chest.'

That was too good a chance to miss. 'I'd love it,' I said.

Her next statement surprised and delighted me. 'Come in the house,' she said, looking about to see the street was deserted.

Opening the gate for me, she added, her voice quite calm. 'I've been standing outside feeling horny this morning. My Hector doesn't give me what I need. I saw you coming and thought "I bet that young Dominic wouldn't turn me down".'

I'd never heard a woman so bold before. I already had a hard-on.

In her living room, I reached out to feel her tits. 'Would you like to see them?' she asked, as excited as I was. She unzipped her dress at the back, pulled her arms from the sleeves and drew the dress down to her waist. She wore no slip and stood before me in just her bra with two lacy cups overflowing with luscious creamy mounds.

'Forty inches,' she giggled. 'What could you do with them?' She unhooked and tossed the garment aside, giving her tits a shimmy that made them shake like jellies.

'Play with them, I like them played with,' she told me as I stood fixed to the carpet in admiration, mesmerised by the huge pair. She held them in her hands, offering them to me. 'Go on, they won't bite you,' she teased.

But *I* could *bite* them, I thought, advancing with my hands cupped. She allowed me to heft and squeeze them, to weigh them and pull them apart. I kissed and sucked on each nipple, in absolute heaven all the while.

'Have they ever been titty-fucked?' I asked. 'They'd give a marvellous ride.'

She laughed. 'You dirty sod,' she said. 'I didn't know you were like this. You'd better try it then, seeing as you want to. But I'll want more than that later. Here, I'll get on the couch for you—' Before she did that, however, she stepped out of her dress and drew off her panties. Gloriously naked, she sat up before me, great tits thrust forward. 'Take off your clothes as well,' she said. 'You've seen me, I want to see you—'

My raging cockstand pleased her. She took it between her tits and pressed the cleavage tight around my shaft, rolling the mounds around and bending her head to suck the knob.

'Now kiss my cunt and then fuck me,' she ordered. 'I want you to come inside me, not over my tits.' The offer was a good one, even as much as I was enjoying the tit-ride. She lay along the couch, knees raised, presenting a well-furred cunt, the kind with inward-turned rolls of flesh and not the outer lippy kind. I kissed it lingeringly, tasted the sweet scent of her juice and started to tongue it, but she was impatient.

'Later, later,' she moaned. 'Fuck me now, Dom. Don't you come till you've brought me off! I haven't come with a man for ages. Hector's no bloody use. You fuck his wife for him—'

I did my best, screwing her in long and short strokes, trying not to shoot, hard as that was with my iron-hard dong gripped by her warm silky cunt. It was almost a relief to hear her cry out that she was *there, there, coming*! Her body jerked in a frenzy so I let myself go too, filling her cunt channel with the boiling contents of my aching balls. 'Oh, you sod, you've fucked me rotten,' she sighed as we rolled apart.

That's how it started and that's how it continues. I keep Isabel happy while her hubby has his own interests. I've never met a woman like her for wanting cock and it sure takes the edge off being unemployed.

Dominic, Glasgow

Lady Boss

When my firm was taken over I was made redundant from a well-salaried position and took a job as a typist. The people in my new office were so unpleasant that I thought of leaving. They set out to deliberately make me miserable. I put this down to the fact that I was far more experienced than them – three middle-aged women and a young girl of sixteen. Also, I take pride in my appearance, being tall with the figure to carry a thirty-eight inch bust, and I dress smartly in business suits. All this made them resent me, adding to the fact that the firm, although with good order books and making money, seemed to be run by accident. The office systems were out of Charles Dickens.

The owner and managing director liked me – so what's new? In the few jobs I'd had since starting as a sixteen-year-old filing clerk (I am now twenty-four) all my bosses had made advances. Mr K, my new boss was no exception. He was in his middle forties and handsome in a flamboyant way. He dressed well but ruined the effect with a slight belly. By the way he looked at my tits and touched me when leaning over to explain something, he obviously had a letch for me. He greeted me every morning in over-friendly fashion, which annoyed the others. He had inherited the business from his father but was lazy, I felt, taking days off to go sailing.

Sometimes in his office I'd almost be chased around the desk. The remarks he made were just as crude. 'You could do me a lot of good, Evelyn, with that curvy body you've got! How about it?' he'd say. He was hardly suave in his approach. 'Tell that to your wife,' I'd reply. Once he laughed and said, 'That bitch. Spending my money is her only interest. A good screw would kill her.'

'Charming,' I said coldly, refusing to call him Freddie as he'd asked me to. All the other office staff referred to him as Mr K. As for his wife, I grudgingly had to admit he was right about her, she was a snooty hawk-faced bitch. The marriage had been one of convenience, her family business being added to the present one. I knew she talked about me to the other women when she called and did all she could to humiliate me. I was made to carry parcels out to her car and take her poodle for a walk once when she visited, even though Jean, the sixteen-year-old office junior, was sitting reading a pop magazine. Still, I needed the job, so I continued, managing to change the filing system and greatly improve the style and grammar of Mr K's letters. To my surprise, he noticed all this and called me into his office one day to congratulate me.

It so happened his wife had just left, leaving me fuming as she'd sent me out on an errand. The others had smirked as I tried to keep calm. Inside his office he regarded me as ever, mentally undressing me, his eyes boring into my blouse as if baring my breasts. He said the filing system was a great improvement, as were his letters – and for once the post was going out on time.

'I'm putting you in charge of cash flow,' he said 'Old Mrs Dean is built in here with the bricks – but she's about as much use as the Pope's balls. Take over, clear out that unused office and get what you need to make it habitable. Chase up our customers to make sure their payments are on time. You'll get a commensurate increase of salary, of course.'

I was still raging inwardly from his wife's visit and the promotion did little to assuage my temper. 'They won't like it out there but I can deal with that,' I said grimly.

He laughed. 'I'm sure you can, I know they've been giving you a hard time. Kick ass all you want, I'll stand by you.'

It was the opportunity I'd been waiting for. 'I could make your office into an ultra-efficient operation,' I told him. 'Change the whole system for the better—'

'I might well consider that,' he said cunningly, rising from his desk and coming to stand close, my breasts almost touching his chest. 'With cooperation from you, of course, Evelyn. What do you say?' With that he put his arms about me, pulling me tight to him, my tits pressed to his jacket, his belly warm against mine. He stood like that as if awaiting my agreement.

I felt his prick stir and start to rise directly against my crotch. I did not feel excitement but realised it was a classic case of killing two birds with one stone: being in charge of the office administration and getting one up on his hateful wife. I therefore forced a smile and nodded.

'Gawd,' he exclaimed forcefully, 'have I waited for this! You won't be sorry.' I felt I was in the hands of an impatient lecher and wanted it to be over quickly, in fact that was what I expected.

How wrong can you get? He kissed me lingeringly, pushing his tongue into my mouth while his two hands cupped and rolled my boobs around sensuously and gently. For a big man his touch was light and erotically titillating. His mouth was expert too, open and moist and his breath was sweet. I returned the kiss, somewhat bewildered by the sudden surge of passion aroused in my lower depths.

'Let me see them,' he said. 'I've always longed to. Show me your gorgeous tits—'

I helped him take off my clothes. My blouse and bra were cast aside and he buried his face in the warm flesh of my cleavage, kissing all over the rounded flesh, sucking my nipples until I gave out little moans and held each breast up in turn for his attention.

'Let's both undress,' he said, leaving me to turn the key in his office door. I stepped out of my skirt and took off all I wore, noting him eyeing me hungrily as he threw off his jacket and pushed down his trousers. Nude, he was a mass of hair, reaching from his chest down to a thick and upright penis as big as any I'd encountered.

He swept away the clutter on his desk and lowered me across it – it was a classic boss and secretary scenario, but I didn't care. Now I was as eager as he was, reaching out to grasp the thick pulsing girth of his manhood, wanting it so much that my cunt was opening like a flower and actually throbbing with the sensations that coursed through it. I straddled the desk, my bottom on the edge, legs wide apart and bent up at the knee as I gladly offered my sex to him. He bent to suck and tongue it, making me grasp his head. I came off with jerky motions, thrusting into his face, and then he stood between my legs, poised upright with his menacing prick directed to my cleft. My arms about his neck, my legs circling his waist, I told him urgently, 'Yes, oh yes, give it to me. Fuck me!'

Its thickness filled me, its length penetrated to my deepest recess. I jerked my hips madly to his shafting, aware I was being gloriously screwed by a master cocksman. Not until I had climaxed so many times that I lost count did he grunt and thrust faster, soaking my cunt with a lasting volley of his hot emission.

'When did you last have it?' he asked cheekily as we dressed after the bout. 'Or are you always so hot for it?' It had been some time, I admitted.

That I was his mistress from that moment on I gladly accepted. I slept with him on business trips, on his cabin cruiser, in his bed when his wife went to a health resort and we fucked at odd times when the letch was on us in his office, his car and at hotels. As for being in charge of the running of the office, after that they all sucked up to me and trembled when my eye was on them.

Jean, the office junior, stopped reading her teenage magazines and took over my old post as typist, showing great promise. At least she did after I caught her wasting time and ordered her to my office. I really can be a brute. After threatening her with the disgrace of instant dismissal, I offered punishment instead. I didn't think it was in me, but I enjoyed having her raise her skirt and draw down her knickers so I could give her smooth bottom several good whacks with a plastic ruler. She left tearful but thanked me for not dismissing her. After that she improved in her work and I became aware that she had a crush on me.

As you can tell, I run a tight ship. Only the boss tells me what to do and I love it when he does!

Evelyn, Southampton

Some Other Man's Wife

My name is Jonathan. I am twenty-seven and have a shop that sells flowers, an unusual occupation I guess for an ex-paratrooper. My family owns a market garden and we grow blooms of all kinds as well as vegetables and fruit. As a kid I learned to make wreaths and floral decorations, so on leaving the army I took over the family shop. It's not really much more than a one-room place with a flat above, where I live. It suits me and the work is profitable. I'm single and I've had a few girlfriends up in my pad. Best of all was a married woman I'll call Lena, which is near enough her name. For fucking and allowing me to do everything a kinky young stud likes, I've never met her like and that's the plain truth.

She came to browse in my shop one morning. I reckoned she was about thirty or so. She was lovely, no common piece, dressed smartly in a short jacket and summer dress with a silk scarf knotted carelessly around her throat. Her figure was shapely and slender with curves in all the places I liked: breasts that swelled out of her dress and a fine round arse. I sat at the back of the shop and let her look around, thinking how much I'd love to fuck her. She was married, no doubt, probably with a couple of kids. At last I went to attend to her, thinking what a sweet face she had. Then it struck me that I'd seen her before, looking in the shop window but never entering.

We chatted and, after discussing roses and such, she

said it was unusual to find a fit young man like myself in a florist's shop. Usually women did such work. I told her I'd seen her looking in several times, feeling there was something about this lady that intrigued me. She didn't leave, even when other customers came and went, and I didn't want her to. She said she'd been married ten years and had four children, all at school. I said I was a bachelor. The atmosphere became tense as we talked. Was she hovering about for me to make an advance, I thought? Surely not a nice respectable woman like her?

I closed the shop for my lunch break, taking the chance to ask her up to my flat for a coffee. She agreed readily. Up there in my sitting room, I pushed it, saying if I was still single it was because I hadn't found a woman like her. 'Do you think so?' She said, her eyes lowered to the coffee cup in her hands. 'In that case, do you want to make love to me?'

You could have knocked me over with the proverbial feather. 'More than anything,' I told her. 'God, yes! Why me?'

She said simply that she'd seen me unloading the delivery van and had liked the look of me. Lucky old me!

I didn't argue but led her into my bedroom where she let me undress her and kiss and fondle her. 'You undress too,' she said, 'I want to see you naked.'

I had nothing to worry about there, I thought immodestly, my army training leaving me with a good physique. The rampant chopper I revealed when I kicked off my Y-fronts matched most I'd ever seen. She sat up on the bed watching me undress, her lovely milk-white boobs sticking out, a dark mass of hair at her crotch. I saw her look at my cock, impressed I could see by its thick eight inches. I bent to kiss her and she clasped my dong, and stuck out her chest as I fondled her tits. She parted her

73

legs and my hand went to her split, pushing sticky fingers into her moistness.

'What position would you like me in?' She asked. I told her to get on her back to begin with so that I could suck her nipples. She fell back on the bed, still holding my prick, stroking it delightfully.

She was fantastic, telling me in throaty tones that she loved the feeling as I fucked her, the feel of my big prick slipping in and out of her cunt. We merged together as if we were one person, our bodies thrashing up and down, pubic bones clashing, groaning out our lustful pleasure, urging each other on in the lewdest terms.

'You're fucking me, fucking another man's wife!' she cried out, which no doubt gave her a thrill. 'Never mind about Richard, he's not here! You fuck his wife for him—'

I realised then that she had a 'thing' about being unfaithful to her husband, even with a comparative stranger like me. The idea turned me on too.

'Does he fuck you like this then?' I cried, shafting her strenuously. 'Is his prick as big and hard as mine? You come here any time, I'll fuck his wife for him!'

It made her lift her whole body to mine, every inch of my dick embedded up her lovely quim.

'Yes, yes, tell me that!' she screamed out. 'You fuck his precious wife for him. I love it, love it—'

Then she was helpless in her climax, gripping me as if for dear life, urging me not to stop, the middle finger of one hand up my bottom hole to the first knuckle, driving me insane with lust. I was unable to prevent myself shooting wads of hot spunk up her passage. She flopped about below me, still having an orgasm as I was withdrawing.

We lay and talked. She said she wasn't a bit ashamed of what she'd done. Now she would go home and prepare the evening meal with a blissful feeling, even look forward to having sex with her husband that night.

'Two men in one day tickles you, doesn't it?' I teased her. 'Not that I'm complaining. Does your hubby know you go in for a bit of rough on the side?'

She told me frankly that she couldn't resist having other men – it was a craving she had. 'At times I wonder if I'm not a nymphomaniac,' she confessed.

Her husband had no idea of her sexual adventures. With him, her children and her friends she was considered perfectly normal.

I don't know how long our association will last, but I'm more than happy to satisfy her extra-marital desires while they last.

P.L., Oxon

2. LADIES' CHOICE

Not Hard To Beat

I've always had what you'd label a strange desire, that is, I often think and dream about being spanked. When I was nineteen, outwardly a normal pretty girl working as a secretary, I had my share of boyfriends of my own age. I'd lost my virginity at seventeen and had sex with two other boys, but none of them had made me come – let alone suggest that they'd enjoy smacking my bottom. It was a nice round bum and made for it too. In all my sexual fantasies, when I masturbated, I thought of being placed across someone's knee and well spanked.

Then one night I was at a party and one of the men present was older than the rest of us, about thirty-five or forty. He chatted me up and danced with me, but I had my eye on another boy so I tried to ignore him and was quite rude. However, all the girls and boys present paired off and I was left alone until Steven approached me again.

'I'm leaving,' he said bluntly. 'If you want a lift home, I'll take you.'

I suppose I've always been the submissive type. It was the way he offered the lift – take it or leave it – that made me say I'd get my coat and go with him.

Once in his car, he said to me, 'You're an arrogant little bitch, Judy. Were you mad because you didn't get off with that pimply-faced boy? You want to live in the real world, my girl, and learn that you can't always have what you want. You need to be taken down a peg or two.'

79

'And you think you could do that?' I said, a bit intimidated by his masterful attitude but intrigued all the same. 'You're too old for me anyway. Why don't you go back to your wife—'

'I haven't got one,' he snapped, 'and if you were my wife I'd soon tame you and teach you better manners. You're a pretty thing, I could do things to you.' With that he pulled up his car and reached for me, kissing me hard on the mouth and rolling his lips over mine lewdly, his tongue probing within.

I was left breathless when he stopped, my tummy churning, wishing he had continued. He put the car in gear and moved off, saying, 'My place or yours? You've got possibilities I'd like to explore.' I still lived at home with my parents, so I heard a weak voice say, 'Yours.'

He drove to a smart block of flats while I sat shaking, wondering what I'd let myself in for, yet dying to find out. Once in his lounge he gave me a soft drink and poured a gin for himself.

'You're too young to hit the hard stuff,' he said sternly when I complained.

'You know nothing about me,' I shouted, infuriated by his manner.

'I know you are a headstrong silly girl who should be put across my knee and taught a lesson,' he answered coolly.

That, of course, silenced me and I think he knew he'd touched on a subject that fascinated me. 'You'd like that, wouldn't you, Judy?' he said in his superior way. 'Put across my knee with your lovely little bum bared to receive the punishment it deserves. Take off your clothes, we'll do this properly—'

As if hypnotised, I started to undress. He pulled up a chair and patted his knee. God, there was I naked, with my boobs trembling and my cunt on view before this complete stranger, yet I obediently went across his lap.

'Never done it before?' he enquired, his strong palms smoothing my bottom cheeks. When I murmured no, he said, 'But it's what you've always wanted, I can tell. Naughty rebellious Judy having a big nasty man smack some sense into her.'

I knew he could sense my excitement as I lay across his knee. 'This is probably going to hurt me more than you,' he joked crudely.

I clenched my bum awaiting the first slap, excited yet petrified. 'Don't hurt me,' I wailed, starting to cry but, whether in ecstasy or fear, I wasn't sure.

As if to increase my trepidation he kept me waiting. He parted my buttocks and peered into the crack, his light touch gliding over my anus and then my cunt, making me shudder with anticipation.

'Very pretty,' he announced. 'A sweet little cunt, tight as a mouse's ear. I shall take pleasure in fucking that, once I've warmed your bottom. What do you say to that, girl?'

Then the first smack descended and I squirmed, crying out, smarting, but loving it.

I received a good dozen or so slaps, then he let me off his lap and made me turn round so he could admire the pink bum he'd given me. Then he sent me to bed like a naughty girl, saying he'd be through later. I'd never met a man like him. I lay on his bed impatient for his arrival and he appeared with a drink in his hand and began to undress. His prick looked menacing and thick. He told me to kiss it, then he was beside me, fondling my tits and sucking my nipples and even going down to lick my cunt. In my excitement I wanted him to do all these things. I returned his kisses and grasped his prick.

'Turn over,' he ordered. 'We'll do it from the rear.' I was on my hands and knees for him in a second. Then I felt his

81

hardness enter me, pushing right to the farthest depths of my cunt.

How he fucked me that first time! His belly hard against my raised bottom, he went quick and slow in turn until I was crying out in my first shuddering climax and bumping my bottom back to him for more. I came two or three times until he withdrew, having drenched me with his spunk.

I lay face down on the bed utterly spent but never happier, having my first bottom-smacking and first orgasm all in the same session. Both my arse and my cunt felt on fire as never before. Before I left I asked him if I could call again – for more of the same, of course.

On subsequent visits it was routine to get my panties pulled down and my bare bum spanked until it throbbed. We then fucked in his bed, sometimes throughout the night if I'd told my mother I was staying with a friend. And so I was, in a manner of speaking though hardly the sort of friend she would have approved of.

Steven gave me what I wanted over the next two years until I got married. My husband thinks spanking is a perversion and refuses to do it. So it was not too long after the honeymoon that I called on Steven again. Needless to say he's always glad to oblige.

Judy, Essex

82

Out of the Window

When Justin and I got married we returned from our honeymoon to stay with my parents. That didn't work, kind as they were, as we wanted privacy. I saw an advert in a shop window for a top flat to let so I went to see it. It was a large Victorian house with three storeys. I'm quite a big girl and the man who answered the door was tall and broad, a retired policeman in his fifties who made no bones about staring at my boobs filling my tight sweater. He showed me over the rooms at the top of his house, all the time making me feel he was mentally undressing me, his eyes boring through my clothes, picturing my tits, cunt and bum. Anyway, I got the tenancy and Justin and I moved in.

Our landlord was called Grimes and whenever we passed on the stairway or in the hall his hand always seemed to brush my hip or bottom. I knew he lusted after me but the rent was reasonable and, as Justin was just learning his job as a double-glazing salesman, I put up with his sexual remarks and touching. I was just starting my first pregnancy too. One day I went into Mr Grimes's living room on the ground floor to pay the rent and he waved it aside. Straight out, he said he fancied me and I could keep the money if I did him a favour – join him in bed that afternoon. I was tempted, being a saver and liking nothing better than depositing what I could in our building society account. As I was in the first month or so of being pregnant he couldn't put me in the family way. He was also a strong

83

and handsome man who towered above my Justin.

I shook my head, however, deciding not to take up his offer, though the thought of earning money as a prostitute was something of a turn-on. The next day I was going downstairs to go shopping when he called me from his bedroom on the second floor. I went in to find him still in bed and asked if he was ill. 'Just having a lie-in,' he said and asked me if I'd bring back his daily paper. 'See what you do to me, lass?' he said suddenly, drawing back the duvet.

He only had a pyjama top on, so I saw his hairy legs and between them a massive prick that reared up from large balls, a lengthy shaft of a size and girth I'd never imagined. It seemed to throb and pulse it looked so engorged, with an uncapped red helmet as big as a hen's egg. My God, it looked twice the size of Justin's equipment and my knees went weak and my cunt twitched at the sight of such a monster.

'How would you like to sit on that, Mrs B?' he enquired. 'You'd love it and I'd make it worth your while – a week's rent. What do you say, just between us?' I fled out of the room, but thought about that huge cock all the time I was shopping, wondering what that would feel like up me.

A day or two later he came up to my flat to lend us an electric kettle. I made him tea in the kitchen, then stood at the sink washing up the cups. Directly before me was a window overlooking the side of the house and a narrow alleyway that ran alongside it, much used as a shortcut by people going through to a nearby shopping centre. I could see my mother and aunty approaching at the far end so I raised the window and called out to them as they passed below. To speak to them better, I leaned over the sink gripping the taps, my head well out of the window.

'Watch you don't fall out, our Daphne,' warned my

mum, as I gave an involuntary leap as I felt Grimes's hand slide up my leg below my skirt.

I got my quim felt through my knicker gusset, his big hand cupping my cunt bulge and his middle finger stroking my outer lips slowly and provocatively through the thin cotton material. Still trying to maintain a normal conversation with my mother and aunt, my throat tightened and my cunt wept with the effect of the touching-up I was getting.

'You like it,' Grimes whispered lewdly from behind me. 'You're soaking your pants, gel. Let's get 'em off and have a real feel—'

'Can we bring you back anything from the shops?' my mum called up to me. I shook my head. All that I needed right then, excited as I was by the intimate titillating I'd received from the hand of my randy landlord, was a continuation of the same. That I was to get it was certain for, as I'd made no protest and indeed my cunt had given me away further by moistening so copiously on his hand, Grimes was now in the process of drawing down my panties.

He had lifted my skirt and draped it over my back so that, as he pulled the briefs clear of my bottom, I presented him with my bare buttocks as I leaned forward out of the window. Naughty me! I got a tremendous thrill imagining just what he could see: my plump arse cheeks and the bum cleavage that he was even then parting with his hands to reveal the tight puckered ring of my bottomhole and the hanging split bulge of my cunt with its surrounding mass of hair.

I'm sure my voice was a mere croak as I thanked my mother and said I didn't need a thing from the shops. I was lifting each foot in turn at the same time to allow Grimes to discard my knickers completely. His hands stroked both bum cheeks slowly and sensuously as if savouring the feel. He was taking his time.

'Lovely arse,' he was muttering from behind me, 'I could eat it. In fact, I bloody well will.' His face pressed into my bottom as he knelt down and I automatically parted my legs for him. A warm tongue lapped and licked me, the tip teasing my opening, making me wriggle and stick my bum out for him.

'What's up with your voice?' my mum called up from below. 'You sound so throaty, have you got a cold coming on?'

Something else was coming on, a surging eruption in my lower stomach that was transmitting quickening tremors to my tongued cunt – the helpless beginning of a shattering climax! Grimes stood up just as I was beginning to jerk my rear, desperate for the come he'd brought me to the verge of. Then I felt his prick, so big and stiff, nestle between my cheeks, poking its bulbous knob to my cunt lips. How I wanted it!

'What a pretty cunt you've got, it's just begging for the prick,' I heard Grimes grunt from my rear.

'Fuck it then,' I urged him through gritted teeth, still facing down at my mother and aunt in the alley. 'Fuck my cunt! Do it! Fuck me—'

It was with an audible gasp of relief that I felt his hard length slide right up me, touching the sides as they say. I lost all attempts to control myself as he began shunting it up to the hilt before withdrawing and thrusting into me again. His balls pummelled my bum cheeks, his hands gripping my hips as he stood behind me, fucking me like I'd never known. At one end I tried to keep my head and shoulders still, at the other I gyrated and tilted my rear to gain every lovely inch of his cock. I came powerfully, my body racked from end to end with shuddering spasms, and felt Grimes buckle against me and stifle his gasps as he flooded my cunt.

'Daphne's got the flu, I think,' my aunt said from below. 'I could see her shiver from down here. Off to bed with you, girl, and take something for it—'

Off to bed I went, with Grimes joining me, quite shamelessly allowing him to do what he liked and loving it every minute. Much of what he showed me I determined I'd get my husband to do – I was sure he'd like to try such rude things.

As for Grimes, until we managed to find our first house and got a mortgage, the rent book was duly stamped as paid-up into the final week of my pregnancy. And I can't deny that, after we moved, I called on our old landlord once or twice for old time's sake.

Daphne B, Stepney

Auntie is No Maiden

I'm a seventeen-year-old Asian girl and I live at home with my widowed mum. I hope to go to college so I spend a lot of time studying and have little to do with boys. My mother works in a shop owned by my Aunt Koomi and I help there at weekends. Aunt threw her husband out some years before as he gambled away her money. Unlike many of us Asians, auntie is not conventional. She likes a drink and a good time. Last summer she booked a holiday in Spain and treated my mother and I. I'm sure she felt sorry for us.

At first the almost complete nakedness at the beach and around the hotel pool surprised mother and I. Even older women bared their breasts and what they wore below, often a mere thong, showed all their buttocks. Soon we were in for an even bigger surprise. When we went down to the pool after arriving – my mum and I wearing long beach robes with decent one-piece swimming costumes underneath – Aunt Koomi took off her robe and stood bare-breasted, with just the tiniest triangle covering her sex. I saw men around the pool looking at her. She does have nice brown skin and her breasts were full and uplifted, with dark purple nipples so different from the fair-skinned women sunbathing topless around us.

She teased my mother and I, saying that we should show more. She said my mum had a lovely figure and I had a girlish body I should be proud to show off. Men came up to talk to us, complete strangers, and Aunt Koomi joked and laughed with them as if they were old friends. Two of the men were German and they brought us drinks and then sat with us. At dinner that night they hung about and later danced with my aunt and mum. Both women wore their saris and looked elegant. I left them to watch the film show in the lounge but noticed them at the bar, drinking, between dances – which was unusual for mother who rarely touched alcohol.

When the film ended I watched people swimming in the floodlit pool and had a coke and a hamburger. I talked to some young people my own age and agreed to meet them the next day. They were all English.

I went to the room I shared with mum and found it empty. She must be with auntie, I thought, so went to the next door along the corridor, expecting to find her there. It wasn't locked and, as I turned the handle, I heard unusual sounds coming from the room. I peeked in and got the shock of my life. The two German men were in there with my mum and aunt, all of them naked. Mother was face down on the bed with her bare buttocks raised and the man standing behind her was obviously penetrating her that way. His white skin and mother's brown body made it look very erotic. I heard her giving whimpers and moans as if extremely excited.

The other man was standing too, with Aunt Koomi on her knees gripping the erect stem of his penis and sucking the head of it with her mouth. While I watched I felt the most curious sensations surge through my stomach and my vagina pulsed and throbbed. I tore myself away before I was noticed and went back to bed.

Thinking of what I'd witnessed, I found myself playing with my sex and I had a strong climax. I couldn't get to sleep for a long while but my mother never returned to the room. She was there when I awoke next morning. She asked if I minded her going off for the day with aunt and some new friends. I knew who she meant, the men they had been having sex with.

I said nothing about what I'd seen, feeling that I was just as bad, having masturbated over it. I met my new friends. The girls were topless at the pool and I felt out of place in my one-piece. That morning I bought two bikinis and went on the beach that afternoon, with my breasts bare like every other female. Later, back at the hotel pool I saw my mother and she was topless as well, sitting at the poolside bar with my aunt and their lovers. The holiday in the sun had changed us completely.

Surgit, Yorks

Insatiable

A young man at my work came on strong and hinted he'd love to have sex with me, even though I'm over twice his age. I'm a forty-four-year-old married woman and had never been with any other man but my husband. I considered he was just having me on, me being what you'd call comfortably built and he a handsome boy who could have had his pick of girls. I refused him but secretly regretted it when he didn't approach me again. Then, at an office drinks party, I plucked up courage and asked Ken if he'd drive me home. He jumped at the chance.

I knew what he'd expect and it made me tremble with excitement and feel like I hadn't felt for years. We drove out of town and parked and began a heavy-petting session. He got me terribly worked up as we french-kissed and I allowed him to put his hand inside my blouse to fondle my breasts and squeeze and tweak my nipples. It was like being a teenager again and I loved it. But when he put my hand on his stiff penis and attempted to feel between my legs, saying we should use the back seat to make love, I took fright and asked him to drive me home. He was obviously very disappointed but agreed to stop and deliver me to my house.

My husband was asleep in bed when I went up. I was a shaken woman and aroused as never before. I undressed, finding the crotch of my knickers soaking from the flow of moisture between my legs brought on by Ken's kissing and cuddling. I wished then that I had let him go all the way with me, that it was his youthful body I was getting into bed with. I was heady with the memory of how long and hard his penis had felt in my hand. I deliberately left off my nightie and slipped in beside my husband, pushing my breasts and crotch against his back, reaching into his pyjama trousers. He complained that he was tired and promptly went back to sleep.

I had never felt so frustrated in my life. Lying apart from my husband, I thought back to the delightful petting session with Ken; how it had got me so excited that I'd been kissing him with a wet open mouth as if I could swallow him. My hands cupped my breasts and I pulled my nipples just as he had done. They were still stiff from his touching. I felt down to the moistness of my cleft and did something I had not done for years – I masturbated. On my back, with my husband sound asleep beside me, I parted and stretched my legs, stifling my moans and sighs as I fingered myself to orgasm. My thoughts ran riot, imagining it was Ken's young cock inside me, that he was at home bringing himself off by hand just like me.

The following day, my mind full of what might have been, I took a chance and surprised myself. It's amazing what a strong sexual urge will make a normally quiet and respectable woman do! I told my husband that an audit was taking place at my work and I'd be late home. He was going to his indoor-bowls meeting anyway. Then at finishing time I waited by Ken's car. My standing there in the dark was enough. He held open the car door for me and, once inside, we kissed as if desperate for each other. This time, I told him, I was his to do with as he liked. I wanted it! He nodded eagerly and drove off to his little flat, saying how he'd fancied having me and longed to get the chance.

Once inside, I noticed the untidy room and unmade

bed but didn't care. I was in his arms as soon as he closed the door. As we kissed I told him how I'd regretted not allowing him to have sex with me the night before, that later I'd wished he'd forced me, for I had really needed his hard young prick. As he guided me to the bed, he said he had often pictured me naked as I passed his desk, my blouse bulging with my large breasts and my skirt moulded temptingly round my buttocks, that he'd ached to reach out and pull my clothes off.

I couldn't remember being talked to like that and it made me go weak at the knees. Suddenly I had to let him see everything – my full breasts, the thick thatch of hair covering my pussy mound and my curvy plump bottom. My husband hardly noticed me any more. Ken looked at me with eyes alight with joy and gratitude. He had me lie across his bed while he played with my breasts and made a close inspection of my vagina. Then he wanted me to roll over on my hands and knees, bottom raised with legs parted, while he made a close investigation of what one can see from that position. It was while I was so placed that he fondled and fingered me internally, making me wriggle on his hand and give little squeaks of pleasure.

'Put it in that way,' I suggested in a lather of tremendous arousal, knowing only what I wanted and not caring how it sounded for a woman to offer herself like that. 'Go on,' I urged him. 'Please! Please fuck me.'

'That's just what I'm going to do,' he said almost in a growl, directing his hardness between my cheeks and entering me, the full length penetrating and filling my channel until I felt his soft balls nestling in my bottom divide. I glanced back to see him standing naked, then he curled over me, his hands reaching around to grip my breasts.

'Oh, yes!' I heard him grunt. 'What a tight cunt you've

got. Thrust your arse back, Stella. Have I looked forward to screwing you! Fuck! Fuck! I've wanked myself silly thinking about shafting you. I just knew you'd love the prick up your cunt—'

His hot words and the iron-hard bar of flesh probing so deeply, had me yelling out with pleasure. It was heaven, pure heaven, made all the more exciting by the way I was being taken. I felt wide open and defenceless against the buffeting I received, powerless to do anything but be used and enjoyed, stripped of all shame and dignity in my lust. Had there been other men in that room I would have let them all have their way with me, such was my abandoned lust as Ken thrust into my now-insatiable cleft. I came and came again, screeching out my delight.

Of course, once initiated to these pleasures, I wanted more. My visits to Ken's flat continued throughout the winter and we made good use of his bed. So, I had a toy-boy and returned to my husband sated after evenings supposedly spent working late or visiting friends. Of course the day came when I called at his flat and he had a girl of his own age there. I returned home and cried, glad my husband wasn't there to witness the scene. Then I took a long bath, followed by a stiff brandy, and decided that I would share Ken if that's the way it had to be. And that's the way it is. These days, I'm just insatiable!

Stella, Wolverhampton

Co-respondents Course

For years my husband and I felt guilty about sex. Then one day I came across his secret horde of girlie magazines. I sat and read through the letters and realised my long-repressed desires were normal – in fact, others wrote of things I'd never imagined! Reading about them made me bring myself off by hand. For once I didn't feel bad about it. Then I told my husband I'd found his mags, and wanted to share them with him. I well remember his delight when I offered to take his erect penis in my mouth. I loved it, the way I made him squirm and groan. Though he said he would not come in my mouth, I carried on and swallowed his spunk. Then he licked my cunt for the first time.

From that we began to share new delights in the privacy of our bedroom, the living room, the kitchen – wherever the urge took us. I found going about naked most arousing and flaunted my breasts and cunt before him, making him reach for me. To make up for lost time we tried all the variations and positions – even anal sex. The 'forbidden' nature of it made me wild with excitement and we repeated it at times.

All of this was too good not to want to share. I passed over the magazines with some of the better letters to my best friend, Myra, a woman who had also admitted that her sex life with her husband was not all that terrific.

When I called on her some days later she agreed with me that reading the sexy letters had been quite a turn-on, saying that some of the activities were what she had always dreamed of. I confessed that I'd always been ashamed of my fantasies. We had a laugh about it and talked frankly about our likes and dislikes. It so happened that we both became randy with all the sexy talk.

'I feel like having it,' Myra admitted shyly. 'But Doug would wonder what was up if he came home and I draped myself around his neck and told him to fuck me. After fifteen years of marriage you wouldn't say our sex life was a wild romp. I don't mind admitting that some afternoons, when my work in the house is done, I go up to bed and bring myself to orgasm.' She smiled when I showed surprise. 'I do it regularly, Diana, I enjoy a good come. I even sent away for a couple of vibrators I saw advertised. They're a great advance on using your fingers—'

'I've seen pictures of them,' I said, full of admiration for Myra's initiative. 'But I've never seen a real one.' That, of course, was almost asking her to produce the objects. You never know, do you? There was Myra, a long-time close friend, and I never dreamed that she pleasured herself with sex-aids.

Myra told me to follow her upstairs. In her bedroom, she unlocked her jewel case and brought out a vanity bag, opening it to take out a pair of phallic-shaped objects. One was black, the exact replica of a male penis, some seven inches long and complete with raised veins and a perfectly shaped plummy helmet. It had big balls too. The other one was even bigger, a white plastic vibrator with ribs on the side. Myra showed me how the end came off to insert batteries.

'My lovers,' she said laughing selfconsciously. She cradled the dummy prick in her hands, gently massaging its thick length between her slim fingers. 'It makes me want to do it now,' she confessed. 'Just the sight of it gets me aroused. Unlike my Doug, it always gives me satisfaction.'

You could have cut the atmosphere with a knife. Her look at me was hopeful, as if begging my permission. 'Use it if you want to, Myra,' I said in a small voice, shaking with emotion myself. 'I'll leave if you want me to—'

'No,' she said firmly, obviously determined that we were at the stage where we had nothing to hide. 'It would be more fun for you to be here. I've imagined people watching me while I masturbate and it always gets me terribly excited. Shall I show you my usual routine—?'

'Yes, do,' I agreed, 'I may learn something.'

'Well,' she said, 'when I've finished my housework my mind turns to relieving myself. I try to resist the temptation but I always give in. What the hell, I tell myself, what harm is there? So I come upstairs. I undress completely and stand before the long mirror admiring myself and holding my breasts and touching myself down there. Is it all right if I say *cunt*?'

'That's what it is,' I giggled. 'Tits and cunt is what we have, isn't it? Geoff uses those words now when we fuck. It does add to the occasion using rude words.' My cunt was flowing with lubrication at that moment. I *wanted* to see Myra naked too. Some of my fantasies included females – especially a form mistress I'd once had a crush on. By now I was trembling outwardly. 'Go on, undress then, Myra,' I said shakily. My excited state could hardly pass unnoticed.

'You too,' she said, her voice sounding as strained as mine. 'Join me.' She began to strip, hurriedly draping her clothes over a chair, at last facing me in the nude. Her breasts were bigger than mine and they thrust out temptingly.

I hesitated before undressing, feeling a poor match for Myra's voluptuousness. But when I did she praised my figure. I felt almost shy when she took my arm and guided

97

me before the long mirror. Staring back at us were two thirty-something women with tilted breasts and hair-covered mounds at the forks of their thighs. Myra slipped an arm around my waist, her touch electric on my skin. She half-turned to me and, as if it was the most natural thing in the world, our lips met and clung, her tongue sliding wetly into my mouth. When we drew our faces apart she cupped and lifted one of her large full breasts. The nipple seemed to darken, swell and direct itself at me. With a long sigh, I sucked upon it greedily.

Thus we stood, bodies touching, while I suckled until she offered the other nipple, her hand meanwhile searching between my thighs and a finger insinuating itself into my cleft.

'You're so wet down there,' she murmured. 'Come to bed with me, my darling. Let me love you properly—'

My mind was in turmoil as she led me to her bed, but my body was unable to resist. 'You've done this before?' I asked, feeling now that Myra was in complete charge and I was her passive subject.

'Not for some years now,' she said. 'Before I married Geoff there were two special women lovers. I'm bi-sexual and I want to do it with you so much—'

She laid me on the bed and kissed and caressed me, her touch so much lighter and gentler than a man's. I returned her kisses, madly aroused, reaching for her breasts, my fingers in her warm wet cunt. Then it was I felt something firmer and rounder gliding over the outer lips of my cunt. I looked down over my breasts and stomach to see Myra with the black dildo in her hand.

'Try it, Diana, you'll love it,' she encouraged me. 'It's worked for me so often. I'm really awful, I lie back fucking myself and fantasising that some big black stud is up me. Use your hands, open up yourself, you can take it all—' She inched it into me until I felt the whole length filling me, then she moved it back and forth until I was rearing up my bottom, urging her to give it me faster.

We stayed together all that morning and into the afternoon, pleasuring ourselves and discovering the delights of our bodies. For the first time I looked properly at another woman's cunt, parting the lips, fingering her clitoris, then going down to suck it. Myra did as much for me in the sixty-nine position – at which we soon became expert.

My calls became frequent and she visited my house to return the favour, while my life at home and sex with my husband seemed to get better and better. The more you get the more you want, I suppose. Myra too was likewise affected, informing me happily that she'd got Douglas interested in her again by being the initiator in their sex life – and that now he was doing his stuff with her almost nightly.

Myra and Doug came to dinner one night. The soft lights, sweet music, wine and dancing soon made us all amorous. Before the night was out, I was on my husband's knee, kissing and fondling openly while Myra and Doug did the same. We two wives further encouraged the men with a striptease, then we were fucked on the rug by our husbands, Myra and I lying side by side and holding hands as we were laid. Later we swopped partners and, with Doug's prick up me, I watch Myra squatting up over Geoff, working herself up and down feverishly on his shaft. Later, when the men had been exhausted by their efforts, Myra and I gave them a demonstration of female loving. Neither minded, in fact they applauded us for a good show. Little did they know we'd been expert at it for almost a year by then.

D. J., Leics

The Silent Type

My boyfriend gives me the silent treatment in bed. He doesn't utter a sound when he fucks me. I know he enjoys sex and is very skilful, always making me climax – often twice – before he comes himself. He's not shy, but is a manly type, a bit bossy. I don't mind this, I rather like being made to do as he tells me, but his silences when we make love is alien to me – I like being worked up with dirty talk – but he kisses, sucks and fucks me without a word.

We are both twenty-six and have had other lovers. In my case, I've had two who used to tell me how much they loved fucking me and what it felt like to be up a juicy cunt, even that I was a slut and a whore. I loved it. It made me wildly responsive. I want this with Alan, but when I urge him on during sex and beg him to tell me how he loves fucking my cunt or sucking my tits, he tells me to shut up and concentrate. Not that he's not good at it. His bigger-than-average cock touches my deepest recess, poking its plum head right back to my cervix, giving me body-sapping undulations as I come. Isn't that enough? he says.

One afternoon, playing naked on our bed, I sucked him off and he hardly made a sound. I liked it with other lovers who used to call me 'a dirty cocksucker' and 'a filthy cow' as I made them shoot in my mouth. I mentioned this to Alan, complaining that, apart from a few suppressed grunts

100

as he drenched my throat, he didn't seem too excited by my gobbling his cock.

'You bloody bitch,' he told me, 'I said I don't like talking when I'm fucking. Can't you get that through your head?'

When I argued further he grabbed me and drew me over his knee, using the hard palm of his hand to belt my bum, giving it a proper smacking until I was crying out for mercy. I got up and went to the wardrobe mirror when he'd finished, to look at my pink bottom. I felt very aroused and – there was a warm glow in my cunt. I went back to him on the bed and snuggled up, begging *his* forgiveness.

It was the first time that I'd been smacked by a man and I found it terribly exciting. I know I'm the passive type and that I enjoy humiliation. Although Alan wasn't interested in insults and crude talk, I found him terribly horny because he put me over his knee and slapped my bum.

Within seconds he had thrust his prick up me with a vengeance and fucked me savagely. We were both out of control and he didn't object as I screamed out to him to 'Fuck me, fuck me harder, you cruel beast!' When we had both come we lolled apart, steaming from our exertions.

Maybe I had a strong silent type but I found that doing small annoying things was the excuse he needed to drape me over his knee with my panties down. Thereafter I had my bum smacked regularly and he seemed to like me crying out that he was a beast or a swine. He always had a huge erection after punishing me and we had lots of good fucks.

Our little games have now proceeded to mild bondage. He ties my wrists and ankles to the bedposts and smacks my upraised bottom before mounting me urgently. I may miss out on vocal encouragement with him but I'm quite happy to settle for our bottom-paddling session before we fuck. Still, it's a pity I haven't got both and I tell him that just to hear him order me to take off my knickers and bend over his lap. I know what it always leads to – a great session of screwing.

Pamela, Croydon

Taking Matters in Hand

I know I shouldn't have, but I read my daughter Justine's diary one day when tidying her bedroom. I discovered that she had had sex with several men, two at a time, when on holiday in Greece that summer. It was so descriptive that I couldn't put it down, full of lurid details of what she had done and how the men compared. She was a nineteen-year-old nurse so I didn't expect that she was still a virgin but, my goodness, she appeared to be a nymphomaniac. She had done things I'd never tried, even with my husband. And reading about her doing such things with so many men gave me a totally unexpected feeling of excitement. Any man who had entered that room could have had me there and then. Mid-morning though it was, I lay back on her bed and masturbated for the first time in years.

Ashamed, but helpless to resist, I hitched up my dress, put a hand inside my knickers and fingered myself. All the time I was fantasising about what my daughter had done – like being naked at a party on holiday and sucking the sperm from two men who later slept on each side of her. I tried to imagine what it would be like, with two mouths and four hands at her breasts and vagina, both taking her throughout the night. I brought myself to a gasping, shuddering orgasm, the most strength-sapping I had ever experienced. When I had recovered, embarrassed and shocked at my actions, I had to admit that it had been a tremendous thrill, even if only brought about by my own fingers.

It would not happen again, I promised myself, but the pleasure I had obtained filled my thoughts. My husband rarely gave me any kind of orgasm and I didn't expect him to any more. That same night, my mind still full of the thrill of satisfying myself so delightfully, I actually cuddled up to him in bed and asked him to make love to me. He had the surprise of his life, especially when I played with his penis and shyly asked if he would like me to suck it – something which I'd never agreed to do. The poor man got so excited he ejaculated into my mouth. I discovered that I liked that too and the way he was helplessly out of control while I sucked him. Before morning I approached him again, much to his delight. He asked me what had come over me but he was not complaining! That time we had full sex and, while he was penetrating me, I thought of all the dirty things I'd read in the diary and came off strongly, pleasing my husband no end.

So, a sneaky look at Justine's diary has made me a changed woman. I suppose it had always been in my nature, but I had dismissed it as 'not nice'. I have not given up pleasuring myself. I do it several times a week and it really does relieve stress and is also great fun. More women should try doing it for their health and wellbeing. I told my husband I do it 'occasionally' and he was tickled pink. He said it's like having a new wife and insists I do it while he watches. I've acquired one or two vibrators and they give me multiple orgasms, which I would never have thought possible. I've certainly taken myself in hand this past year!

Doreen, Notts

Inside the Wendy House

I was forty-two years old, married with teenage kids and could be described as pleasantly plump. Hardly the type, you would say, to allow a young stud to have his wicked way with me! To help the family income, I went to work in a local estate agents. Tim was one of the staff, a brash youth in his early twenties who spent a great deal of time chatting up several young girls on the payroll. He even teased me about my big breasts, asking me what size they were. The other girls in the office all avoided him. I heard he'd taken them all out at times and afterwards gave broad hints he'd seduced them.

We were handling the sale of a new estate and it was arranged I would take charge of the fully furnished show house. Tim took me there in his car to show me how to fill in the paperwork if someone wanted to purchase. He also pointed out the features I should inform buyers about. We were in a bedroom when he suddenly put his hand on my bottom, cupping my cheeks and giving them a squeeze. I should have been annoyed, but the most curious feeling was kindled in my stomach. I did tell him to keep his hands to himself, but that only made him laugh and take me in his arms.

'You're so cuddly, Wendy,' the young flirt told me. 'I've fancied you in the office. God, I'd love to see your tits, they're real handfuls. I bet your old man likes to play with them.'

105

'Don't you dare speak to me like that,' I said, but the feeling in my stomach persisted, I even felt my – all right, I'll say it – cunt moisten.

'Go on,' he said cheekily. 'Those tits were made to be fondled. I'll bet you like your nipples sucked, eh? Has he ever had a titty-ride? I would—'

'I don't know what you're talking about,' I said, telling him to let go of me. He held me close and I was further embarrassed when I felt his stiff penis pressing through my dress into my crotch.

'Let me go, please,' I said again, but this time in a small voice that gave my feelings away, making him chuckle.

'Come off it, Wendy,' he said. 'What a chance we've got alone in here. A bit of what you fancy does you good, I say. I'd just love to fuck you—'

'My husband doesn't speak to me like that,' I protested, but it was strangely exciting to hear crude talk. Then Tim kissed me hard on the lips, pushing his tongue into my mouth, making my knees go weak. A hand came between us to squeeze my breasts and I was guided back to the bed and laid across it.

Then he was undressing me, pulling off my dress and unclipping my bra, drawing off my tights and knickers. He stood back then, nodding his approval. In the wardrobe mirror across the room I saw myself laid back, my huge breasts lolling apart on my chest, a dark mass of hair covering the fork of my thighs.

He threw off his clothes, his penis rigid and threatening, leaning over me to hold my breasts and kiss them, sucking hard on my nipples. Then he sat me upright and did what he promised, putting his manhood between my cleavage and moving against me, 'titty-fucking' my breasts. This was the first time for me. When he pushed me back, he put his head between my legs and actually licked me there and put

106

his tongue inside. It made me even weaker, my tummy turning to jelly, knowing I would let him continue and wanting his big thing inside me.

'Don't you dare ever mention this in the office,' I said, raising my knees. When his cock slid into me I just held him with my arms and legs, letting him fuck me, hoping he would make me climax. Tim was not as excited as I was, taking me slowly with his thrusts.

'Oh, Lord, what are we doing?' I cried out as I began to lose control and push myself back at him, lifting my bottom from the bed, wanting it all inside me. 'Fuck me harder,' I told him. 'Make me come. Don't you dare leave me unfinished.'

'Wendy, I'll fuck you silly,' he promised. 'What a lovely buttery cunt you've got! What fabulous tits! You just lie back and enjoy it. I always bring my girls off before I shoot my load—'

He was in me so deeply, our naked bodies slapping and his balls buffeting my bottom, and I just let myself go, urging him to 'fuck me harder! Put it all up me!' Then I was gasping, juddering, throwing up my pelvis as I came and came several times.

'What a fuck, what a fuck,' I heard myself shout, then Tim was bucking faster and coming into me with great spurts.

Afterwards he brought me a glass of water from the bathroom, I was so fucked out.

That evening I couldn't help looking across at my husband doing his crossword puzzle, wondering what he would think if he knew his wife had been fucked by a young man that day. Naughty me! I had to chuckle. As for Tim, I thought that as he had had me, I was simply another notch on his gun. However, he made regular calls to the show house during my tenure there, cheekily taking my arm and leading me up to the bedroom to fuck me. I have to admit it gave me a lot of pleasure over a few months and I was sorry when all the houses were sold.

Wendy, Norfolk.

Woman to Woman

My daughter Teresa never seemed to have a boyfriend. Then she became close to a woman at her work and moved in with her. I noticed they both wore wedding rings and, although they never admitted it, I was sure they were lovers. They do often visit me but never accepted my offer to stay overnight. This made me think they liked to sleep together. I wasn't happy about this. Being a married woman and still enjoying regular sex with my husband, I just couldn't think what two women could do for each other that was as enjoyable as what a man and a woman could do. I didn't understand it at all.

I'm a skilled dressmaker and had made Teresa a dress for a special party she was going to – an all-woman affair, I was sure. I suppose it was just noseyness on my part, but I decided to deliver it to the flat where she lived with her friend. It was a large house divided into flats and a nice-looking woman of about my own age, came to the door and invited me into her downstairs flat. She said Teresa and her companion were out and offered me a sherry. What a nice woman, I thought. She said she owned the building and her tenants were all nice young females. We chatted and, thinking she would know, I asked if she thought my daughter and her flat-mate were lovers.

'All my tenants are gay,' she said easily, 'and I find nothing wrong with that. I'm the same and always have been. Have you never made love with another woman? I can assure you it's every bit as passionate as heterosexual love. Don't worry about your daughter, she's a lovely girl and perfectly happy. Of course, if you know nothing about lesbian love, I suppose you wonder what it's all about. You should try it—'

Somewhat shocked by her frankness, I froze in my chair and she came over to me and stroked my cheek. 'I can see where Teresa gets her good looks from,' she said softly. 'She's such a sweet thing—'

'Has she . . . has she been with you?' I stuttered. 'I mean, you know—' The glimpse into the lesbian world had me both puzzled and intrigued. I imagined orgies and all sorts of lewd things taking place.

'Goodness, no,' smiled the woman. 'Teresa and Janet are very much in love and faithful to each other. Have you no idea how sweet it can be to be made love to by another woman who finds you very attractive?'

She bent her head and kissed my lips, startling me, but with her soft mouth on mine, I felt confused. Within me I felt the stirrings of lust and was almost sorry when she drew her mouth away.

'There,' she said. 'There's nothing distasteful or sordid about that, do you think? I should like to make love to you. I'm sure that you would enjoy it too. Do I shock you, dear? I find you most attractive. It could be fun for both of us—'

'I don't think so,' I said, all of a tizzy. I left in a hurry.

Back at home I tried to get on with my housework but kept thinking of that woman's mouth on mine. It had been a sweet kiss and her warm tongue had penetrated to meet mine. The woman had tried to seduce me, I decided angrily, but the memory lingered, further arousing me despite myself. I felt an itching feeling in my vagina and it got awfully moist. I hadn't felt so worked up for years, and with the feeling came wild imaginings of what would have happened if I'd let her continue. I was fantasising, something I'd never done since I was a young girl. The urge was so strong that I had to lie on the bed I'd just made. I could not prevent my hand rubbing at my crotch. In a surprising short time, I had a tremendous climax, all the while thinking of that soft hot mouth on mine.

Of course, when I'd recovered, I was angry at myself. I had *masturbated*, something I had rarely done even as a girl. More disturbing was that I'd been so highly aroused by that woman's kiss and suggestive remarks. Was I that way inclined?

She phoned a few days later and I trembled with weakness just to hear her voice. 'I've been admiring your dressmaking skill,' she said. 'I've seen the dress you've made for your daughter. I'd love you to make one for me and would pay whatever you charge. Could I pop around to your house for you to measure me—?'

It was on the tip of my tongue to say 'Definitely no', but the words stuck in my throat. 'Yes,' I said weakly, feeling like a shy virgin on her wedding night.

I had to tell myself I was a straight woman with a husband who expected regular sex. So I wasn't short of *that*. Why then was I all of a dither about this woman's arrival, drinking two glasses of port left over from Christmas to steady myself, making up my face to pretty myself for her?

She kissed my cheek on her arrival, thanking me for agreeing to her request. I gave her a glass of port and had another myself while studying the very professional drawing of the dress she wanted. I was impressed when she said it was her work. We went upstairs to the spare bedroom where I keep my sewing equipment and there she peeled off her dress . In just a bra and brief panties, I saw she had an overall tan. I fumbled with the tape measure, finding her shapely figure quite disturbing. Measuring her bust and hips, in contact with her soft flesh, it was hard to remain calm.

'Why don't you come to the party?' she suggested. 'You'd be most welcome. I'm sure that with your flair for dressmaking you must have a special gown that you could wear.' I admitted that I had. She followed me, still in just her undies, when I went to my bedroom and brought the dress out of my wardrobe.

'I want to see it on you,' she said. Shyly, as if undressing before a man, I got down to my bra and panties. As her eyes roved over my breasts and thighs, my tummy flipped and my nipples and vulva tightened.

'It's perfectly lovely,' she said as I held the dress up. 'But then so are you, my dear. May I kiss you? I do want to so very much.'

To my great agitation, I was taken in her arms and her mouth clung to mine as if desperate for the kiss, her full lips rolling over mine, her tongue probing deeply. Our body contact too made me all of a flutter, our breasts squashing together, bare stomachs and pubic mounds grinding. I was lowered to the bed directly behind me and smothered in long passionate kisses which I found myself returning.

Her hands came around my back and unclipped my bra. 'Yes,' she said pleased with my bared breasts and pink perky nipples. 'They are so firm and tempting.'

I held her head as she nuzzled them and sucked on each nipple. 'Oh yes!' I encouraged her, brought to the highest pitch of wantonness I'd ever known.

I was willing to allow her to do anything with my body. She pulled down my knickers, parted my thighs with her hands and dived between them with a heartfelt moan. I felt her breath on my sex, her lips sucking on the outer lips. Then a stiff tongue entered me.

'Such a sweet cunt,' I heard her murmur as she probed

112

to find my clitoris and drive me into realms of wild ecstasy as she swirled and flicked her expert tongue over the sensitive nub. I screamed out. 'I'm coming! Oh, God help me, you are making me COME!' My thighs clamped about her ears and I bucked and heaved against her mouth.

She slid over me then, her breasts on mine, belly to belly and cunt to cunt, our pussy hair mingling. Her slow sensuous grinding against my mound was like a man. On heat, I rotated my sex back against hers. She kissed me lingeringly, her mouth wet and tasting of my own juices.

'Now you must do the same for me, my lover,' she whispered. 'Lick me. Use your tongue as I did.' Unthinkable as it was, suddenly this became an irresistible and compelling desire. She lifted her knees and offered me her cunt. She tasted like honey.

It was the first of many such encounters. I looked forward to her visits and often called at her house to make love. A complete beginner at the joys of female love, under her tutelage I was an eager pupil. I was the passive partner and she the dominant one, a skilled performer with a strap-on dildo which she used to fuck me so wonderfully with that I'd beg her for it.

Our affair still continues. Outwardly, with family and friends, I'm the same woman but it is lovely to have a naughty secret. As for daughter Teresa and her lesbian love, I don't worry about that any more.

Maureen, Canterbury

Playing Away

My husband, Ray, never gives me a climax when we make love and he gets into a temper about it. He likes to read about couples coming off together every time they make love and, though he gets angry with himself, I feel he's really blaming me. I would love to have a really strong orgasm when doing it with him. I've sometimes pretended to come when Ray fucks me, but if I act like I'm responding then he always has a premature ejaculation, leaving me worse off. He's not very expert at love-making and I'm not all that experienced myself.

I work with a man who is always particularly nice to me. When Mark suggested we go for a drink one night I thought 'Why not?' Life was pretty dull at home. It was the first time I'd ever agreed to meet another man. We had a few drinks and a good meal in a restaurant, then Mark asked if I'd like to see his house. He drove me there and of course I'd wondered if he'd try anything. I complimented him on how neat and clean he kept the place, then he put his arms around me and kissed me sweetly, whispering that he'd always thought me a lovely woman. Ray never said that to me and I allowed the kissing to go on, with Mark feeling my breasts and telling me how he longed to see them.

All of a tremble and aroused as never before, I let him do as he liked. I took off my blouse and bra, feeling shy but enjoying it when he stared at my breasts. He began to fondle them, then kissed very gently all over the mounds before

114

sucking hard on my nipples. All the time he played with them he murmured how sweet they were and how sexy I was. He took my hand down to hold his stiff penis, saying he'd like to make love to me. We stood up and undressed completely. He stood back to admire my body, which I appreciated – Ray never did that. He praised my curvy figure and asked me to turn around slowly so that he could enjoy the sight. It made me terribly excited.

When he lowered me along the couch I expected him to put it in right away. Instead, he began kissing me all over – on my eyes, nose, mouth, breasts and belly – before lowering himself between my legs. It was a shock to think he was looking directly at my pussy, which I'd never thought of as a thing of beauty with its mass of hair and crinkly pink outer lips. But he kissed me there too, as if it was my mouth, saying he could eat it. I'd never had that before, a man kissing me there and I found myself pressing my crotch to his face, feeling his tongue slip inside me. Soon I was begging him not to stop. Then I was arching my back and I had a shattering come. It was my first climax and I had come on a man's tongue!

'Please fuck me,' I begged him, wanting it so much that I didn't care about anything else.

'Yes, I'll fuck you, Jane,' Mark said. 'I've always wanted to. This is a dream come true.'

I was so agitated that I clutched his bottom, pulling him closer. I expected him to jerk about like Ray and come right away. Instead, Mark moved slow and fast in turn, thrusting and withdrawing almost completely, giving me the most delicious thrills. I cried out how wonderful it was and I climaxed twice.

Mark wouldn't let me dress afterwards, saying he loved to see my body, which I had always thought too plump but which evidently pleased him. So I sat on the couch stark

115

naked, showing off my swollen breasts and my pussy which still throbbed from his fucking. I realised that I enjoyed good sex and could climax as well as any woman with the right lover. He made coffee and we sat together naked, talking and drinking without me feeling the least bit shy. Before he drove me home, we kissed and cuddled some more until he said he'd like to make love on the lounge floor. Once again he brought me off beautifully before he came in me. When we parted I kissed him lovingly, agreeing that we would have other times together.

So began an affair that still continues. We have snatched evenings together when all we want to do is make love. It's so good having sex with him that I have no conscience about being unfaithful to Ray. My great wish is to sleep with Mark and make it an all-night session. I'm working on that, trying to find some excuse to be away from home. I don't feel like a wicked woman, just one that has to go elsewhere for satisfaction, like plenty of other wives do.

Jane, Northumberland

Titty-lation!

Although I'm a married woman, I have a girlfriend on the side, so have the best of both worlds. I adore Sheena's long, pointed breasts. I can best describe them as elongated pear shapes with thick inch-long nipples. They are rock hard and although I enjoy fondling and sucking them, they have another extraordinary use. She can use them like a prick to bring me to orgasm.

First she licks my fanny to get me opened up and moist. I lie flat on the bed with my legs wide apart over the edge. She holds one tit and can actually reach my clitoris with a nipple. This of course arouses me further as, first with one hard nipple then the other, she flicks my erect nub. I'm then eager to pull apart my cunt lips and she works the tapered end of her long breast into my gaping cleft. In my excitement I raise my knees and pull my fanny to its widest. Believe me, at times we've got almost all of one of her tits inside me.

It's an unbelievable sensation to have that up your cunt. Sheena pushes into me and I never fail to explode into a climax, especially when I position myself to get the hard tip of a nipple rub-rubbing tormentingly on my clitty. Sheena fingers herself while doing this to me, making herself come over and over again. At other times she asks me to pinch her nipples quite hard, to playfully slap her breasts and squeeze them tightly. We certainly have fun with her tits!

But there's no more erotic sight than when she draws her breast flesh from my cunt after a really good 'titty-fuck' and it is all sticky and glistening with my love juice. To show my deep appreciation I like to lick it clean for her, giving a special suck to the nipple as a thank-you for bringing me off so nicely. On my evenings at her flat, I always go home glowing and give my husband a treat, letting him do anything to me that he fancies.

Joyce, Camberwell

Even Steven

It was most embarrassing when my parents caught me having sex with my boyfriend on the carpet on their return from an evening out. We were fucking like mad when they walked in, just at that frenzied stage of starting to come and thrusting at each other. Moreover, we were both absolutely naked, with our clothes strewn over the floor. Dad went wild, screaming at my boyfriend and pulling him off me. Steve was leaping up anyway and his cock came out of my cunt with a plop and stood up like a flagpole. My mother saw it and shouted I was a dirty little bitch as I grabbed for some clothes to cover myself. What a situation! Although I'm nineteen I was ordered up to my bedroom, while Steve was practically thrown out of the house.

My next move was to find a flat where I could live a more private life. Steve and I broke up soon after, he was just a passing fancy. I remained close to my parents, of course, despite our differences and I got on better with them by living away from home. Steve and I used to get together again on an occasional basis, nothing serious. To tell the truth, he had such a lovely big cock I missed his fucking. So, after a night out together, I'd go with him to his little ground-floor bed-sit and sleep with him. On weekend afternoons if I was shopping in his area I'd see if he was around and pop in for a good fuck. After, I'd doll myself up to meet my latest boyfriend who, I felt sure, was on the verge of asking me to become engaged. To show

119

him what a 'nice' girl I was, so far we'd only petted!

One Saturday, I parked near Steve's place. From an overgrown path you could see into his room. He was usually watching the sports programme on telly with a can or two of lager, so I'd rap on the window and he'd look up and let me in. We'd get down to it at once and, afterwards, I'd proceed home with a satisfied glow. For variety, me on top or doing it doggy-style or having a sixty-nine, Steve was indeed a great stud. But that day, as I raised my hand to tap his window, I saw my mum talking to him. Then she was in his arms and they were kissing deeply, clinging together like vines.

My ma, by God! I drew back and crouched down, fascinated and tickled pink. She who had gone on at me for being such a slut! How did they get to be so chummy? I watched in amazement as they stood beside the bed taking off their clothes! Steve helped her, undoing the clip of her bra, kissing her inside leg and inner thighs as he pulled off her tights and knickers.

Then he stripped off, his huge erection bobbing before her face. I could see it all and grew excited at the sight, all the more so I'm sure because his partner was my mother. She sat up on the bed as he stood in front of her, his hands cupping her tits, which I must admit were bigger than mine. I saw her take his cock and bend her head to it, sucking on a whole mouthful. I didn't know she did that and wondered if she did it for dad. Then Steve was pushing her flat, going to her tits and sucking them before sliding lower to mouth her cunt – a routine I knew so well. Mother grasped his head and raised her knees, bucking her hips, obviously in the throes of great pleasure. Then she pulled him over her and guided his prick to her cunt.

I don't think dad could have been satisfying her, the way she raised her body to Steve's thrusts, his arse working away as he shafted her lustily. I could hear her moans and cries from outside the window, such was her pleasure in the poking she was getting.

By her agitated spasms, I'd say she came at least twice. When it was over she dressed quickly and hurried away. There was no fond goodbye kiss or lingering farewell. It was clear to me they were just enjoying each other's bodies for sex. Steve didn't dress, he just put on a dressing gown.

Eager to know just what was going on, I rapped on the window and he looked up a little startled. He let me in by the door and I said straight away, 'You rotten sod, Steve, I saw my mother in here with you. How long has all this been going on?'

As I sat on the rumpled bed on which he'd just had my mum, the pair of us chuckled over the situation. 'It must have been when she saw you and I at it,' he said. 'She always spoke to me in the street after that, asking why you and I had broken up. I had the feeling she was horny for it. She's a good-looking woman, your mum. I saw her out one day and took her for a drink, then she came back here for coffee, only we had more drink. That settled it, I tried my hand and got there.'

He sure had, I agreed, and as I discovered they'd fucked for several months, in afternoon and evening sessions when dad thought she was out with friends. Good for her, I had to say, for getting a bit of extra pleasure out of life, dad being a stay-at-home type. After all, I was using Steve for the same purpose and his dalliance with my mother hadn't affected his performance. To prove it, before I left he fucked me across the bed like he had my mum. He said we were two of a kind, fond of the dick and he was happy to supply it. Speaking for myself, I was only too happy to get it.

Pippa, Newcastle.

Sweet Vengeance

When I broke up with my latest boyfriend after I'd found him kissing my best friend at a party she told me it was a fuss about nothing. I'd gone into the kitchen of her house and found Gail and my boy in a long embrace and clinging kiss. She said it was just in the spirit of the party and didn't mean a thing. Not from where I was standing. She'd been my best friend since our schooldays and was a married woman with a hunk of a husband. I seethed inside while outwardly remaining friendly. I was determined to get back at her.

So, my revenge affair with her husband, Terry, began soon after at a dance. I'd had a few drinks and when he led me onto the floor it was one of the few slow dances the band played. We clung close and, as I'm a well-built girl, Terry had my big tits against his chest and my belly hard against his crotch. He said he couldn't understand why a girl like me didn't have a steady boyfriend. On a whim I rubbed my cunt mound against his prick and felt it, hard and rigid, through my dress. When the music stopped he went directly to the gent's instead of returning to the table, no doubt to conceal that he had a big hard-on.

For the next slow dance he took me onto the floor again and held me close. On the crowded dance floor no one could see that we were almost having a dry fuck. As Terry was a policeman, I asked if that was his truncheon I felt pressed up against me? His face was against my cheek so I

122

whispered sexy things in his ear to further turn him on.

'I'd just let you do anything to me, the way I feel,' I told him. 'What would you like to do to me, Terry?'

With his pulsating prick jammed against my crotch, he answered, 'Just give me the chance, Dawn. Can I come to your flat tomorrow evening when I finish duty?'

I whispered, 'If you want to,' and my cunt was soaking wet at the thought.

The next evening I was slightly apprehensive about what I was getting into. I'd intended to get back at Gail, but this was going all the way – Terry was no doubt expecting to fuck me after what I'd said at the dance. So when he came in, I asked if his wife would wonder why he wasn't home.

'I called her from the station,' he said. 'Working an extra shift is quite usual.' With that he took me in his arms and kissed me, his tongue darting into my mouth. I returned his kiss eagerly.

'Where's the bedroom?' he said. 'I've been desperate to fuck you all day.' Obviously Terry spoke his mind, and as we went through to my bedroom, still clinging to each other and kissing, he added, 'I've always fancied you. I can't wait to see if your tits are real. I bet you've got a lovely cunt too – just made to lick out and take my dick—' The voice was hard, his crudeness strange to me but exciting.

'Do you talk to your wife like that?' I asked as Terry pulled at my clothes.

He laughed and said, 'Not any more. Now I'm lucky if the bitch comes across once a week. Take off your bra, Dawn – by Christ, what a pair of beauties!'

He buried his face between my tits, mumbling his pleasure, seeking my nipples, sucking on them in turn. I was then lowered onto the bed and my panties removed to reveal my cunt with its bush of thick hair. He fastened his mouth over it like a starving man, sucking in my lips before inserting his tongue. It was the first time a man had gone down on me. I was out of my mind to think someone actually wanted to lick out my cunt. I pushed against his mouth, jerking in lust, and came off at once.

'That was heaven, just absolute heaven,' I gasped out as he stood up and pulled off his uniform. 'Let me do the same to you,' I offered, seeing the upright prick and, for once, eager to give head. Terry stood with legs apart as I sat up to cradle it in my hands, kissing the knob before engulfing the thick shaft.

'If only Gail could see us now,' he laughed lewdly as I sucked him, enjoying the taste on my tongue. I was excited to think of what I was doing and further aroused by his groans of pleasure and the mention of his wife. He held my head and his stomach was hard against my forehead as he began moving his hips, thrusting his prick down my throat. He's fucking my mouth, I thought. I sucked harder and he shouted as if in agony that he was coming.

'Swallow it!' he cried out and I felt his cock give several leaps and spurt jets of come into my mouth and I sucked and swallowed his load.

Then he fell across me on the bed, fondling my breasts and kissing my mouth, saying over and over how good it had been and how fantastic I was. I held him and kissed him in return. We were two lovers delighted with each other's bodies and our greed for each other.

His hand went down to my pussy, fingering me, making me impatient to take his now-limp weapon. 'You do it, you play with yourself, that'll get me going,' Terry suggested. Like all single girls I masturbated at times, but I had never thought in my wildest fantasy that I would do it while being observed. Such was my eagerness to please him, I stretched out on the bed and put my hand on my already wet and receptive cunt, using my other hand to part my outer and inner lips, showing the pink pearl of my clitty. I stroked and rubbed the taut little nub, finding myself terrifically randy, my hips moving in time with my fingering.

'Yes,' said Terry hoarsely. 'Go on, wank yourself. That's something every man would like to see a woman doing.' He stood beside the bed, rubbing his own prick as he watched, making it stiffen. By then, with his eyes glued to my wet folds, it was already half erect. I moaned and writhed, worked up to a previously unknown state of lust.

'Aren't we such dirty things?' I cried out in my agitation. 'Animals, beasts, that's what we are—' I stared at him wild-eyed. 'You've made me like this. Now fuck me, for goodness sake, Terry. Fuck my cunt before I bring myself off. Fuck me!'

It was with a great cry of relief that Terry gave me what I craved, his fully erect prick sliding into me, going deep and filling me up.

How we thrashed about on that bed, our bodies humping and crashing in our mad thrusts at each other. I felt the blunt crown of his prick buffeting the depths of my channel, its girth blocking me, loving the sliding as it shunted up and down. We were both crying out in our passion but such furious fucking was too hot to last. Terry bucked and spent himself in a last rapid flurry of jerks, while I squealed and came in continuous spasms, shaken to the core.

We did not speak for a long time after we fell apart, gulping air. 'You fucked me, you dirty devil,' I teased him, as he sat up and looked down at my heaving tits and parted legs.

'It won't be the last time either,' he grinned. 'That was the best screw I've ever had.'

I wondered how I would face Gail after that no-holds-barred session with her husband, but it is amazing how one can pretend when pushed. I found I could act perfectly

normally with her even though Terry and I were having
it off several times a week. Once she remarked to me that
he wasn't demanding sex so much of late, adding that she
wondered if he had a bit on the side. 'He's not that sort,' I
told her with a straight face. It just shows what you can get
away with.

Dawn, Norwich

Joan's New Look

I'm having a completely unexpected affair with another woman at work. This is after believing for years that lesbians must be sick. It started when I was put to work next to her in our electrical factory. We became friendly and I wondered why she'd never married, being so attractive. I'm married myself, with two teenagers at school, and always glad to get out of an evening, so I accepted Rhona's offer to go for a drink. I thought what a nice person she was and found myself attracted to her in a curious way.

At the end of the evening she asked me back to see her flat. She made coffee and sat on the arm of my chair. 'I'm glad we work together,' she said, 'I've grown really fond of you. May I kiss you?'

Her words made me tremble. After all, I enjoyed sex with my husband and never had trouble in climaxing when he fucked me. I liked his hands and mouth on my breasts and the way he touched up my cunt. Yet I wanted this woman to kiss me so I simply raised my face. She kissed me long and passionately, slipping her tongue into my mouth. I held her close and returned her kiss, unable to resist. Then her hands were clasping my breasts through my dress. She murmured against my mouth, 'They are lovely, so firm and round. Let me see them—' and then she was drawing me to my feet, leading me through to her bedroom.

I never thought it could happen to me, such sudden

excitement at another woman's touch. Standing beside her bed, we kissed passionately, breast to breast. Then she was undressing me and I helped her. At last I stood naked before her and she nodded her appreciation as she slipped out of her clothes. I stood awkwardly, waiting for her next move.

I couldn't resist looking at her sharp-ended breasts and pointed nipples, so different from my rounded heavy teats. She was shaved clean at the join of her legs too, her cunt a mere slit dividing the mound.

She pulled me into her arms again and I was thrilled by the soft womanly skin pressed against mine. I was so used to my husband's hard hairy body it was erotically exciting. What we were doing was what I'd always thought of as perverted. But her mouth was sweet and her touch was so light and sensual that I was lost.

Rhona laid me across her bed and kissed me repeatedly, all the time telling me how sweet I was, how lovely – things my husband had long given up saying. Her hands snaked over my whole body and she bent her head to suck on my nipples in turn, making me sigh and thrust out my chest while she suckled.

'You should shave there,' she whispered as she moved lower. 'It's so much nicer to kiss and tongue a cunt that's prepared for a lover.' She said this while her fingers explored my cleft, then lowered herself between my parted thighs to peer into the mouth of my cunt. I looked down between my lolling breasts to her head, poised as it was over my forested mound.

'Don't, if you don't want to,' I said in a trembling voice, hoping she would.

'Oh, but I do,' she uttered. 'Very much. I want to taste you, eat you—' Her mouth fastened wide open over my cunt as if she meant to suck it all into her mouth.

'Yes, please,' I heard myself saying weakly. 'Oh, please—'

Without hurrying she licked and lapped at me, swirling her stiffened tongue around and using the tip to nudge my throbbing clitoris until I was lifting my bottom from the bed in a torment of ecstasy. I came strongly, then came a second time, thrusting myself against her, wanting that tongue to continue its probing. I cried out, gripped her head, and bucked shamelessly in my throes. I began to sob with the utter pleasure of it, calling her my darling, my love. I had never been so beautifully licked out. My belly and cunt churned with lust and I came so many times I lost count.

She drew her mouth away to fall over my body full length, kissing me deeply, the taste of my sex on her lips.

'You *do* like it, Joan,' she said triumphantly. 'I hoped you would. Open your legs, dear, let me in between them.' I did so still extremely aroused and willing to let an experienced lesbian lover guide me. I felt her cunt mound and pubic bone press directly on mine, our vulvas mashing together. As if it was the most natural thing in the world, I curled my legs around her back, lifting myself to meet her cunt as it pushed and gyrated against mine. My hands went behind her to grip her bottom cheeks, unused to the smooth silkiness of a woman's buttocks. Gasping and muttering, we rubbed our quims together until at last we were crying out and coming simultaneously.

I drove home a disturbed and shaken woman, having to come to terms with the fact that I had been seduced by Rhona. It had been such a beautiful and erotic experience. I knew I'd be back for more and wondered if I wasn't already in love with her!

Indoors, my husband and two boys were preparing for bed. I was surprised how normally I behaved in front of them, having just come from a sexual romp with another woman. I said I wanted a bath and lay back in the warm water looking down at my breasts that had been so expertly kissed and sucked by my female lover. My cunt still throbbed from her loving.

When my husband came into the bathroom to use the toilet, a sudden urge took me. I raised my hips out of the water and showed him my pussy.

'Have you ever thought how this would look with all the hairs shaved off?' I asked him. 'They say it's more hygienic and cooler in summer.'

His interest was immediately engaged. 'Never seen a shaven haven,' he laughed. 'If you want to try it, I'll get the soap and my safety razor and do it for you.' I didn't tell him that it wasn't really for my own satisfaction.

On my next visit to Rhona's flat, a regular occasion now, she was delighted with my new look. I'm still a good wife to my husband and a willing bedmate, but I feel that, with Rhona as well, I've got the best of both worlds.

Joan K, Sheffield

Role Reversal

When my husband told me that he wanted to come to bed with me wearing my suspender-belt and stockings, I tried to treat it as a joke. We had been married only a few months and he was all man in bed – or so I thought. It knocked all the sexy feeling out of me as he begged me to let him. He said he'd always fantasised about it. I demanded to know if he was a secret transvestite. He hung his head and admitted he'd tried on my undies and dresses while I was out.

I didn't know what to think and started to cry. He took me in his arms and said it was harmless, something between man and wife, something he thought would make our sex life more exciting. I told him it was exciting enough already.

I'd been a virgin until we became engaged. He held a responsible job with good pay and was everything I thought a nice husband should be. True, he had shocked me on our honeymoon by licking my pussy, which I thought was not decent even though I got aroused and came. I flatly refused to suck his penis. As for sexual intercourse, I never had a proper climax unless he used his tongue afterwards. Now, it seemed, he wanted something else – to wear my clothes.

He held me close and kissed me tenderly, until I felt sorry for him. 'All right, Robert,' I said. 'Just this once, but if I don't like it, you must take the things off.' His face brightened up immediately and he promised me all would be well. We went up to bed with me feeling apprehensive

131

and strangely disturbed. Is this what all wives have to put up with? I wondered.

In our room, I handed over the stockings and suspenders as he got undressed. I saw he had a huge erection, his penis sticking out like a poker as he put on the garments. My strange feeling grew.

'Please don't wear your nightdress tonight, love,' he said as I reached for it. I always wore one, I didn't think it was right to sleep naked. I was a prude.

I got under the covers and he joined me, clad in suspenders and my stockings. He was really very aroused, pulling me to him much more ardently than usual, kissing my mouth and then my breasts, sliding down in the bed to lick my sex. When he came back up, I felt his penis stiff against my stomach.

'Tell me to fuck you,' he said. 'Go on, I want to hear you say it.'

In a weak voice I told him 'Fuck me, Robert,' wondering what had got into him. But I wanted him to do that too, my tummy was all fluttery and I knew I was moist. When he penetrated me I not only felt his hardness inside me, but the suspender-belt against my skin and the silkiness of the stockings sliding over my legs. Then it seemed I wanted all he could give me, thrusting against him and crying out for him to fuck me. Then I had a very strong orgasm.

Of course, he was delighted. In the morning I awoke to feel him touching me, his fingers inside me, and I said, 'Put it in then,' wanting him to. I thought all day while he was at work about how nice it had been and how hard I had come both times.

That night he came to bed as normal in his pyjamas, surprised when he got in beside me to find I'd left my nightie off. 'You horny little thing,' he teased me, and that pleased me. I went into his arms, thinking I'd have another climax, but he came before I could.

The following night when we went to bed, I asked if he didn't want to wear my suspenders and stockings. He was in seventh heaven, being much more passionate than usual and so was I. He fucked me and made me come quickly – because of what he was wearing, I decided. Then I was feeling wicked, so I whispered to him that I wanted him to kiss my pussy and lick me out. Again I had a strong climax and I realised how much I enjoyed fucking. Robert seemed like a new husband after that, attentive and fawning over me all the time.

In return, one night after a good fuck, I teased him about wearing my clothes. 'I'd like to see you dressed like a girl,' I said. 'I'll help—'

So we got out of bed and I took him to my wardrobe. I chose the bra, panties, suspenders and stockings, and he stood rather self-consciously before me like that.

'No titties,' I said and put some of his socks in the cups to round them out. All the time he had a huge erection, which I fondled with my hand. I picked out a dress and he put it on, the skirt bulging against his hardness. Then I kissed him. It was almost like kissing another girl. It led to us going back to the bed and Robert having me again still wearing the dress.

We've advanced since then. Robert has long hair so I've styled it like a girl's, applied make-up and had him sitting with me some evenings as if I had another woman as a visitor. I see no harm in all this now, finding it good fun and harmless. He doesn't want to go out as a woman. Some nights we sit and cuddle and kiss, which always leads to our making love there on the couch, almost two girls together. It has had its funny moments, such as when my parents called unexpectedly and Robert had to bolt upstairs and I lied that he was out. To wives who find they have the same situation at home – a husband who gets a kick out of dressing as a woman – there are worse things. Robert doesn't drink or gamble and provides me with a nice home. We are the only ones aware of his secret and it will stay that way.

Oh, by the way, I have now learned to enjoy sucking him off, often having to raise the hem of his dress to take him in my mouth.

Robert's wife, Ealing

The Babysitter

Though I'm over sixteen I'm not allowed to go out with boys. My dad is very strict and trusts no one since my mum left him for another man. But where there's a will there's a way. The only bloke he trusts, his best mate, made love to me while I was babysitting his children. I know it's wrong of us, but it's far too nice to stop it! Every Saturday night, Dad, his friend Ken and Ken's wife go out and I babysit. Usually, they return so late that I sleep in a spare room in Ken's house. The two girls are tucked up by eight o'clock so I sit and watch television until late, then go to bed.

A few weekends ago I heard Ken and his wife come home. After a while I heard someone look into the kids' room. I thought it would be his wife, so I got out of bed to tell her all was well. On the landing I saw Ken standing there absolutely naked, his large cock dangling over his balls. I was no virgin, despite my dad's confining me to the house. I'd held a few boys' pricks and even been fucked by one. The very size of Ken's prick made me giggle. He was about forty and well-built in every way. Not at all put out by me seeing him naked, he chuckled and asked me what was so funny. Had I never seen a real man's chopper before?

I myself am a well-developed girl, my tits are quite big and I've a good bush of hair on my quim. More to the point, I was standing in my shortie nightie, which was thin cotton and barely reached my thighs. The shadow of my nipples and cunt hair showed through plainly. I saw Ken eyeing me.

'I'll tuck you in, Trace,' he said, leading me back to my room. I was suddenly aroused but fearful too.

'What about your wife?' I whispered.

He gave a quiet laugh. 'She's out for the count,' he said. 'I've just put her to bed and she's had plenty to drink—'

I got under the duvet and he bent his head to kiss me good night. Only it got longer and more passionate, with his tongue slipping into my mouth. 'I bet all the boys fancy you,' he said. 'I bloody well do myself, seeing you in that short nightie.' Then he drew back the duvet to look at me. 'Yes, you've got all a man needs, I reckon—'

I glanced sideways and saw that his prick had risen mightily, looking absolutely huge to my eyes. 'What are you going to do then?' I said, my wicked glance at his erection not going unnoticed.

'Game little bitch, aren't you?' Ken told me. I felt his hand slide up my leg, pushing up the hem of my nightie, revealing my cunt. When he trailed his fingers over my pussy lips it felt so good. 'Get that silly nightdress off and let me see you properly,' he ordered.

Well, he was naked and in truth I was keen to let him see all of me. I pulled off the nightie and lay back. 'Nice tits,' he said. 'Very nice.' He took both of them in his hands and I arched my back to offer them to him. His thumbs flicked over my nipples and I shivered at his touch. He kissed each in turn, then fastened his mouth over them, sucking them right into his mouth.

I saw his big prick bobbing near as he bent over me, so I reached out and held it, gave it little rubs, feeling the loose skin moving under my fingers. It felt so stiff and hot. Then his mouth moved down over my tits, over my stomach to my quim. I turned towards him, opening my thighs,

136

and he tongued me there, making me squeak like a mouse as I tried to hold down the noise because his wife was only two bedrooms away.

I writhed about on his tongue, loving the feeling. He stopped and said, 'Your old man would kill me, but I'll chance it—' and he lay between my legs.

'I'm not on the pill yet,' I told him, which was as good as saying do what you want but be careful.

'Then I'll get off at Crewe instead of Blackpool,' he joked gruffly, directing the bulbous head of his prick to my cunt.

'It's too big,' I giggled. 'It won't go in—'

He laughed again. 'All cunts stretch a mile before they tear an inch. Don't worry, Trace, I'll go easy to start with – then you'll love it.'

Actually, despite its size, it slipped inside me beautifully, Ken inching it up until I was taking it all. I felt strangely full and eager for him to start fucking me. Then his hips thrust and the big tool bulldozed into my grotto.

'No problem,' Ken grunted, increasing his thrusts. 'You're really juiced up. Wrap your legs around my back now, Trace, grip my arse with your hands and heave into me.'

But I didn't need instructions. By then, with that hot shaft of stiff flesh up me, I was gurgling with delight, raising my bum off the bed to take his all, telling him to shove it all in. I came in a series of bumps and grinds and felt a complete loss of control, gasping and coming a second time, holding him in a vice-like grip. He uttered low grunts and pulled away from me, shooting thick gouts of warm spunk over my stomach up to my tits, filling my belly button.

'I'd have loved to let that go,' he said as we recovered, 'but better out than in – there was a baby in that lot, I reckon.'

The following Saturday night the crafty sod made sure

his wife got really pissed. My dad had to help Ken get her to bed before he went home. I lay waiting for him and was not disappointed. He slept with me for most of the night, initiating me into different positions and different ways, all of which, naughty girl that I am, I loved. Now I look forward to his visits every Saturday night. I'm on the pill now as our loving is too intense to take chances. One thing I do know. When I marry, I'll make sure that my husband is as good a lover as Ken is – not that I think we'll stop our secret meetings even when I'm someone's wife. It's just the way I am.

Tracy, Lancashire

Christmas Stuffing

A year ago my neighbour was involved in a car accident. Her husband was killed but she was not injured. After the death we consoled her and had her in for meals to alleviate her loneliness. That made her take advantage of our kindness, often dropping in on us uninvited, saying she was bored. My husband Fred got fed-up, saying we hardly ever had an evening alone together. After the kids were in bed, Janice always seeming to be sitting with us. Despite this, I really liked her. She was very kind and gave us all lavish presents at Christmas.

We could do little else but invite her to spend the big day with us. She bought the turkey and helped me cook it, the pair of us dibbing at the sherry bottle, and me glad of her assistance. When the kids were at last tucked up in bed, the three of us sat drinking. Again, she had been most generous. Fred and I were not broke but we had kids to provide for and a large mortgage, so it was a great help that she stocked our drinks cabinet with wines and spirits. I'm not a regular drinker but I tend to overdo it on special occasions, and when I get tipsy I get randy. If Janice hadn't been there I'd have tempted Fred into fucking me in the living room as a Christmas treat.

As it was, when Fred left us to go to the kitchen to get more crisps and nuts, it was the other kind of nuts I was thinking about, my cunt all in a lather. I followed him out there and cuddled up to him, kissing him with my tongue in his mouth and saying that as soon as Janice left he was to fuck me. I pressed my pubic bulge against his prick and felt it harden. Fred rubbed his prick into me, telling me just what he intended to do. I suppose we forgot about Janice as we enjoyed a randy dry-rub with my bum pressed against the sink. It was then that Janice, tired of waiting for us, walked in. Fred and I jumped apart.

Janice said, 'Don't stop on my account. I've been watching you for several minutes. The thing I miss most about being a widow is not getting regular sex. My Tom was always at me and it's very frustrating doing without.'

I couldn't suppress a giggle as the very proper Janice admitted she missed having a fuck. I remembered her Tom as a quiet bank-manager type, which shows one shouldn't go by appearances.

We went back into the living room and I sat on Fred's lap, squirming my bum into his erection while Janice watched. I liked her watching, it increased my excitement.

'I'd better go,' she announced at last. 'It's obvious you two can't wait to get to bed, lucky things.'

With a suddenness that surprised even myself, I said, 'Then why don't you join us, Jan? I'd like to see if my Fred can manage the both of us.'

Fred said eagerly, 'Why not? I've always fancied three in a bed. Here, Liz, start the ball rolling. Let Jan see how well you strip—' I rather fancied myself as a stripper, often giving Fred an eyeful after a few drinks. He'd put on smoochy music and I'd disrobe in what I considered to be the most seductive way.

'Yes, that would be fun,' Janice said. 'I'd like to see that—'

I wiggled in time to the music Fred selected, pulling off my dress, bra and panties, waggling my tits at Fred and flashing my bottom. Then Janice did the same, throwing off her clothes and standing with her arms thrown wide to show her all. At the sight of her strapping frame, with full tits and a cunt so much hairier than mine, Fred's eyes boggled. We headed for the bedroom and my husband stripped off to reveal a raging cockstand while Janice and I lay side by side on the bed awaiting his pleasure. He had probably been dreaming of such a moment all his life!

Holding hands and giggling like schoolgirls, Janice and I offered our breasts to be sucked by Fred and his hands wandered all over our bodies, before he went down to kiss our cunts. I wanted very much to see him mounting the strapping Janice and told him to get on with it. She gave a long sigh of satisfaction as he went up her, moving his hips slowly to give her the full measure and making her squeal out in pleasure.

'Leave some for me,' I cried, enjoying the sight of the pair of them writhing about beside me. I was proud of him when she bucked her hips and cried out loudly that she was coming. But Fred had come too and I had to wait until he was aroused again, this being accomplished by Janice and I sucking him in turn. We offered him our tits and squashed him between our two naked female forms until he got it up again.

At some time in the night, Janice cuddled up to me and it seemed only natural that we should kiss and touch intimately. It was the first time I had felt another woman's breasts and fingered her cunt. She did the same for me, which delighted Fred, who sat back on his knees egging us on.

I awoke on Boxing Day morning to find myself alone in the bed, wryly wondering if last night's orgy had really happened. But it had and Fred turned up with a cup of tea, saying it had been his best Christmas ever.

'I suppose Janice is not a bad sort after all,' he admitted, with a broad grin on his face.

Liz, Barking

3. BOYS WILL BE BOYS

By Mutual Consent
Completing the Double
Three Into Two Will Go
Birthday Treat
Lust in the Library
Keeping Mum
Swallows in Winter
Night-School Nookie
The Milkman Cometh
Every Boy Should Have One
An Ill Wind
The Lay of the Land
The New Member
Sandy Lands the Big One
New Balls, Please
Danish Open Sandwich
Object of Adoration

By Mutual Consent

I've just spent a marvellous hour or two fucking my younger brother's wife. Before you say 'Rotten sod,' or 'Lucky bastard,' I must add that my brother Don was busily working a stiff prick into my wife's cunt at the same time. The four of us were panting with lust – lost to all but our pleasures. It's a perfect set-up, with no outsiders who might boast around town of our sessions. The four of us love all types of sexual play. Don and I have always considered 'fuckability' in a wife far above 'fidelity'!

Both girls are good-lookers with fine figures, but Don's wife, Jean, is fair, while my wife, Pat, has long dark hair – there's a forest of it around her beautiful quim. Jean loves sport – tennis, golf and swimming – and has the big firm breasts and plump round muscled arse of a sportswoman, supported by two shapely strong legs just made for wrapping around a man's back. My wife is more the model type: slim, with long legs and lovely tits with nipples like strawberries.

It turned out that Don and I had admired and secretly fancied each other's partners for too long without doing anything about it. Nothing more than kisses had been exchanged at parties until the four of us took a holiday together.

On a remote cliff-sheltered beach on the south side of the Isle of Wight we discovered we'd ventured onto the local stretch of shore used by nudists. All around us were men and women as bare as nature intended and seemingly unconcerned by the assortment of tits, cunts and pricks on show. Our two wives were persuaded that when in Rome one does as the Romans do, and the way they giggled between themselves it was obvious they found the idea of baring their bodies intriguing. With their big tits and curvy bums on show, they attracted many a stare.

Of course, Don and I, seeing our respective spouses nude for the first time, began to sport erections and made a quick dash for the sea. When we emerged, cooled-off for the time being, the girls ushered us behind a large rock where they'd laid out towels and picnic gear. The sight of these two naked girls soon resurrected our horny tools, much to their huge amusement. Four shapely tits bobbed enticingly as they laughed at us. They did not improve matters by parting their thighs to reveal the beauty of their moist pink cunts. As if by unspoken agreement, each wife took her husband in hand, making derogatory remarks about our lack of control.

Later, when swimming, Don and I admitted that we'd love to screw each other's wives. In the hotel bar that evening we heard the girls admit they'd enjoyed going naked and wanking their husband's cocks, so Don and I suggested we go a step further and swop partners for a session. The girls weren't too sure and that night I slept as usual with my Pat. We fucked like rabbits, however, and I worked her to a frenzy as I told her how much Don would love to be up her tight cunt. 'Yes, yes, I'd let him fuck me. I *want* him to fuck me,' Pat moaned as she writhed below me.

I learned later that Don had used the same ploy on his wife while screwing her from the rear doggy-style, saying in crude terms how his brother would like to fuck her and getting a throaty response that she'd love it, love it!

The next afternoon on the beach, a sweltering day, four

hot naked bodies lay hidden behind our rock. As if by mutual consent I was beside Jean and no comment or protest was made when I kissed her. Don and Pat watched and then kissed passionately too. I fondled Jean's tits and explored her moist cunt. Pat had Don's erect cock in her hand while he sucked greedily on a nipple. To my great delight, Jean lowered her head to take me in her mouth, sucking hard at my stalk. Looking aside, I was thrilled to see Pat laid back with knees drawn up and Don lapping away noisily at her love-nest.

'Put it in me!' I heard my wife say and she squealed as his prick penetrated her to the balls. Jean meanwhile had manoeuvred herself over me and was directing my engorged tool to her juicy cunt, thrusting down to impale herself on its length. Thus we fucked in unison for the first of many times.

That night Jean came to my room and slept with me, my wife sharing a bed with Don. I discovered that Jean was not only a wanton fuck when roused but that she was mad keen on oral sex. She loved a dick in her mouth and demanded her turn too, urging me to 'Lick me out, lick me clean!' after each bout – no doubt her routine with my brother. Don told me next day, while comparing notes, that Jean had been an avid cocksucker at college where he had met her. He was full of praise for Pat's sensuality, her lovely smooth body and the way her tight cunt muscles could grip and 'milk' an invading prick. He had also been allowed to have a 'titty-roll' with his prick held in her cleavage, coming in spurts that covered her neck and chin. So a good time was had by all and what's wrong with that?

Four's Company, Hants

Completing the Double

It was during my service in the Royal Navy that I first heard the expression 'completing the double' which referred to a chap who had fucked his wife *and* her mother. It was, among shipmates, considered just about the highest accolade conferred upon one of a randy bunch. But the 'double' is not so rare in my experience. Not a few frustrated and neglected middle-aged mothers-in-law have had it off with their daughter's horny husbands. I have always been intrigued by the sexual sharing of the same man by mum and daughter. I learned about it at an early age.

I lived near a busy shipyard and a young welder from Scotland came to work there, taking digs in our street with the widowed Mrs H, a comely woman of about forty who had a pretty sixteen-year-old daughter, Peggy. Sandy, their new lodger, was a strapping lad who spent a deal of his spare time tinkering beside the pavement with his motorcycle. After a few months, rumours became rife about Sandy and the mum and daughter he lodged with. Little wonder, for both Mrs H and Peggy became 'great with child' as the biblical term has it – or well in the pudding club, the pair of 'em round of belly from taking the dick.

There seemed little doubt among my parents and neighbours who'd got them in the family way at about the same time – their young lodger! My mother was shocked, but dad chuckled wickedly as they discussed it. I had a feeling my old man felt nothing but admiration for Sandy the randy lodger who had evidently made himself at home. The thought excited me too. What great digs he has found, I thought, with two shapely females to screw in turn. Did they do it all together, I wondered? My lurid young mind pictured a naked three-in-a-bed romp, always a scenario that led to me jerking off.

I walked by the welder as he polished his motorbike, staring at the lucky bastard, and, as if aware of what I was thinking, he gave me the broadest wink. One day, I determined, I'd do that – have a mother and daughter either singly or together. Both ways would be great.

Came World War Two and a ship in which I served was mined, towed to an east coast port and most of the crew sent on leave. I was one of those left to maintain the ship while it was being repaired and I met a girl at the local dance hall who fucked like it was going out of fashion. We did it in cold fields where her tits were like ice when I got them out, in shop doorways in the blackout and even in her kitchen when her mother had gone to bed. She was about seventeen and a matelot's dream, giving me my first suck off, and so sexy she allowed almost anything. That Christmas Day she invited me home after my duty watch to spend the evening with her mum and herself. I'd have sooner taken her out to a pub and fucked her later, but I couldn't refuse.

I took along a bottle of rum I found in a pantry locker in the deserted wardroom, thinking it would add to the festive fare. I was introduced to May's mum, a plump woman of early middle-age, who had plastered on the make-up, like her daughter, for my visit. On the mantelpiece was a framed picture of her husband, well out of the way on a minesweeper based in Malta. We hit the drink and I danced with the women to gramophone music in their cosy living room. The three of us became tipsy and May sat on my lap, kissing me lewdly with open mouth and tongue in front of her ma. Of course I got rampant. May got off my lap to go upstairs to the bathroom, so her mother put on another record and hauled me to my feet to dance.

Right away she felt my big hard tadger pressing into her crotch as she held me close. She giggled and jiggled her cunt mound against my prick. 'Kiss me, lad, it's been so long,' she said. We stood still, moving our hips sensuously in a 'dry rub' and out of this world with randiness, our mouths glued together, when May came bouncing back into the room.

She wasn't taken aback at all, saying, 'I thought you two would be at it as soon as I left the room!'

She joined us, making a circle, and I kissed her and her mum in turn, my tongue in both of their mouths, my hands groping their tits.

The pair of them undressed me with great merriment. I insisted that they got down to the skin, too, and they stripped before me giggling at their naughtiness – a big-titted mother with a forest of hair on a fat cunt mound with an arse to match, and May, slimmer but with all the signs she'd turn out like her ma. I was like a kid let loose in a sweetshop, grabbing tits, kissing bums, feeling up cunts, and in turn being smothered, smooched and rubbed up. It was May's mother who drew me down over her on the couch, my prick in her hand directed to her cunt. We fucked like rabbits, me bouncing up and down on her cushiony flesh, coming early but continuing to fuck her as she bucked and jerked to a climax. May sat on the edge of the couch, encouraging us and shouting, 'My turn next!' She pushed at my arse with her hands to bang it faster into her ma.

'Oh, Lord, I'm fucked, I feel all queer,' said the mother as we separated, almost falling off the couch. She crawled on her hands and knees, presenting a magnificent arse as she crossed the carpet and sat on the floor with her back against an armchair. Her tits lolled, round udders lengthening as her shoulders drooped. Her legs spread uncaringly and her well-fucked cunt, still pouting and parted, showing pink through the mass of hair.

I had taken care not to imbibe as much as the two females, not intending to get so pissed that I'd miss out on a marvellous mating game. While May's mum sat up on the floor and tried to focus her bleary eyes on what we were doing, I was prone on the couch as her daughter tried to regain my erection first with her hand and tits, then sucking the limp dick back to life with her mouth.

'Dirty little bitch,' her ma hiccuped from her vantage point. 'I don't do that to your father—' All the same she crawled back to us, her head on the edge of the couch to get a close-up. My free hand reached out to cup one of her tits and, with the vigour of youth, I felt my prick responding in May's warm mouth. Her mum sat by while I turned May round to shove it up her doggy-style. Then the three of us went up to bed to continue the orgy.

It was to be many years later that I was privileged to 'complete the double' again. I was working in Saudi and a backstage electrician for the local European amateur dramatic group in my spare time. Zelda was a young nurse who worked backstage too in the costume department. For all the twenty years age difference between us, we began to kiss and cuddle for the fun of it while the play took place on stage. Thereafter we fucked regularly in her flat. I was lucky to have a nice young bed-partner to lick out, suck on her nipples and screw regularly. Then she met a steady boyfriend at her hospital and it was over.

Some time later her mother came out to visit her. We met at a dinner party, danced and got friendly. The following morning, a Sunday, I'd got up late and was wearing just my pyjama trousers when a knock came to my door.

It was Zelda's mother, Celia, in a linen frock that accentuated a curvy body.

'I was out for a walk on this lovely sunny morning,' she said, giving no other explanation for calling. 'Wasn't it a nice party last night?'

I asked her in for coffee. The atmosphere grew tense as we chatted and as she stood to leave I took her hand. She knew what I was after, saying as I took her in my arms, 'I've a husband at home, you know.' Such are the wiles of women! She had visited me knowing full well I would be tempted and saying that she had a husband no doubt added to her feeling of being wicked.

I decided that if this nice respectable married lady wanted a holiday fling, I'd give her the full treatment. She didn't know, of course, that I'd been screwing her daughter. That only added to the pleasure I felt in having the mother.

Our kisses were long and passionate. We stood there with my tongue deep in her mouth and my prick hard against her cunt. 'Phew!' she said as our mouths parted, pretending to fan herself as if overheated. 'I don't know if I should allow you to do this to me.' Typical, I thought – she was as randy as I was. 'I've never done anything like this before—'

'Well, you are now,' I said, deciding to take charge, certain she would prefer it that way. I started to unbutton her dress and she let me. 'Must you?' was all she said.

I had it open to her waist at once, pulling the garment off her shoulders to reveal her pretty bra and its contents, two nicely rounded tits. 'I don't know what my husband would think if he knew you were doing this to me,' she said in a low voice, but I could sense the excitement in her tone. It turned her on to think about it.

'Who cares about your husband,' I said, sneering. 'I want

you and I'm going to have you, and you are going to let me, Mrs S. Unhook that bra and let me see your tits. While we are at it, take off everything. I want to see it all. Do it now!'

She regarded me for a long moment, then lowered the dress and stepped out of it. All she was left in was her bra and tiny briefs. I ogled her shapely body, so white and smooth. 'Please,' she said, begging me. 'Must I take more off?'

'You know you must,' I told her. To make her feel it was an even trade, I lowered my pyjama trousers and stood naked before her with my prick rampant. She unhooked the bra and her tits were lovely, I could see her nipples were taut with her excitement. She hesitated and then slipped down her panties, standing shyly and exhibiting a neat bush. I walked around her as if inspecting her, enjoying every moment of my mastery. This one liked it.

I trailed my fingers over her tight rounded arse, and she gave out with a surprised 'Ooh', so I gave it a friendly smack. Standing before her I lifted each tit, tweaked her nipples, then had a quick feel of her cunt. 'Please—' was all she said. 'Walk through to my bedroom,' I said sharply.

She stood by my bed, apprehensive. 'What are you going to do to me?' she asked, as if she didn't know. 'Why so coy?' I demanded. 'You've nothing to be ashamed of. Pretty tits and a sweet little cunt I shall enjoy eating out later. You've got a cheeky bottom too, madam. Has it ever been punished? From the look of it, it deserves a smacking—'

'Certainly not,' she said quietly. 'You're not going to do that, are you?'

'Only if you don't do exactly as I want,' I told her, drawing her down to the bed and parting her thighs with the palms of my hands. I was looking directly at her crevice with its light down of hair. From above me I heard her say 'No—' so I rasped my tongue over her outer lips then licked inside her, finding warm moist folds and the hard nub of her clitty. In moments she was squirming her bottom to my tonguing.

'You dirty thing,' I heard her moan, but she was wriggling her arse. I stopped just long enough to have her groan, 'Please—' as if now desperate to continue. Her hands sought my head and held on to it, pulling me into her thighs.

'Does your husband do this to you?' I taunted her. 'You love it, don't you?' I don't know if he was satisfying her but the way she suddenly jerked and cried out it was evident she was coming. Then I stood over her with my dick upright like a flagpole. I saw her eyes take it in. 'Yes, it's all for you,' I told her.

She averted her eyes. 'It's so big,' she whispered.

'All the better to fuck you with,' I answered, then penetrated her cunt in one go, sliding to the hilt, finding her juicy and receptive. Her legs and arms folded about me and she returned my thrusts.

'Oh God, what am I doing?' she moaned. 'This man is fucking me! What would my husband and daughter think of that?'

I could have told her precisely what Zelda might say – seeing as how she'd already taken my prick. As it was, I concentrated hard on giving the lady the screw of a lifetime.

It's my main enjoyment to pleasure women so much in a good screw that they mouth obscenities as they take my prick. This one was no different. She lifted her body so that only her shoulders were on the bed and cried out, urging me to fuck her, fuck harder, deeper, all the while shifting her arse about so that my angle of penetration touched the spots she liked titillated. She came at least four times before I allowed myself to shoot up her. When we had both subsided she nestled in my arms, grateful for what she had received.

'You're a wicked man, doing all that to someone else's wife,' she said shyly, harping back on the theme that intrigued her, being unfaithful to hubby at home.

'And you are naughty too,' I replied, 'letting me see your tits and arse, taking my prick up your cunt. I say naughty girls deserve punishing. Over my knee with you.'

I had this desire to give her bottom a few smacks and she got over my knee as if in full agreement. I'm sure she enjoyed the smacking as much as I did, her full bottom reddening as my palm thrashed it.

On future visits she allowed me similar liberties in our romps. She stayed two weeks, during which time my bed saw a lot of sexual action, our closeness so evident that her daughter accused me of fucking her mother. As if I would! Celia was all for anything I suggested. She loved having her nipples sucked and her cunt licked, returning the favour by sucking me off. She delighted in all the new positions I fucked her in too, which made me sure that her husband was no great shakes in the boudoir department. That was a pity, for she was a natural when given the chance and randier than her daughter, bless her.

So I've had the pleasure of completing the double twice over the years, making it among my fondest memories.

Charles, Weymouth

Three Into Two Will Go

My latest girlfriend had had lots of three-in-a-bed sessions before we met. I fell for her hard and it annoyed and even disgusted me, for she loved to discuss what she had done and was evidently proud of her sexual prowess. Although it made me very excited and led to some epic sex sessions, as a young man in love I wanted to believe she was mine alone.

So I was confused, having found a lively intelligent girl with a good sense of humour and a lovely body who enjoyed revealing to me all the lurid details of her sexy past. When I suggested we might get engaged she said she loved sex and I would have to accept the fact she liked more than one partner. In other words, the sex romps would continue if we got married. I felt this was tearing us apart, so she insisted we try it out to see if I could live with it.

Much to my amazement, on the night in question she arrived at my flat with a girlfriend. Patricia introduced her as Gloria and, after a drink or two with them openly discussing previous nights spent with men, the pair led me off to the bedroom.

'He might be shy,' Pat said as the two of them stripped before me, 'but Bill can fuck better than anyone when he's horny. Shall we give him the treatment?'

Gloria, I noticed, was a plump fleshy girl and her tits jiggled as she cast off her bra. She laughed and said, 'Let him get undressed then, or shall we do it for him, Pat?'

Of course it was impossible not to have a solid hard-on with these two vixens prancing around me stark naked. The sight of my upright prick caused lewd giggles when I stripped. I lay on the bed, as directed, and at once I was buried under soft scented flesh. I didn't know whose tits were pressed to my face, whose hand was rubbing my engorged cock or whose tongue was in my mouth.

Then Pat decided my erection was too good to be wasted and Gloria agreed with her that it was indeed a beauty. Flat on my back, and privately admitting that one was fun but two was better, I was putty in their busy hands. Pat straddled me, directing my knob to her cunt and gliding her bottom down until I was fully sheathed. As she began her up-and-down motions I almost crowed with delight, urging her to grind down faster, my pelvis straining up against her thrusts, gloriously embedded up a warm wet cunt channel.

'Sit on his face, Gloria,' I heard Pat instruct her friend. 'Don't just play with yourself. Let Bill bring you off too—'

Gloria immediately hefted her ample arse over my face, knees planted each side of my ears, parting her bum cheeks and lowering a lippy quim to my mouth. In my frenzy I sucked and tongued it while Pat rode me with quickening thrusts.

'Fuck me!' she cried out and her friend yelled, 'Suck me too!'

As the pair of them lost control, it was marvellous to think I was bringing off two females at the same time. The sensations were incredible and I bucked and sucked, shooting my jism in great heaving spurts up Pat's cunt. Both girls were uttering wild cries as they climaxed too, falling off me in a crumpled heap.

What we did for the rest of the night left nothing untried, and with two comely and randy females restoring my erections with their lips, tits and hands, I gave a good account of myself. I loved it all.

In the morning when Gloria left us, I admitted to Pat that threesomes were special. She looked me over with a serious face. 'So you see, darling,' she said, 'why I like it as a special treat. And if you found it so good with two girls, you can imagine what it is like for me with two men. Would you object if I asked Philip, an old friend of mine, to join in once in a while, just to add to the excitement?' I nodded my agreement, though I was still unsure how I would react to see another man fucking her.

As we drove to Philip's house, Pat filled me in on her relationship with him. He was divorced and had been her first employer when she'd started as a secretary some years before. Handsome and suave, she'd been flattered by his attentions, which culminated in his fucking her across his desk and taking her virginity at seventeen.

'Lucky bastard,' I mumbled as I drove my car into the driveway of a large house. Pat had visited often and Philip had taught her to love sex in every conceivable fashion. I told myself that I couldn't complain. Through him I'd gained a completely uninhibited girl, one always eager for sex.

'Don't worry, I love you. This is purely physical,' she assured me as we rang the bell. Philip received us in a dressing gown, obviously prepared. He shook my hand, saying I was a lucky fellow to have a girl like Pat and allow her added sexual pleasure. He was middle-aged, big in bulk, but I noted with pleasure when we all stripped in his bedroom that my prick had the edge on his for thickness and length. When Pat stood naked before us, he walked around her, his hands fondling her breasts and bum.

'Just look at these lovely tits,' he enthused. 'Such nice curves to the swell of her bottom too. And what a sweet little pussy with a pretty nest of hair around the lips. Bill, my boy, you and I are going to make the most of that naughty slit tonight!'

He was right, for Pat took all we could give her and I'm sure would have welcomed another prick between times had one been available. She was sucked, fucked and taken simultaneously by us, revelling in being the object of our lust. Seeing Philip fuck her excited me too and she knew it, smiling up at me as I stood beside the bed watching her, a hand reaching out to grasp my cock and pull it towards her open mouth. By the morning she had been thoroughly used and abused in every way by the two of us and still wanted more.

Our strange courtship continued, with regular visits to Philip's house to share Pat with her old boss and with her friend Gloria calling on us frequently. So it went on, quite happily, until Philip decided to live abroad in the sun of Florida, and Pat couldn't resist going with him. At present, Gloria and I are consoling each other very well. We've even discussed making it a permanent arrangement and, with that in mind, she has banned all further threesomes. Girlfriends with marriage in mind are like that, I suppose!

Bill S., Essex

Birthday Treat

For as long as I could remember we had stayed at the same south coast hotel each summer. The woman that owned and managed it became like an aunt to me and good friends with my parents. I'd always had my birthdays there as it coincided with the holidays. My sixteenth was a special occasion, but at the time I thought it kid's stuff: the cake with candles, paper hats, everybody singing 'Happy Birthday', all of it laid on by my 'aunt', Margaret. I thanked everyone for the party, but said it would be the last one as, the next year, I thought I would go on holiday without my parents. I'd been listening to my mates, who had gone to a holiday camp, boast of the great time they'd had with no end of spare girls to chat up – even ones of twenty and older. All my pals claimed they'd fucked some of them during the fortnight.

I was desperate to lose my virginity. I'd felt girls up in dark lanes, had a handful of tit in the cinema, done plenty of french-kissing and even been wanked off. But I'd never scored, dipped my wick or got my leg over – though, like boys do, I'd boasted I had.

At my birthday party I was allowed a sherry and, just for the fun of it, I poured half a bottle of vodka into the punch bowl on the dining-room table. The thing was a mixture of fruit juices with dash of gin and bits of orange and lemon floating on the surface. We all drank a lot of it, my father complimenting Margaret on making such a splendid punch.

I got a bit tiddly, but I wasn't the only one. The tables were cleared and we danced. All the women kissed me, some of them quite passionately, as if to say, 'Let's give the lad a treat', for I've no doubt that in their heart of hearts the idea of seducing a virgin was a fond desire. As it was the accepted thing to do, to kiss a young fellow on the verge of manhood, I got a few good smackers from the ladies – one or two lingering for that long second which turns a simple kiss into a passionate one. They knew it, breaking away from me giggling naughtily, pretending to be breathless. I knew it, enveloped as I was in warm female flesh, getting the first stirrings of a hard-on. My mother knew it too and watched with a most disapproving eye. Of course, we were all rather merry.

The only one who hadn't kissed me was our hostess, Margaret. In the past year or so, I had matured and looked quite the young man. I saw her in a new light. She sometimes came swimming with us and I couldn't help but notice how her tits and rounded arse moulded to her swimming costume when wet. She had auburn hair, the colour of horse chestnuts, which she kept swept up on her head. I thought she was too busy to kiss me as she was attending to her guests.

She gathered up glasses and plates to take to the kitchen and handed me a tray, saying, 'Here, birthday boy, make yourself useful and help me carry these.' I followed her to the kitchen, ogling the waggle of her fine arse cheeks, each full moon rounded out under the material of her dress.

'Happy birthday, Eric,' she said. 'Come here and get your birthday kiss from me. All the others have had a turn.'

We went into each other's arms and her full lips closed over mine, her mouth open and her breath sweet with alcohol. I took the chance to kiss her back. After a moment, I pushed my tongue into her mouth and she sucked it.

Alone, with the sounds of continuing merriment sounding from the dining hall, we clung together and kissed again and again. My dick rose automatically, pushing into her. Then she eased out of my grip, holding me off, her lovely chest heaving.

'Good God, young Eric,' she said, surprised at the intensity of our clinch. 'You are growing up!' I was hoping she referred to the iron-hard cylindrical bar of flesh she must have felt rubbing up against her stomach. 'Phew!' she added. 'What happened there? It rather got out of hand, didn't it?'

I told her like a love-sick boy, or perhaps just one who wanted more of that sensual body to nudge my prick against, that it had been marvellous, she was beautiful, wonderful – she put a hand over my mouth to stop me rambling on.

'Yes, well,' she said, composing herself, for I could see she had been affected by our torrid smooch. 'You mustn't say those things and it shouldn't have happened. Your mother would certainly not approve. I don't approve of it either.' With that she took a deep breath, as if shaking off the arousal she felt, and headed back into the dining room. 'You'd better hang on a minute,' she said, turning at the door, a wicked smile on her full lips, 'and let *that* go down again—' I almost crowed with delight, as I realised that this splendid woman was referring to the big bulge in the front of my trousers.

Of course, I couldn't think of anything else for the rest of the evening. I looked across at her frequently and often found she was looking at me. I had turned her on! I was thrilled. She was the most desirable creature in the world. I went to my lonely bed wishing she were in there with me.

Finally, all went quiet below, my parents went to their room and I guessed Margaret and her staff would be clearing up. In my excitement I couldn't sleep, my hand was on my tool, stroking it slowly, savouring again those mad moments with my desired one. I'd kept my bedside light on and thankfully it shone under the door. It was past midnight when, in answer to my most fervent prayer, Margaret looked around the door, saying 'Can't you sleep, Eric? What's the matter?'

'You,' I said moodily. 'I can't sleep thinking of you.'

She advanced and sat on my bed, her chestnut hair loose over her shoulders. She wore a dressing gown and I looked down the neck, hoping to see a hint of swelling tit, but she wore a frilly nightdress.

'You are a silly boy,' she said. 'I'll give you one kiss and then you must sleep.' But I noted the catch in her voice, a nervous huskiness and took heart.

As she leaned over to kiss me I held her close, kissing her fiercely with my tongue in her mouth to let her know exactly what I wanted. She tightened her body for a moment then reciprocated as if unable to resist. I clutched one of her hanging tits, and her hand went under the bedcover to seek out my prick. 'Come in beside me,' I begged her.

Never did a youth lose his virginity in a more ardent night of sexual activity. 'We must be quiet,' was all she said as she slipped in my bed, shedding the dressing gown. After several wracking kisses, I was allowed to draw off the nightie and she was gloriously naked in my arms. Like her pretty face, her lovely big tits were freckled too, and at the fork of her legs a mass of reddish hair covered the raised mound of her cunt. She it was who pulled me across her and fed my rampant prick to her hot moist pussy mouth, my length going up her as if tailored for her channel.

'Don't rush,' she begged, 'fuck me slow, my darling boy. It's been a long time, too long. Oh, it feels so lovely up

163

there, so stiff – don't move for a moment – let it soak there, let me feel it in me—'

I was enchanted by her low moans, her whispered pleas, all this from a mature woman because my prick was up her! I was thrilled when she bucked beneath me wildly, mouthing out that she was going to come. Then I could hold off no longer, shooting my load up her in my final thrusts. We kissed lovingly and explored each other's bodies. She asked if I loved her and kissed all over my face, then held up her breasts for me to suck. Best of all, later she bent over to have a suck herself, this time at my semi-erect dick. With the energy of eagerness of youth, I screwed her at least four or five times before she slipped away at dawn, leaving me with a last kiss and a fondle at her tits before she covered them up.

The following year I was back – and the year after that. Holidays with my parents, I concluded, were not such a bad deal after all.

Eric, Gloucester

Lust in the Library

As an eighteen-year-old college student, I was glad of a part-time job on my campus as a library assistant. The money was useful but the real bonus was that I shared my work with a gorgeous girl, as slim and pretty as a model, who soon featured in my nightly wanking. As cool as she seemed at first, as time went on we became quite friendly. She saw that I couldn't help staring at her and teased me that she was engaged to a medical student – 'So hands off, buster.' To see her pert arse jiggling under her tight skirt as she walked about gave me painful erections.

'You'd better take a cold shower, Nigel,' she would say when, with her working close by and her scent filling my nostrils, I had a real boner on that tented my jeans. The sexy witch enjoyed flaunting herself to get me going, often asking me to hold the ladder while she fetched books from high shelves, knowing I could see her tiny panties beneath her skirt.

Then came an evening when we were working side by side at a desk, cataloguing books. The room was small and warm and musky. The perfume from her bare arms and neck made me increasingly horny.

'You're beautiful,' I told her, and she turned to me and kissed my cheek. I drew her close and returned her kiss full on the lips. She must have been feeling randy too, for her mouth opened and her tongue slid over mine, wet and warm. More kisses followed and, to my great excitement, she took hold of my hand and put it down the low rounded neck of her sleeveless blouse. My fingers came in contact with the soft yielding flesh of her pointy tits, the nipples stiffly erect. Under the desk her hand sought and squeezed my rampant prick through my jeans.

She pulled at my zip and delved in to pull out my cock, massaging it expertly. 'It's so hard,' she whispered. 'Did I do that to you?' Of course, the bitch knew she had so, for good measure, I went up her skirt and found the damp crotch of her panties, rubbing her cunt mound while she caught her breath and pushed her crotch against my hand.

'Go on,' she said. 'I'm on the pill. You've always wanted to, haven't you?'

I was keen to shag her but I was greedy, wanting to see her naked as well. I got the blouse off while we kissed, drew down her skirt and knickers, laid her across the desk and licked her tight little slit of a quim with its wispy hairs. Pushing my jeans down to my ankles, she pulled me urgently between her legs and I felt my cock gripped and directed to her cunt. It was pure heaven sliding up the tight channel, my bursting tool embedded in moist flesh, my arse clenching and lifting as I gave it to her. She was all for it, circling my hips with her legs, thrusting back at me, urging me to fuck, fuck, and then crying out 'Oh, give me a baby, put a baby up me, you bastard!' – which I hoped was just her horny sex-talk.

I was working away, feeling her body jerk in quickening spasms, shooting hot jism in helpless spurts up her fanny when in walked the senior librarian, a middle-aged woman married to one of our tutors.

'Just *what* do you two think you are doing?' she bawled furiously. I should have said it was obvious, what with my bare arse thrusting in my last tremors and a girl below me

166

with her legs spread. We certainly weren't checking in the new books!

Never did two fuckers separate so quickly as we apologised and tried to cover ourselves. The librarian turned on her heel and left, leaving me thinking I was out of a job. However, apart from the girl and I being put on different shifts, I continued working in the library, under the eye of Mrs P, the lady who'd caught us.

Actually, she appeared quite friendly, as if willing to forgive my lapse. I worked late one night in the same room where I'd enjoyed that unexpected fuck, all alone until the boss lady looked in. She perched on the corner of my desk, regarding me as if undecided about something. Mrs P was what one might call attractively buxom, big-breasted and well-fleshed with a curvaceous figure.

'Have you been seeing your girlfriend since that time I blundered in on you?' she said. 'Are you engaged to Janine? I'm sorry I was angry.'

I saw a curious look on her face. 'She's not my girlfriend, in fact she's engaged to someone else,' I said. 'It just sort of happened between us and I don't blame you for being shocked. I'm grateful that you didn't dismiss me. I need the money—'

'Do you always,' she began, still a little hesitant but with playfulness in her voice, 'make a habit of having sex with engaged girls, or married women even? I think you are rather naughty, don't you?' She paused, as if taking a deep breath, coming out with, 'Would you make love to an older married woman, like me, for instance?'

I stared up at her, realising she was offering herself to me, fearful of refusal perhaps but unable to resist the temptation. She was a frustrated wife, I supposed, turned on by what she had seen Janine and I doing across the desk. Her apprehensive look and the fact that she had braved a rebuff made me admire her. Why not, if she fancied a fuck with a young man?

Anyway, seeing her looking hopeful I thought what an attractive face she had. And those tits! She was broad-shouldered with the kind of breasts that go out sideways and curve out to their frontal prominence. I'd never had an older woman, but now I had a strong letch to see this one nude, with bare tits and hairy cunt. My cock was already rising in my jeans as I arose to take her comfortable form in my arms, determined to have some fun.

We kissed and she smiled, embarrassed but pleased. My erection nestled against her cunt mound nicely. 'You must think I'm an awful woman,' she whispered. 'It's just that, well, seeing you with Janine, it's been on my mind. Never out of my mind to tell the truth.'

'I'm glad you let me know,' I said, placing little kisses on her lips. 'See, you've got me hard for you, I want you. Let's take off our clothes. I want to see all of you, your tits and cunt and arse. You're lovely.'

'Ooh, such plain talk,' she said, giggling, and I guessed that a little crudity turned her on. We both undressed and I was confronted by a plump expanse of soft pink flesh. I buried my face between those magnificent mammaries, sucking on the long rubbery nipples while fingering her moist pussy. I bent her over the desk and was up her like a ferret, shafting away slowly at first to bring her to the boil, talking into her wide-eyed face as I fucked her. 'Oh, it's so good,' she burbled. 'I haven't had any satisfying intercourse for such a long time—'

'The word is *fuck*,' I told her, revelling in my mastery, for the normally assertive older woman was suddenly very passive. I'd got used to girls of my own age who screwed on equal terms. Evidently frustrated mature ladies were more grateful and conditioned by age to let the male be the dominant partner. I found it a refreshing change and I loved lording it over a willing subject. 'I'm fucking you, that's what I'm doing. Say it—' I ordered her. 'Say it and tell me what it's like!'

Mrs P was panting out moans and sighs, cradling me in her thighs, her strong legs gripping my back like a vice, her hands pulling at my arse. She was well into the eruptions of a violent climax, heaving up to me and out of control. 'You're fucking me! Oh God, yes, you're fucking me!' she screeched wildly. 'Don't stop! Fuck my cunt more. Please, please—'

For my part I delighted in holding back, playing her like a fish on a hook; altering my angle of penetration, going deep only to withdraw to the knob, which made her thrust against me in desperation to get the full length back up her. I wanted to bring her off several times at least to show what a good fucker I was – if only I could restrain the boiling fire in my balls. To my joy she let out an abandoned cry of 'Aaaargh – I'm coming!' and thrust her hips against me in an absolute frenzy.

She came twice more at least, her body in continuous shudders as I pounded her cunt until it was too much and I had to let fly, emptying my bollocks deep in her with lusty thrusts. When I climbed off her, she lay back as if paralysed, eyes glassy and huge tits heaving as she regained her breath. 'My boy,' she managed to gasp, 'that was heaven, I didn't know where I was. It was really so *good*—' She put out a hand to clasp mine as if in thanks.

It had been bloody marvellous for me too, all that comfy rounded flesh under me, and she'd been so uninhibited, eager to fuck for the sake of the pleasure alone. I could well understand why toy boys loved their older mistresses. There must be a vast array of horny mature ladies out there wanting young cock for their full satisfaction. As if knowing what I was thinking, she said with a content sigh, 'You were so *hard*! I'd forgotten how stiff and erect a young man can get.'

'Your husband can't fuck you like that, I'll bet,' I said boastfully, and she nodded. I toyed with her dangling breasts, lifting them and kissing them. 'Don't dress yet,' I told her. 'We can do it again. Suck me. That will bring it up.'

'I never have,' she whispered, but bent her head to take me in her mouth, sucking inexpertly but soon getting the hang of it. I resisted the temptation to come in her mouth, meaning to do that on a later occasion. When I pulled out from her lips my prick stood flagpole erect, glistening with her saliva. 'I quite enjoyed that,' she said shyly, 'I didn't want to stop. Are you going to fuck me again, Nigel?'

What I had in mind was going in from the rear in doggy-fashion. Her plump arse looked built for a man to have her that way. When I told her to bend over the desk she complied with her back dipped and bum raised, looking back over her shoulder to inform me we were doing things her husband had never done to her. She gasped when I went up her well-juiced cunt full length, but rolled her comfortable bottom hard back against me as the shafting commenced. I gripped her tits, rose on my toes to gain the extra inch and told her to reach back and part her big cheeks for added depth. Then we were going at it like a dog and bitch on heat, crying out together as we climaxed, my belly slapping loudly against her tilted arse. When she left me later I was kissed fondly by a grateful woman.

The little ante-room saw a fair bit of action on future evenings, but best of all was when her husband was absent, lecturing elsewhere, and we made full use of the double bed in their campus flat, even if it meant I had to sneak out at dawn. She proved all woman, willing to experiment and

170

allow me all the lurid things I'd fantasised: tit-fucking, woman-on-top, the sixty-nine position, a bit of bondage, even some playful spanking. She was making up for lost time and I was making a beast of myself. I'm happy to write this in praise of older women. Pay them proper attention, lads, you'll find it well worth your while!

Nigel, Surrey

Keeping Mum

Don't think it's only in this so-called permissive age that sexy activities take place. I well remember the war years when tens of thousands of husbands were away from home, leaving lonely and frustrated wives. My dad was one of those absent men and by 1943 he had been some two years overseas in the Middle East. I was seventeen and not much company for my mum, who was in her late thirties and who did everything for me, like doing my washing, making my bed and having my dinner ready when I came home from the aircraft factory.

She seemed to me to be just an ordinary housewife and I never thought of her as having sexual feelings. Her life consisted of sitting at home, the radio her great source of entertainment. The only evenings I stayed in was when my best mate Arthur called and we played cards. My mother loved that, enjoying the company and games of whist. 'Bring your friend home any time,' she said. 'Arthur is such a nice boy. It makes a break from sitting here by myself every evening.' Arthur, by the way, was a good-looking lad some months younger than me – athletic and well-built. He seemed to greatly enjoy coming to our house.

One evening playing cards, cheating as usual, the ace I'd secreted on my lap slipped to the floor. Bending to pick it up quickly under the table, to my surprise I caught mum and Arthur holding hands! Of course, they instantly let go of each other as I bent down, looking a bit guilty as I sat up in my chair. Are they being soppy with each other? I thought. Surely not! Anyway, I carried on as if I'd noticed nothing. But I was suspicious, even amused to think the unthinkable – that Arthur and my mum were lovers. No, I couldn't imagine that, only that she was fond of him. I mean, she was old enough to be his mother and though she was attractive, I supposed, she wasn't like that.

All the same, I kept an eye on them, tickled pink to think what might be going on. As a randy youth myself who had fucked a few girls, I didn't blame anyone for enjoying some nookie wherever it was to be had.

It was Arthur who suggested we take my mum to the pictures one evening as she'd expressed a wish to see the film. She sat between us with her coat over her knees and, glancing across, I was sure that she and Arthur held hands. Coming out into the night, which was pitch dark in the blackout, I dallied to talk to Eunice, the usherette I was having it off with. When I hurried out to catch mum and Arthur up, my eyes getting used to the dark, I was sure they were walking with arms around each other's waists. Of course they separated as I drew near.

Back home, mum said she'd make tea and Arthur immediately offered to help, going in to the kitchen with her. I waited in the living room, giving them some minutes together, then went through to join them. The door was slightly ajar and the inch or so was quite enough for me to see them by the sink, clasped to each other tightly, kissing really passionately, their mouths fused together. So they were at the kiss-and-cuddle stage! I stood and watched as they kissed several times more before parting. Both seemed quite agitated and breathless from their clinch, so I returned to the living room and waited until they came back with the tea cups and a pot covered by a cosy. I bet, I thought, if I wasn't here the pair of them would go at it. I could tell by

173

the way they snogged each other, their bodies rubbing together.

One weekend we went to a variety show in a nearby town, getting back late on the bus. It had been arranged that Arthur would stay overnight in the spare room. All seemed normal and my friend and I went up to our bedrooms, leaving mum downstairs to tidy up. I lay in bed, not able to sleep. I decided to go to the bathroom along the landing but, on the way, I paused, sure I was hearing noises from downstairs, voices in the still night.

It was just murmurs, almost my imagination, but barefoot and in my pyjamas I tiptoed down. All was dark in the passageway, but I distinctly heard muffled sounds from the direction of the front room, the Sunday-best lounge with the three-piece suite. Low groans, muttered words, the squeak of springs of the couch issued as I cocked an ear outside the door. I risked a gentle push at it and it swung open silently for an inch or so.

Peering in cautiously, the first thing I saw was the glowing red bars of the electric fire in the grate, which gave a ruddy illumination to the room. I made out a pile of clothes as if discarded hurriedly. My eyes transferred to the couch, seeing it from sideways on. Bathed in the red light of the fire, Arthur was stretched out on top of my mum's naked body. The randy sod was fucking her!

He was fucking her good, too, the way his slim arse was bobbing up and down. She wasn't complaining either. Her legs were clasped around his waist and her hands reached down his back to clutch at his bum cheeks. Her thighs rose to meet his thrusts and I could actually see his prick disappearing up her cunt on his forward lunges. As if in ecstasy at being penetrated so lustily, my mother muttered and rambled on while the shafting proceeded. 'Oh, my darling, yes, yes!' I heard her groan. 'Keep fucking me, don't stop yet! It's heaven, lovely – oh so *good*. Push harder, Arthur! Fuck me do—' and her hips bucked as she lost all control, her breasts wobbling on her chest as Arthur loomed above her, shagging away like a demon.

So help me, I watched fascinated, hardly daring to breathe. I saw them pause and guessed they had both climaxed. Mother reached up and drew Arthur's face down to kiss him lovingly. Then she held a nipple up to his mouth and he sucked it, going to the other one in time before she sighed loudly and pulled his face between her cleavage. At that moment, too engrossed in watching the lovers, my shoulder touched the door and it creaked open wider.

Mother sat up like a scalded cat, pushing Arthur away from her, then leapt to her feet. For a brief moment she stood full-frontal before me in the nude, her large breasts and the triangle of thick hair at her crotch on full view, a full-bodied curvacious woman. She snatched up her clothes from the fireside rug and bolted past me, dashing upstairs to her bedroom. That left me standing with a mortified and frightened Arthur.

'Oh, Frank,' he pleaded, blurting out what scared him most. 'Don't ever tell your old man you caught me with your ma. He'd bloody kill me—' To his relief he saw me laugh.

'Don't be so bloody silly,' I told him, grinning. 'What you two do is up to you. I don't blame anyone for having a bit. I bet you enjoyed that, didn't you?' For my part I would have loved to have a nice older woman to fuck. 'How long have you two been shagging?'

Assured of my compliance and relieved by my apparent unconcern that he was doing it with my mother, Arthur relaxed and giggled with me. 'A few weeks now,' he said proudly. 'I thought she liked me. One night she saw me to the door when I was leaving after our card game and, with

175

you still in the living room, she kissed me goodnight, saying she thought me a nice young man. So I kissed her back and she was all for it. Next day I called when you were out and she wasn't so sure, saying it was wrong and all that. But I got kissing her and and she let me get her tits out to play with. Next time I felt her cunt and she rubbed my dick. On about the third or fourth visit she let me fuck her. We've been at it ever since—'

'Rotten sod,' I told him in admiration. 'She's probably up there feeling miserable because I caught you screwing. We'd better go to bed in case she thinks we're talking about her. You can tell me all about it tomorrow.'

I went to my room and got into bed, not surprised that mother came through to me soon after, her eyes red from crying. 'That was a terrible thing for you to see me doing,' she sobbed. 'It's just that I've been so lonely and I've made a fool of myself.'

I felt really sorry for her in such a miserable state and was about to tell her that I didn't mind and that I understood, when she added sorrowfully, 'It was the first time and I feel so ashamed.'

That was a blatant lie, I knew, but I nodded consolingly. 'It will never happen again, of course,' she swore. 'You'll never tell your dad, will you, son?'

I assured her I never would and said, 'Cheer up, mum, I've forgotten it already. Go to bed and forget it as well.'

Next day I cross-questioned Arthur closely, interested as I was in all matters sexual. By then he was quite proud of himself. First I warned him he'd better not boast about it to the village boys and he hastily assured me he'd never do that in case it ever got back to my father. Once that had been cleared up, he delighted in relating all the lurid details of their affair. As the story unfolded I forgot it was my mother he was talking about. It had the ring of truth but I would never have believed it of a sensible and respectable woman like her! After all, I'd seen her being strenuously rogered and loving it, using the 'fuck' word I'd never heard from her lips and telling young Arthur to keep going, push harder, that it was absolute heaven with his stiff prick up her quim!

With me out most evenings, working shifts too, it seemed Arthur had been a regular visitor. I'd noted I hadn't seen so much of him lately. On his arrival no time was wasted, he said, it was down to it right away on the front room couch – or even in her bed when time allowed. Of course, they were in the first flush of their affair so, before the novelty wore off, they fucked like rabbits, as Arthur put it.

There were more suprises in store. Mum went naked and unashamed all the time her boyfriend was with her, lying back on the bed with him and allowing the lad free rein with her body. She had let him rove his hands all over her body, sighing gratefully, even guiding his fingers to her clitoris for her pleasure when he felt her up. He had not only sucked her nipples, which she encouraged him to do, but had suggested that he put his prick between her breasts for a titty-ride. She had said there were other ways of doing it too, rolling over with arse upraised for him to inspect what lie between the valley of her bum cheeks and their first doggy-fashion fuck had resulted. She had taken him in hand right enough, and I reckon he was lucky to have such a tutor. He recalled with delight how she had mounted him, impaled on his prick with her tits bouncing as she rode to her climax.

She had told me it would never happen again but it did, frequently, and Arthur kept me informed. It seemed she was too fond of it to stop. He screwed her in the house and in the nearby wood when spring came. I even caught them once again, coming home from a rained-off Home Guard parade to find them up in her bed – at least that's where they'd been for they came down the stairs double quick and highly embarrassed. Once again mother pleaded that she was a lonely woman, this time saying she couldn't help herself but she had fallen in love with Arthur. True, by this time the pair couldn't keep their eyes off each other.

They got careless, I suppose, and in the heat of their passion Arthur didn't always take the precautions he should have. Whatever shortages there were in the war, there was no shortage of rubbers, condoms or frenchies, as they were variously called. I came home one night to find mother staring into the fire, her eyes red-rimmed.

'Lord help me, son,' she said in utter misery. 'I'm going to have Arthur's baby. The shame of it. What's to become of me? What will your father say?' Soon she grew big with the child, her belly rounded and Arthur's visits stopped dead. The local people put the blame on some unknown soldier from the army camp nearby.

Well, mother wasn't the only village female to get in the family way in those days. Many a local lass and married woman was put up the spout by the squaddies stationed around us. Mum was quite happy to let everyone think it was a lapse with a serviceman that had caused her downfall, preferring that to them knowing it had been a lad younger than her son. A daughter was born in time and dad returned from the war to find an addition to his family, having already been told in a remorseful letter. Susan was a year old when he came back and a delightful love-child. To the old man's credit, he picked her up and tickled her, accepting her as his own. That's how it had to be as many lonely wives had babies while their husbands were away. The Yank troops left a good few souvenirs behind them.

I went for a drink with dad soon after his return. 'So you've got a sister,' he said to me. 'I can live with it, your ma must have had a lonely rotten time of it while I was gone. Did you ever see her with a bloke, some soldier or other?' Never, I told him, and he didn't mention the matter again. He made up for lost time by putting another baby into his wife right away.

Arthur joined the Merchant Navy on completing his apprenticeship and married a New Zealand girl, never to return to the village again. Mother went on living her life as a good wife and mother, reaching a good age before she died. It was her one fling, I believe, and I don't blame her for getting some joy in a dark time. So it all went on years ago, and no doubt this true account of a wartime affair was duplicated all over the country wherever wives were left to fend for themselves and starved of a little warmth in the night.

Frank, Derbyshire

Swallows in Winter

When my firm sent me to work away from home, I took a bed-sit in a large house divided up for that purpose and befriended a woman on the same landing. Miranda was twenty-eight to my twenty-two, a plain type with spectacles and straight hair but a curvy figure. It started when I offered to carry her bags of groceries upstairs. One night she invited me into her room for a meal. Later that week I cooked a chicken and, there being more than enough, decided to ask her to join me. I was knocking at her door when she appeared from the bathroom along the corridor, carrying her soap bag and dressed only in her dressing gown. She must have seen me looking at the clinging divide of her big breasts, for she gave me a little smile.

She came to dinner and helped me wash up the dishes, then stayed to chat. We'd seen off nearly two bottles of wine and while I was pouring more drinks at the sideboard she rose to inspect my untidy bookcase which was overflowing with books and magazines. Some of these were porn that I'd collected and, to my horror, these were the ones she picked up and began to flick through. When I rejoined her, wondering what to say, she held up a double-page spread. In glorious colour there were several pictures of a very well-endowed man having his prick sucked by a lovely girl.

'That's a lovely cock,' she said admiringly. 'Do you enjoy oral sex? These photographs really are a turn-on, aren't they? Would you like me to do that to you, Michael?'

180

Two reactions occurred at her words: one was that I gasped in surprise, the other was an immediate thickening of my prick. I stood before her with the two full glasses in my hand, muttering that I would love that – if she wanted to – and she reached out a hand to unzip my fly and draw out my tool. By then I was very aroused and her cupping my balls in one hand and wanking my shaft in the other had me trembling.

'It's so warm and hard,' Miranda said. 'You don't mind me doing this, do you? It's just that I'm into this sort of thing, I do enjoy it, and you seem a lonely young man. Why shouldn't we please each other?'

Why not indeed? I thought, spilling wine as I hastily put down the glasses. I'd never met a woman so refreshingly honest about her desires. The main thing was she was doodling my dick delightfully, so much so that I had to restrain myself from coming over her wrist.

It was mid-winter, so what with the roaring fire I'd made for her visit plus my aroused state, I was boiling over in more ways than one. To my groans of pure pleasure, she pulled my prick to her lips, gobbled the circumcised crown and then sucked me into her mouth. Buckling at the knees, I started to come quickly. She swallowed but some dribbled down her chin. She gathered it with a finger and licked it clean, as if savouring a delicacy. 'You're quite salty,' she announced.

'Would you do the same for me now?'

It would have been churlish to refuse, besides the fact I was eager to see her cunt and lick it, something I loved doing to my girlfriend at home. Miranda rose and rucked up her skirt, drawing down scarlet knickers and crossing to my bed to lie back with her legs over the edge. With her skirt up, bare thighs parted and bottom raised on one of my pillows, she offered a hairy mound with a pouting gash.

181

I fell on my knees on the threadbare carpet and rubbed my nose and mouth against its soft moistness, kissing it hungrily and inserting my tongue to savour its sharp piquant flavour.

'Lick me clean,' I heard her mutter. 'Tongue-fuck me! Make me come! Yes, there – flick your tongue there—'

I really reemed her out and she came with great heaves of her broad arse. When she laid back to recuperate, I leapt on top of her, my fingers fumbling at her blouse, eager to bare her big tits, my mouth seeking hers. She turned her face away, saying, 'No, no, Michael, we mustn't get too close. Be satisfied with what we've done, please—'

I paused, with several buttons of her blouse undone, gazing at the white swelling mounds of her tits as they bulged over her bra.

'I'm a married woman. I'm only living here until I can join my husband in Canada. I know you want to fuck me,' she said compassionately, 'but I don't take the pill and I can't risk getting pregnant, can I? Not with an excitable young man like you. We can suck each other, I'd like that, but we can't be proper lovers—'

Of course, through licking her out I had regained a mighty hard-on. I had noticed she wore a wedding ring, but thought she must be separated or divorced, living as she did in a bed-sit. I stood in front of her to let her see my engorged tool. She smiled kindly and trailed her fingers over it. 'We can do something about this, of course,' she offered. 'What would you like? I could suck it again—' As I stood there, not daring to say what I wanted, she added, 'Don't be shy, tell me. Anything but fucking—'

'I'd love to see your breasts,' I said through a dry throat. 'Is that OK?' She nodded, pulling her blouse out of her waistband and removing her bra. Her tits were huge and shaped like melons, the small nipples dead in the centre of the rounds.

'Come here,' she said, 'I know what you want – it's a titty-fuck, isn't it? It doesn't do much for me, but you can if that's what you want. I'll sit up and you stand before me. There, put it in my cleavage and I'll push my breasts together for you—'

It was warm and soft between her tits. I went up on tiptoe to thrust my prick into the channel thus formed. 'Tell me when you are coming,' Margaret warned. 'I'll finish you with my mouth.'

That was about all I could take and, aware of my agitated jerks, she bent her neck to suck greedily on my knob, accepting the series of spurts I shot into her.

Over the next month or two until she left for Canada, we sucked and wanked each other all the time. On certain nights that cold winter we slept together for warmth and company, but never was I allowed the ultimate pleasure. However, I wasn't complaining!

Michael, York

Night-School Nookie

Like every other husband, I suppose, I considered my wife Wendy would be the last one to take up with another man but you can never tell, even after years of marriage. I mean, we got on great, with rarely a cross word and our sex life was fine. Come one winter and as usual she took a course in the local adult education centre – Drawing and Painting being her choice. Now our daughter had left home, my wife had time on her hands and experimented with canvas and oils. She looked forward to her two nights a week at the class, bringing home quite presentable portraits and landscapes.

I watched television most nights waiting for her return, the supper ready, and she would breeze in looking elated and starry-eyed, getting later each week. She explained that the students would discuss their work after class and time just flew. It was often well after eleven before she returned but I was pleased that she had such an interest. She enthused about a young chap called Elwin whom she said was brilliant and had helped her more than the tutor. I'd seen him around our small town in his ponytail and jeans. He looked like a typical student layabout, very arty.

Wendy returned home one night with her latest painting, a bowl of fruit which was going to be hung in the town's library along with other class efforts. Of course Elwin had several of his in pride of place and I must admit he was good. I went with Wendy to the exhibition and was greatly struck by a full-length nude by the star artist.

It was priced at seventy-five pounds and I would have bought it except that I didn't know what Wendy would say about having such a picture hanging over our fireplace. The model looked familiar, although she had her face turned away, her hair across her cheek. The rest of her – the skin suffused pink by the glow of a fire, the ample breasts, the curve of the rounded hips and the dark triangle of hair at the fork of slightly parted legs – all reminded me of how my wife looked when nude. Of course, I'd never seen her laid out like that before a glowing fire, and the model looked slightly less mature than my Wendy, but it could have been her double. The left arm and hand lay languidly beside an open book, beautifully painted, and I noted no rings on the model's fingers. Wendy wore several rings and never took them off. I moved on to view other pictures, still wishing that I had the nerve to buy it, not even mentioning to Wendy how it reminded me of her. Of course I only saw her naked those days undressing for bed or getting out of the bath.

On the last night of the exhibition I stayed at home. There was a party for the local arty-farties with cheese and wine and lots of chat. Wendy came in near midnight excited and flushed. Someone had actually bought her still-life painting. She drew off her coat revealing her big shapely tits and the rounds of her curvaceous arse. Surprisingly she plonked herself down in my lap. She'd had a few glasses of wine to celebrate, no doubt, and couldn't contain herself. She kissed me long and passionately, the pliant weight of her bum squirming down on my dick, which of course gave the first few twitches of arousal.

'What was that for?' I grinned, sensing a good fuck in the offing, the kind of session a husband doesn't often get after a few years of marriage. She was no doubt on a high.

I cupped a tit and squeezed it, my tongue meeting hers. 'I like it. What have I done?'

'You've let me clutter up the house with my paints,' she said. 'And never once complained about me coming home late. I've been neglecting you, dear.' Then she paused, smiling wickedly, as if unable adding, 'Have you wondered why you haven't had it so much lately? You know, *it*! What we do in bed—'

To tell the truth, I hadn't. I thought we had made love as usual – not as much as a man likes, but on most weekends. However, her impish smile made me suddenly aware she was dying to tell me something. I played along with her. 'Damn right,' I said, getting a tremendous feeling of excitement that my quiet and conventional Wendy had been playing away from home. 'I *have* noticed that we haven't been at it so much lately—'

She kissed me again, giving her bottom another wiggle into my groin, smirking as our mouths parted. 'It's that Elwin,' she giggled. 'He's *fucking* me. Tonight after the art show. I want you to fuck me now—'

To my recollection this was the first time I'd ever heard her use the word and, together with her admitting to screwing the young painter, it really got me horny. Mixed with it was a feeling of betrayal, a bitter-sweet humiliation that only added to the thrill. I thought of Elwin making free with her lovely tits, his prick going up her moist cunt and her parting her legs willingly for him. 'You randy bitch,' I said, more in wonder than anger. 'Slut. Tart. Whore—'

'Yes, yes,' she agreed feverishly, her arse grinding down on my now fully engorged prick. 'Call me those things, love. That's what I've been—' I'd never known her so completely wanton and, mixed as my feelings were about her fucking Elwin, it turned me on.

'You like it, knowing I've been with him,' she whispered.

'I can feel you're hard. Why don't you fuck me, Graham.'

'Fuck is it?' I said as we kissed again and again, our bodies squirming into each other. 'Fuck. I've never heard you say that—'

'That's the word, isn't it?' she said. 'Fuck. Elwin fucked me. Now I want you to fuck me. Fuck me. Fuck my cunt—'

'And how long has he been having you?' I had to ask. 'Not just tonight, I'll bet.'

But now she was standing before me, pulling off her dress, throwing her clothes aside in her eagerness. 'You too,' she said. 'Take me on the carpet naked. Let's fuck. I never wanted it more.'

Stripped in moments, I mounted her, going straight up her juicy cunt first thrust. In my excitement I came at once. Thankfully, such was her excitement that she came off with me, almost bucking me off her in her throes. We lay side by side, recovering, and I reached for her hand to squeeze it.

We kissed and cuddled and she told me that Elwin had been fucking her at least twice a week for several months. Something like over a hundred fucks at her, I reckoned. However, I felt it had made a new woman of her, bringing out an uninhibited nature that had been dormant. It was the fact that she'd had two men wanting her that had made her desire for sex so intense. She had wanted to share her newfound lustful feelings with me and that night had seemed the perfect chance. Who was I to complain? She bent her head to suck me and we had a longer fuck on the carpet before we went to bed to continue making love. Looking back, it was well worth her having an affair at her time of life to awaken her passion.

My one regret was that I didn't buy that nude painting. She agreed it was of her when I asked, saying Elwin had actually painted it in our home on afternoon visits and, after posing, the randy pair would retire to bed. What I did get to keep as a souvenir was a sheaf of pencil drawings her lover had made in preparation. They showed Wendy nude in a variety of positions, standing, sitting and prone, her big breasts and pubic hair featured in each one. I've had them framed and they have pride of place on the wall of my den.

Graham, Middlesex

The Milkman Cometh

My sexiest experience is an unusual one, I think, and goes back some years when I was nineteen and a student at a well-known university. I couldn't live in the college but was supplied with a list of addresses of people who took in student lodgers. I settled for the first one I tried, the woman who answered the door being a handsome and welcoming female of some thirty years, so darkly attractive that it was no surprise to find she was Italian. Maria made lovely meals, great pasta dishes in particular in the days when they were not so common as they are now in Britain. Added to her friendly nature and carefree outlook, she had a truly magnificent pair of tits. She was plump and short but very shapely, with flaring hips and a lovely round arse.

Her husband was English, having met his wife when she came to work as a cook at the university. We all got on well. Tom was an engineer and often worked overseas on the building of hospitals and airport runways in under-developed countries. He sought out these kind of jobs as they were well paid.

Maria was careless about bolting the door of the bathroom and I'd often barge in to find her there. Sometimes she'd be having a wash just in her overflowing bra and knickers and she'd laugh and wave me away.

I spent hours wanking over the sight of her rounded arse and lovely big tits. Seeing them wobble about under her dress was enough to turn me on. One day I went into the bathroom and she was actually in the bath, sitting up with her two bounteous boobs in full view, thrusting out like a pair of full-sized rugby balls. Their weight and fullness seemed to defy gravity. They shook enticingly as she giggled at my embarrassment. Those ripe teats had me stumbling out with glazed eyes at the sight, necessitating a retreat to my room to toss myself off.

Tom, the lucky swine, put Maria in the family way, much to their joy. This was no surprise to me as I well knew how fond of fucking they were. I often heard them going at it like the clappers and would pause enviously outside their bedroom door as I went upstairs at night. Oh, how I would have loved to have had Maria naked in my bed! Maria bloomed with pregnancy, her tits bigger than ever and her belly ballooning. Just before she was due, Tom was offered a trip to the oil-rich Arabian peninsula.

'Don't worry about Maria,' he told me on his departure, handing me the keys to his car. 'Where she's from they have babies like rabbits. Her ma had fourteen of 'em.'

Sure enough Maria took it all as a matter of course. The night before she was due she informed me casually that she'd like a bath, but would need to be helped in and out. Just like that! I ran the hot water for her and she emerged from her bedroom in a dressing gown. Right there beside me she slipped it off to stand naked and pregnantly beautiful, her great tits thrusting out with rubbery big dark-brown nipples like thumbs. The enlarged curve of her belly pressed against my hip, the satiny skin as tight as a drum. She laughed at my unease, holding out a hand for me to help her into the bath. As she cocked a leg to step in, I saw the forest of hair surrounding her cunt.

She told me to wait, saying she wouldn't be long, so I watched her soap her tits, lifting them to wash underneath. Then she asked me to sponge her back. I helped dry her while she stood on the bathmat. Then, with a cockstand straining my trouser front, she asked me to go with her to the bedroom. Still naked, she laid back on the bed with her belly so round and huge she could hardly see over it.

'Rub my tummy with this oil,' she said, handing me a bottle. 'It's what we do in Italy to prevent stretch marks after the birth. Tom always does it but he's not here. You smooth it in, Simon. It's so relaxing.'

Relaxing for her maybe, I thought, as I gazed at her, a cunt mouth staring me in the face. I could have just slipped my cock up it.

Tom flew back next day and was present when their daughter Antonia arrived. After a few days he flew back, not wishing to miss out on the big pay packet and with his wife's full agreement. Therefore I was left alone in the house with her. Like a good mum she breast-fed her tot. At tea-time, when I returned from college, she'd join me at the table with the baby, calmly sitting there with a teat bare, feeding Antonia.

'You don't mind, do you, Simon?' she said the first time. 'In Italy it is natural to feed the baby in front of the family. You are family, so who cares?'

I did, for one, watching as each succulent tit was produced to feed the baby, first on one side and then the other. At times she wouldn't bother to tuck the unused breast back into her dress, leaving both free. As she didn't mind, I gazed in fascination at her two superb udders, the thick nipples running with greyish milk. Well aware of my stare, she teased me by squeezing at a tit, sending the fluid squirting out at me. As the baby's mouth sought the proffered nipple I would think what a lucky little thing she was. Sated, she would sleep at the cushiony breast.

'I've enough milk here to feed a dozen children,' Maria observed. 'My family have always made too much.' True enough, often the front of her dress became saturated between feeds.

One night I returned from an evening lecture to find Maria on the couch with her breasts out, holding one over a basin and squeezing it. Milk spurted from the nipple as she massaged the tit flesh and the basin was half filled.

'I make too much,' she explained. 'Antonia is full and will sleep all night, but my breasts hurt, so I must draw it off. I do this every night. I did not think you would be in. It takes so long and is such a nuisance, but what am I to do?'

I could have told her, right then with her milk-swollen tits bare and nipples dripping, that I longed to suckle such ambrosian sustenance. From her sly smile it was evident that she was thinking along the same lines.

'What would you like for supper?' she enquired archly. 'This takes so long that I've nothing ready. Baked beans on toast, Simon – or would you prefer warm milk?' She laughed at my consternation, jiggling her tits delightfully. 'Come *on*, silly boy,' she said. 'I know what you want to do, so why don't you say so? It would help me too. Come here, come to me!'

As if in a dream, I sat beside her on the couch and she drew me with a strong arm across her lap. I lay face up with a bloated breast before my nose. 'There, there,' she cooed softly, cupping the distended titty and directed the thick nipple to my lips. I closed my eyes and, in a state of ecstasy, I sucked on her too fiercely. My inexperienced mouth lost the nipple and it plopped out, the milk running down my chin.

'No,' she said sharply, feeding the nipple back to my searching lips. 'Suck gently. You're too excited. Relax. Oh, yes, that is right! Now I feel my milk flowing. Suck harder now—'

The warm fluid filled my mouth and I learned to suck and swallow at the same time, as I nestled like a baby to her breast. Her milk was like syrup in my mouth and the action of suctioning at the teat with her big pliant boob against my face was indescribably erotic.

'My *bambino*, my other baby,' Maria crooned soothingly. 'Suck, suck, there is plenty for you. Do you like it?' I had been taught never to speak with my mouth full, and never was my mouth more delightfully filled, so I nodded humbly into the bulge of her tit.

I had, of course, the most rampant hard-on that I'd ever known and it threatened to burst through my fly. Maria too, I noticed, was becoming agitated, emitting little moans and sighs. The hand cupping the tit moved down and sought the iron-hard bar of prick tenting my trouser front.

'Oh, feeding you has made me *loving*,' she said, her voice thick. 'You too, Simon. It feels so *hard*!'

She pulled away to take the nipple from my lips and shifted her shoulders so that the other one brushed my mouth. I drew it in, feeling a renewed supply fill my throat as I sucked. When I had evidently drained the second tit to her satisfaction, she muttered 'Now that is much more comfortable for me, they do not hurt—' She did not cover up her boobs but allowed them to hang before my face, her hand still clasping my rigid cock.

'Now,' she said kindly. 'You have relieved me so I should do the same for you.' My zip was drawn down and her hand delved in to draw out my cock. The sight made her go all giggly. 'Such a big one,' she praised me. 'I would like to have it but it is too soon after having my Antonia. Never mind, there is another way—'

I thought that a woman's hand wanking me off would be the perfect finish to our marvellous session of breast-feeding.

The actuality was even better.

'You fed from me, I shall do the same from you,' she murmured wickedly. 'I like to do it, Tom says I'm very good. It will be a pleasure to suck off your nice big cock.'

She bent her head, holding the upright stalk to her lips for a fond kiss, then sucked on me avidly until I groaned out and shook to my toes, filling her warm mouth with spunk. She sat up beaming.

'So naughty,' she laughed, 'but nice! You are so *slow*, Simon, didn't you know I have wanted you to fuck me for a long time? Now you will have to wait a little while for that!'

What pleasures we miss through not daring to ask for them! Nevertheless in a week or two I knew what heaven it was to be in bed beside Maria's plump nakedness and what it was like to fuck her moist, tight cunt. I shafted her nightly and dutifully fed on the over-abundant milk supply she produced. Tom worked abroad for a good deal of the time I lodged there so you could say I filled in for him!

Simon, Bristol

Every Boy Should Have One

I was lucky enough as a teenager to be taken in hand by an older lady. No doubt she got great satisfaction and titillation by seducing an untutored boy, but who's complaining? Every boy should have a randy mature woman eager to teach him the ropes.

Billy was my closest school chum. We were both six-formers and, like all boys, as horny as we would ever be. I was often at his house and in the company of his good-looking mother. She was busty and curvy, and sometimes joined her son and I when we swam at the town's indoor baths on Sunday mornings. She well knew how I stole looks at her figure in her one-piece costume which when wet, clung to the contours of her big tits and the muscles of her lovely arse. Aware I had a hopeless crush on her and with her husband away at sea, I was sure she teased me on purpose. For instance, when calling one day and leaving my bike in the back garden, I went in the back door to find her doing the ironing in just her bra and knickers. She didn't seem to mind at all. She said Billy was out but I could wait for him and stopped to get me a drink of orange, all the time floating about in her underwear.

Looking back with the wisdom of age, I know she was enjoying flaunting herself before me. I know that bra and panties are no more revealing than a bikini, but it was the thought of her in her undies that turned me on. Of course I wanked later, inspired by her lush womanly body – the creamy big tits overflowing the bra cups, and the hint of a cunt bulge between her thighs.

Billy, his mum and I went on holiday to Scarborough that same summer, staying in a small private hotel. After a swim in the sea, his mother went back to the hotel and, like the love-struck young swain I was, I followed shortly after, leaving Billy chatting to a girl he'd met on the beach. My dream was about to come true.

I dashed upstairs to the room I shared with Billy, which was next to hers. The next moment I was rewarded by her tapping the door and entering, fresh from a shower and in her dressing gown. 'You really will have to stop following me about, young man,' she said kindly. 'It's becoming noticeable. You should find a girl your own age. You're such a nice boy. Would a kiss make you feel better?'

'Oh, yes,' I said, my hopes soaring. 'I think you are beautiful.'

She laughed softly. 'You mustn't think of me that way, Tom. Come here, you silly boy—'

She took me in her arms and we kissed, her mouth soft on mine. Unable to let her go, I held her tight, kissing her back passionately, slipping my tongue into her mouth as I had done with schoolgirls. To my delight, she allowed it to continue, returning my kisses. When she pulled away she sat upon my bed, somewhat flustered and not her usual calm self. I stood in front of her with a raging cockstand which was bulging out of my boxer shorts.

'Please let me—' I begged her. I meant let me continue kissing her sweet mouth.

'This is wrong,' she said, which I suppose has been uttered enough times when an older woman dallies with a boy. 'But since it means so much to you – would you like to see me properly?'

All I could do was nod dumbly as she slipped off the

dressing gown. I goggled at all that shapely flesh: large prominent breasts with thick nipples and plump womanly thighs with a great bush of hair between.

'Have you never seen a woman naked, Tom?' She asked quietly. 'Do you like me?'

I nodded, tongue-tied.

'Would you like to make love?'

Would I? I went for her with arms outstretched but she held me off.

'No,' she said, 'let's do it as it should be done. A handsome boy like you will have his pick, but never forget the woman wants to receive pleasure too. Kiss me first and feel my breasts. Would you like to suck on my nipples? Women like that. And take off those shorts.'

As ordered, I stepped out of my boxer shorts, hoping she would be impressed by my manhood. 'You poor boy,' she said. 'Have I done that to you? It looks so dreadfully stiff it must be painful.' I hadn't said a word so far, nodding my head in answer and feeling overawed. 'Come here, little man,' she said, growing impatient, holding her arms out, her lovely tits bobbing on her chest.

I think it fair to say that I went to her with a strangled sob, kissing wildly at her mouth, neck and breasts. 'Don't be so impatient,' she ordered but, pressed to all that warm flesh, my prick jammed between our stomachs, I gasped and jerked like a landed fish, coming my load all over her. Was I ashamed! I felt I had utterly disgraced myself and let her down.

'I'm sorry, I'm sorry,' I said in my humiliation. To make matters worse, as I got up from her I saw that my come had dripped down the curve of her lower belly and was matted in her thick growth of cunt hair.

She sat up and took my face in her hands. 'Don't worry, dear,' she consoled me. 'I should have expected you'd be

197

too excited. I'll shower again, and you'd better clean yourself up as well.' With that she got up, a very disappointed woman, I was certain. As she walked off, putting on her dressing gown, the glimpse I got of her truly magnificent buttocks only added to my misery. I'd blown it. I was sure there would never be a repeat performance.

Over the next two days, she acted entirely normally towards me, just as if I were a son to her, like Billy. Luckily he'd made friends with a girl and, as we sat at tea in the hotel dining room, he announced he was going out on a date.

'Tom and I will go to see that film we've been talking about,' said his mum. I sat glumly, thinking what might have been, as my desired one went upstairs to get ready for the cinema. Alone with Billy, he excitedly told me he was hoping for a feel of his girl's tits and maybe her quim that evening. I went upstairs to get ready. As I passed his mother's door, which was slightly ajar, my heart flutererd as I heard her call my name. 'Has Billy left?' she said, standing behind the door out of my view. I said he had. 'Would you like to come in?' she added.

I entered to find her standing absolutely naked beside the bed. 'Shall we continue where we left off the other day?' she asked unnecessarily. 'We've all evening now—' I went into her arms and we kissed passionately. I felt her breasts and lowered my mouth to them. 'Take off your clothes,' she said, a catch in her voice.

Naked in seconds, I joined her on the bed, fondling and groping and muttering my love for her. She guided my hand to her cunt and I began to finger her moist folds, she directing my wrist so that I touched her the way she wanted. I'd heard of the clitoris of course. Now I felt its projection, like a stiff fingertip. As I fondled her she began to groan and pull me on top of her. 'Put it in me, my darling,' she whispered. 'You want to, don't you? I'm ready for you—'

She was indeed, randy, eager and well lubricated as I discovered when she guided my stiff dick to her crack and pushed it inside. It was heaven in there, my prick gripped tight between the wet walls of her cunt. I told myself to stay calm, determined not to disgrace myself by coming prematurely. She moved against me sensuously, raising her hips, telling me that it was lovely, just lovely, to keep doing it. I settled into a regular rhythm, hitting her with long strokes, remaining silent as I concentrated hard on keeping from coming prematurely.

The same could not be said for her. Her arse rolled about on the bed, her pelvis jerked, her arms and hands dragged me ever closer to get extra depth.

'Oh, yes,' she groaned. 'Fuck me, Tom, keep fucking me—' Her use of the forbidden word thrilled me. 'This is so wicked, *wicked*,' she cried out in her throes. 'We shouldn't be doing this. Oh, you naughty boy – you are making me COME. Oh, oh, *aaagh!*' Just in time, for I could no longer hold myself back, she went into a wild series of spasms, crying out that she was DONE! In my pride at arousing her to such unruly behaviour, I came with vigorous thrusts, thrusting into her with complete abandon.

She kissed me lovingly as if in congratulation and there was no cinema outing that night. The two of us remained naked on the bed, kissing and fondling, and I fucked her again three or four times. Both of us seemed to be insatiable.

'You must never tell a soul about this,' she warned me several times as we played with each other.

With Billy giving all his time to his girlfriend for the rest of that week, his mum and I fucked at every opportunity. One night, with Billy sound asleep in the bed across my room, I even risked tapping on her door, so eager was I to have her again. She let me in, alarmed at the risk, but after my kisses and entreaties, took off her nightie and allowed me a fuck.

I may have had a crush on her, but she got somewhat infatuated too. On our return home I visited her house whenever I could, taking her in the marital bed, on the settee, in the bath and, at the times when her hubby was home on leave, in the back of her car in the country. The sex we had was almost like a drug to her and she allowed me to do anything. She liked sucking me off and I happily returned the favour. I had her astride me and kneeling on all fours; we even stole kisses in the house when her husband and son were present in another room. It all ended when he caught us smooching in the kitchen. A hell of a row followed and I was barred from coming near her home again. Not that there was much he could do about it when he was away at sea!

Thomas, Suffolk

An Ill Wind

I caught my mother making out with another woman. It's none of my business, really, I suppose. I'm her twenty-year-old son and she is in her late thirties, divorced from my dad who long ago went off with a girl who he's now married.

One night the date I had never turned up. It was pissing with rain so I thought of the cosy fire at home and the telly. I walked into our living room to find mother engaged in a certain sex act with her female friend. Both were naked on the couch. Of course I backed out quick and went up to my room. It was the other woman who got dressed and came up to explain they were long-time lovers. I said what they did was up to them and was invited to go back downstairs for supper. I did but I felt awkward, my mind full of what I'd seen: the two women's naked bodies, my mother bending over the other woman, who was lying back with her legs spread. I had done the same with girlfriends, but I would never have thought—

Once it was out in the open, the woman often stayed the night and I'd lay in bed just imagining what they were up to. Then one night, when I was in alone, I answered the door to a young nurse. She was looking for her mother – my mother's lover – to let her know that she had been called in for night duty in an emergency and wanted to let her mum know she wouldn't be home until morning. I asked her in, saying her mother was out with mine. I'd just made a pot of tea and a sandwich and I made the same for her. As we sat chatting, I thought what a lovely girl she was.

'You know, of course, that your mother and mine are lesbian,' she said matter-of-factly. 'I'm glad they have each other. Your mother is a nice lady.'

'How long have you known?' I said.

'For years,' the girl said. 'Don't tell me you didn't know before you caught them at it?'

When I shook my head, she gave a little laugh. 'My mum told me about it. It must have been quite a shock for you. They're glad it's out in the open now.'

I laughed too and decided she was so nice that a little chatting up was in order. I asked for a date and we went out several times, soon getting closer to the kissing and cuddling stage when I said goodnight. One night we came back from the pictures and I asked her in for coffee. She saw her mother's coat hanging in the hallway beside my mother's but there was no sign of either of them. I sat on the couch with Kay and kissed her. I'd never gone further. She started to giggle. 'Those two of ours are upstairs in bed,' she said. 'What's good for them is good enough for us. Let's go up to your bedroom, Kev, it's about time you and I did more than kiss.'

The chance was too good to miss. We tiptoed up the stairs and in my room she unveiled her pretty body – small pointed tits and a tight rounded bum. She threw open her arms for a moment to let me see her full frontal and then dived under the covers, grinning at me.

It was heaven to hold her in my arms, to kiss her mouth, fondle her tits, and to slide down her squirming body to place my mouth over her twat. When I mounted her I fucked her without restraint and filled her with my come, both of us trying not to make the bed rattle too much with our screwing. Kay was all for it, climbing over me to squat on

202

my dick later in the night, telling me to suck her nipples as she rode me. We sneaked back downstairs before dawn and I walked her home, delighted to have found such an uninhibited girl.

In time we got married and when my mother moved into the house of her lover, Kay and I had a ready-made home. So it's an ill-wind that blows no good, my ma having an affair with another woman led me to meet the girl who became my wife!

Kevin, Bath

The Lay of the Land

OK, so let's get it straight – fucking is the name of my game and I make no apologies. I spent twenty years in Australia and left an ex-wife out there because she didn't go much on my philandering. That's a big word for shagging sun-bronzed Sheilas every chance I got. Divorced and with the wherewithal to pursue my main interest, I decided to return to England to seek out the lay of the land.

No pun intended but I found her. Ginny is short for Virginia and shorter still for Virgin – not that she's been one of those since she wore pigtails and a gym slip, I imagined. I spotted her in a night-club and was immediately impressed. You could say she was ripe, big in all the right places – just my type. I guessed she was in her late twenties, dressed in an evening dress so low-cut that her magnificent mammaries swelled over the top. I gauged her two creamy tits as forty-inchers at least, with a cleavage you couldn't have stuck a coin in edgeways. Though she was well-developed she had not an ounce of fat on her. Her silky dress clung to a flat stomach, and flowed over flaring hips and curvy thighs. I circled about, drooling. Her back view was just as good, more so, if you were an arse-man. The gown revealed an unblemished bare back right down to where the taut moons of a broad backside thrust out. What an arse for a back-scuttle! I thought in awe.

She was with several men and women at the bar, a real beauty with dark chestnut hair framing her face and full lips. Had I gone to her crawling, I'd been on 'all fives' as the saying goes, my prick already as stiff as a post. I edged into the company, free-loaders all, I knew. They accepted my offers of drinks. I took the women, all good-lookers, to be hostesses or whores, enthusiastic amateurs possibly, supplementing their office salaries or housewives earning spare mortgage money. I chatted Ginny up and found her a good-natured and somewhat naive young woman, not a hard-faced pro. I bought her dinner, an outrageously expensive meal she wolfed down as if she hadn't eaten for days, poured wine into her and asked her back to my hotel.

I had met my match. All of Ginny gloriously naked across my bed proved an experience such as I'd never encountered. She put on no act, being as horny as a bucket of randy frogs, a completely uninhibited woman. She let me do everything and I mean *everything*. I made a meal of her great tits, sucked her, fucked her front and back, and she cried out, thrust herself up at me wildly, demanding more. I was drained and spent, not even able to raise a hard with her luscious lips circling my debilitated dong. Ginny actually pouted her disappointment. I left the bed to pour drinks at the sideboard and returned to find that she was lying with her thighs parted, shapely legs over the edge of the bed, diddling her auburn-bushed cunt with her fingers. Here, indeed, was a woman after my own heart. I stood watching until she reared her arse off the bed and came with a strangled groan.

'I couldn't help it, I know I'm awful,' she whimpered. 'I just had to have another come—'

I got to know her intimately (and how!) over the next few days. Once a beauty queen, she'd come to London from a small town hoping to make it as an actress. The only stage she'd managed to appear on was in a Soho strip joint, and the only films the blue kind. Much as she loved a good fuck, she had not liked the type of men such work brought her into contact with. Times were hard for her. She was living in a cockroach-ridden bedsit and considering a career as a whore. 'Not on the streets,' she shuddered. 'That's too dangerous.' She'd had the offer of pimps, but shied clear of them.

The night I met her at the club had been her first venture into meeting a better class of client.

What is money for but to spend? I'd made plenty so I decided to spend some on Ginny. First I paid the rent on a decent flat in a good area, a pad where we exhausted ourselves with lust. Even then she could have carried on. She was truly insatiable and made more so by randy talk. Though intrigued by all kinds of lewdness, even after some of our more experimental bouts she pretended to be shocked. 'You really are a dirty beast, wanting to do *that* to me,' she'd say. 'Honestly, Donnie, you are the limit. Before I met you I wouldn't have thought that possible—' As weeks went on, it struck me that it would take two men or more to satisfy her. I liked the idea.

In the flat above us lived a young chap who I sometimes chatted to when I met him on the stairs. One day in a pub nearby, Billy joined me. He was from the north and was working in a supermarket. As we drank, his shyness faded, finding in me, I think, a soul companion.

'Your wife is a real beauty,' he said in awe. 'That's what I call a woman. She shops where I work and everybody stops to admire her. Lucky you!'

'She's not my wife,' I told him. Looking at his youthful face, I thought, boy, could I do you a favour! 'I'll buy some booze,' I said, 'and we'll go back and have a party. I'll get a Chinese takeaway as well. She loves that. Let's make a night of it—'

When I ushered him into our room, Ginny was wearing

just a kimono and nothing else. She didn't mind me being late and welcomed our guest, who looked at her ripe beauty like a man in a daze. Ginny ate most of the food, chatting happily, hardly aware I was refilling her glass with gin. I sat on the bed beside her while Billy sat in the armchair, his eyes trained on the mounds of her tits bulging her kimono.

Then I slipped an arm around Ginny, cupping a weighty breast and kissing her neck. She turned her face as if to object, but I glued my mouth to hers, tonguing her, and she responded for a moment before pulling away.

'Not with *him* here, Donnie,' she protested, breathless from the kiss and giggly with drink. Across the room Billy almost had his tongue hanging out.

'He told me he thinks you are the most gorgeous woman that's ever walked the earth,' I told her. Ever eager to accept flattery, she smiled across at him. I slipped the loose robe from her shoulders and she shrieked as it fell to her waist, revealing her two beautiful tits. Before she could protest further, I'd pulled her back on the bed, nuzzling her cleavage, seeking the nipples.

'You'll give that lad ideas,' she moaned, but I knew I had her by the way she held my head, pulling my face into the warm depths of her bosom. 'It's not right, you mustn't! Oh, Donnie, no – not now – oh, you beast, you've put it in me—'

Unaccustomed as I was to public shagging, I hitched up her robe, pulled out my prick and buried it to the hilt in her receptive cunt. Ginny groaned and began working her thighs against me, her hands clasping my arse. The first few shoves had her as delirious as usual, thrusting her mound up and wanting every inch.

'You swine,' she uttered. 'You don't care what you do, fucking me with that boy here. Oh God, he's standing over us, watching! It's too much. Oh, now I'm going to come –

oh, save me. Aaaagh, it's there! You bastard, shove it up, all up, don't stop! What dirty things we are – I'm going to come again—'

Indeed she did, bucking like a bronco, crying out wild oaths in her turmoil. Turning my head after I'd shot my load up her, I saw Billy, cock in hand, standing over us. 'Get out of your clothes,' I urged him. 'Take over, Billy. She always wants more. Shaft her. Go on, don't stand there wanking yourself, give her one. She wants it—'

I rolled off Ginny, leaving her with thighs parted and cunt pouting. 'You can't mean him—' she began, but lifted her arse for me to drag the kimono down over her feet. 'Not him—?'

But Billy was not to be denied, and no wonder, with all that ripe nudity facing him. He went between her legs and I couldn't help noticing that she grasped his prick, directing it to her fanny.

'I won't stop you, fuck me if you want to,' she moaned. 'Isn't this awful of us? We're beasts in the fields – oh yes, Billy, push it right up. Oh goodness, what are you doing to me? Go on, go on – it's so nice and hard—'

We screwed her singly and together during the orgy that followed, Ginny more willing and able to continue than the pair of us. I became master of ceremonies, directing them to do this or that, like Billy fucking her tits, taking the sixty-nine position and having her doggy-fashion until the room stank of sex. Still Ginny wanted more. We were forced to try to penetrate her with wilted pricks, she scorning our efforts. In the end we slept, three naked bodies collapsed across the bed. I awoke to find Ginny mounted over Billy around dawn, her tits flying as she ground down on his prick, the lad looking wan and hollow-eyed.

He dropped in regularly after that, and even came to visit us at weekends when I bought a house outside London.

Ginny is still with me, we've been married now for a couple of years. It delights my heart when we holiday in the Mediterranean resorts and men ogle her big tits. They're all *mine*, I tell myself proudly. Two of a kind and well-matched – and that goes for both of us as well.

Donald, Sussex

The New Member

I suppose it's every adolescent boy's dream to see the unclothed female body. When I was a kid we had a medical book in the house – a fat volume illustrated with coloured diagrams. When my parents were out I'd pour over the pictures of the female anatomy. There were excellent drawings of the vagina, clitoris, cervix, womb, and so on, but best of all was a full-page photograph of a naked woman standing full frontal. A well-developed female in her twenties, she faced the camera with her hands at her sides, full thrusting tits and a hair-covered bulge between plump thighs. I thought it the most beautiful picture ever.

It became my obsession to see a real woman in the buff one day. The letch is not unique to me, of course. As a teenager I went out with girls and did all the usual things: feeling their tits and quims, screwing a couple in the local lover's lane – but none in a warm room where I could ogle their charms properly. In my eighteenth year I went steady with Mandy, a pretty girl of seventeen who allowed me to kiss her. I settled for that, however, and we went dancing or to the cinema over a period of weeks. I took her home for Sunday tea and my parents congratulated me on meeting such a beauty.

I'd never been inside her house, only kissed her goodnight at the door. It was a big house in a good area so I didn't think she had anything to be ashamed of. One day we were smooching in my dad's car when she said her parents were giving her a birthday party and friends of the family would be there. I expected her to add that I was invited, but she looked very thoughtful, as if about to say something difficult. 'What do you think of naturists?' she asked. 'You know, nudists, people who like to go about without their clothes on—'

I had long been an admirer of the sun-worshippers' magazine *Health and Efficiency*, envying the pictures of nudists at picnics or on beaches. There was a local nudist colony some miles away, I knew, but the role about single men not being allowed to join had made it impossible for me to enrol.

'I think it's great,' I told her. 'It must be a lovely free feeling to go swimming and sunbathing. I'd like to be a nudist myself. Nothing wrong with revealing the human body, is there?'

Of course, in my case I wanted to be a nudist because I was eager to ogle naked women, but in answer to her carefully phrased query I made it sound decent and natural, feeling she had a point to make on the subject.

'My whole family are naturists,' Mandy replied. 'We practise it in the house as well as being members of the sun club. My mum says I'm not in any way to make you feel you have to join us, but if you come to my birthday party no one will be wearing clothes—'

Fantastic! I thought, my cock twitching – a birthday party with everyone in their birthday suits! I nodded solemnly as if honoured by her invitation.

'Mandy, I would love to be there. I've always considered naturists must be the most sensible people in the world.' My main ambition was to get the curvy Mandy naked and my dream was about to come true. I couldn't wait for the day but I had one worry: that I'd be the only one in the bared throng with a bloody great hard-on!

I presented myself at her door with a bunch of flowers and a special box of chocs, the flowers craftily meant to impress her mother. Mandy's dad let me in, bare as a fish, a skinny middle-aged man with a drooping dick which did not match mine for girth or length. I knew from taking showers with my mates at the football club that I had nothing to be coy about; my prick was fully grown and a good seven inches. Mandy's dad led me to a room piled with discarded clothes, so I undressed.

Then I was led into a large room filled with naked people of both sexes and I tried not to get hard while taking in the massed display of tits and cunts before me. There were some beauties too, large round breasts and heavy pendulous ones, pointy pear-shaped tits and long slack ones that lolled apart. All sorts of female arses were on show too, and cunt mounds bald and hairy. The men's dicks swung as they stood about laughing, with glasses in hand.

Then Mandy came bouncing towards me through the crowd, with another girl and a fine buxom woman beside her, with the biggest bobbing tits I could ever imagine. Mandy was lovely: nice shapely breasts, curvy hips and wisps of hair on a sweet little quim. She kissed me, her tits brushing my chest, bringing an instant erection, this while introducing me to her mother and sister.

I stood in humiliation but they all laughed to see my rigid tool rearing up. 'It's quite normal for a newcomer, especially a young man,' Mandy's mum said kindly. 'No one will take any notice.' This was not exactly true for I saw the way she looked at my upright length, as did Mandy and her sister, who was also a beauty and a bigger edition of my girl.

That then is how I got my wish to see my fill of the opposite sex *au naturel* and, years later, I'm still as keen as ever on the sight. Later, I went to the kitchen to help Mandy wash glasses and she pressed her sweet nakedness against me, her skin like silk and her nipples tracing patterns on my chest.

'We can slip away to my bedroom, if you like,' she whispered saucily. 'After all, it is my birthday. Do you think you could get that lovely erection again?' The washing-up was soon abandoned as we adjourned to Mandy's room. There I fucked her on a bed littered with dolls and teddy bears.

I never married her, though I did become a part of the family in time. At the nudist club her sister showed great interest in my sturdy prick and let it be known that she'd enjoy it up her cunt. She was such a fabulous fuck that I switched sisters. After twenty years, I can assure your readers I made the right choice.

Malcolm, Surrey

Sandy Lands the Big One

My next-door neighbour's son, Sandy, used to help me in the garden for pocket money and I tried to interest him in my great love, fishing, taking him with me on my regular Sunday trips. But Sandy didn't take to it, so I gave up on him. He seemed, as he got into his teens, to enjoy my wife's company more and was often in the house when I came home. The way he looked at her made me sure he had a crush on her. Jean, I might add, is an extremely pretty woman in her thirties, slender with shapely breasts and long legs.

It was often my way when we made love to excite her with lewd talk. She'd often protest at the crude suggestions I made but I knew by the way that her body responded she found it erotic. Certainly she would lose control and urge me to fuck her harder, which a man always likes to hear, and she would have a climax more often than not, especially with me recounting the dirty things she'd like to do if only she had the nerve. Our favourite theme, when I had her going, was to say that she'd love other fellows to fuck her and I'd mention men whom we knew. She never replied but I guessed from her strong reactions that she was aroused by the thought, for she'd rake her fingers down my back and come off over and over again.

One night, after we returned from a fancy dinner, I kissed her as we went up to our bedroom and had a feel of her bottom. I warned her that she was in for it that night. She was in high spirits and responded tipsily, climbing into bed without her nightdress, always a sure sign she was randy too. I went the whole bit, kissing her mouth and breasts, sucking her nipples and cunt, getting her really worked up, before penetrating her cunt with a good hard prick.

She was well juiced up and lifted her hips herself to get every inch, telling me to push harder and work it all up her. For some reason I thought of Sandy, his mooning around her and his looks of adoration. 'I know who'd love to fuck you,' I told her. For once she replied, her body quivering, not far off orgasm. 'Who?' she asked, groaning. 'Who'd like to fuck me now? Tell me—'

'Sandy,' I said simply and, God's honest truth, despite the turmoil in her cunt, she stopped her thrusting as if she had brakes. 'Why do you ask that?' she said, sounding concerned. 'Has he said he'd like to? Has he told you something—?'

I was poised over her, embedded deeply up her cunt but I remained still. 'He's no more than a boy,' she added. 'Why did you say that?' I thought I'd offended her.

'The way he looks at you, that's all,' I said. 'He can't keep his eyes off you when he's here. He's got an almighty crush on you.'

'So you've noticed,' she said. 'It's really embarrassing.'

Her body began to move under me again, wanting my prick. I guessed it was the mention of the ardent youth. I began to poke her, thrusting in, drawing out to the knob, making her strive to keep the whole hot length up her. So responsive were her movements that I resumed my pillow-talk.

'I still say he'd love to fuck that hungry cunt of yours,' I said fiercely. 'Boy or not, he's big enough. Sandy would love to screw you and have you naked in bed with him. Say

215

you'd love him to fuck you, Jean,' I demanded.

She positively shrieked out her reply, bucking her body wildly as she climaxed. 'Yes, yes!' she cried. 'I'd let Sandy fuck me – fuck me – he *does* fuck me! He fucks me and makes me come. He has fucked me—'

In the throes of shooting off into her myself, it was now my turn to apply the brakes. She lay below me as my cock dribbled the last of my jism into her cunt. She regained her breath, her body tense. 'You made me say it,' she complained. 'I didn't mean to, but now you know. It just happened. Sandy hung around so much I suppose I took pity on him, or was tempted, I don't know. Are you disgusted with me—?'

Having digested the information I found it both amusing and exciting. 'Lord, no,' I said easily. 'These things do happen. I suppose with such a love-struck admirer around it was a temptation. I bet the lucky lad enjoyed himself.'

I held her and kissed her. 'I didn't think you had it in you, love,' I said in admiration. 'When did the dirty deed take place?'

She squirmed in embarrassment below me. 'Here, in this bed, when you were fishing one Sunday,' she admitted. 'I'm afraid it hasn't stopped there either. He comes every Sunday when he knows you are away. I tried to say no but he hangs around like a wounded puppy. I suppose I want to do it myself, we always end up in bed—'

So that's how I discovered my wife was being unfaithful. In time I drew more of the lurid details from her and I fancy she quite enjoyed recounting what they got up to while I fished. There was no doubt young Sandy had the better catch. He went off to university soon after but I still have my Sunday outing when he comes home. I return to find Jean looking pleased with herself after a visit from her young lover. Later in bed she tells me what they have been doing and arouses us both tremendously. I look forward to his holidays as much as they do – well, almost.

Gerard, Swindon

New Balls, Please

My first experience of sex with a married woman came just after my eighteenth birthday. A star tennis-player locally, I was invited to play in a mixed-doubles tournament. I was tall, fit and good-looking, though I say it myself. My partner turned out to be a woman called Margaret, who was thirty-four and bloody lovely with it – long fair hair tied in a ponytail and a body that had curves in all the right places. We finished up losing in the final but got a runner's up medal each, which pleased her. I found out while chatting to others at tea that she was the wife of a wealthy businessman. Before she drove off in her big car she invited me to play tennis at her house that Sunday.

I arrived to find her in tennis whites, her tits bulging out of her blouse and her long legs displayed in brief tennis shorts. She said she wanted to improve her game by 'playing with a man' and I told her I was happy to oblige. There was a private court in the grounds of their house and we played until the light faded. Afterwards she made me a snack and suggested I shower before I changed, then she'd drive me home. I was enjoying the refreshing spray when she came in, completely nude herself.

'You have a lovely body, Edward,' she said, eyeing my prick. 'Young men should never grow old.' With that, she stepped in beside me, pressing her lovely body with its full, high breasts against me. I couldn't believe my luck. There was just one snag – her husband.

218

'Never mind him, he's not even in the country,' she said, turning off the water. She bent over my prick and licked it from ball-bag to rearing knob. 'It's always been an ambition of mine to seduce a nice young man,' she said, my cock in her grasp. 'I'm sure you don't mind.' She took the full length of my stalk down her throat and began a rhythmic sucking, making me cry out in pleasure. When she stood up, still with it in her hand, she said, 'I love a big hard prick like yours. Come upstairs and fuck me with it.'

If that was the way she wanted it, I was only too happy to play. I pushed her down on the bed, spread her legs wide and tongued the pouting quim she presented to me. 'You have a tasty cunt, Mrs B,' I told her as she panted and grasped my head urgently.

'Lick me out, lick my cunt clean, you horny young bastard, I love it—' she cried, coming against my mouth with unceasing jerks. I could wait no longer and straddled her, my prick shafting up her love box, poking furiously.

'Make me come again!' she screeched. 'Poke that thing up me harder—' With bellies slapping, we came off together.

We lay in bed fondling each other and I noticed that the room was full of mirrors. There was even one on the ceiling above us.

'I like to see myself being fucked,' she explained, 'seeing a thick prick going up my cunt really excites me. Now put that big tool of yours up me again. This time I'll ride you.' After a bout of sixty-nine, my cock stiffening in her warm mouth, she sat astride me, lowering herself on my prick. She looked in the mirror behind the headboard, watching my length disappear and reappear as she 'rode the pink horse'. Her tits swung heavy and full in front of my face. 'Ride me,' I told her excitedly. 'Ram down on it!'

Later I had her bending over, fingering the split between

her plump bum cheeks and shafting her from the rear. I worked my prick into the suction of her cunt, shouting 'Does your old man fuck you like this? Is his prick as big and hard?' Her pussy muscles seemed to grip my stalk, milking it as I shot the contents of my balls into her. 'Oh God,' she moaned, her arse bucking against my final thrusts. 'That is absolute heaven – you can come and fuck me again – any time you like!'

Well, my forehand didn't improve much that summer, despite my visits to her home with the private court, but my foreplay technique was honed to perfection.

Edward, Bournemouth

Danish Open Sandwich

When I told my mates I'd been raped by four girls, they laughed their heads off. I was on holiday in Greece. On the beach I met four Danish girls who were staying at my hotel. I danced with them and bought them drinks but, because they stuck together, I gave up the idea of having one alone. The beach was topless and all of them had great tits, thinking nothing of sitting and talking to me with their big boobs under my nose. It was fantastic, but I was getting nowhere. I used to wank myself silly when I went up to my room at night.

A boat trip away around the island, was a beach where everyone went naked. The girls told me about it and so I took the trip one morning and was pleased to see that they were also on the boat. When I arrived I kept my swimming trunks on. I noticed that one or two other men did the same and some women retained their bikini briefs, but beneath the bright sun there were dozens of naked people on view. It was only the women I was interested in, of course. There were some fine tits on display and many a pretty pussy mouth. Some of the women lying on the sand had their legs spread and I could see their parted quims. I wore dark glasses so that no one would notice that I was really a voyeur, enjoying the sights.

It was then, walking along to a rocky and less populated stretch of beach, that I saw the four Danish girls. Their tanned bodies were gloriously naked, tits and cunts on display as they lay side by side. I meant to walk past, intending to see all I could on the beach, intrigued by the even bigger breasts of a group of German women who were also staying at our hotel. Anyway, one Danish girl sat up and called my name. The others invited me over and at once taunted me for wearing trunks. 'He is ashamed of what he has between his legs,' one laughed. 'It is so small that he is frightened to show it—'

As a matter of fact, I did not consider myself the best endowed chap in the world. I'd also retained my trunks in case I got a hard-on while deliberately ogling as many naked females as I could. Strangely, I had not had an erection. I sat beside the Danish girls and they challenged me to take off my trunks. When I refused they all circled around me on their knees. Then one leaped at me and the others held me down as I fell on my back. They were strong girls. I felt my trunks being dragged over my bum and pulled free of my ankles. As I twisted and turned to struggle free, I was held face down and one of the girls spanked me viciously with the palm of her hand. The flurry of stinging smacks made me cry out.

There were squeals of delight from my tormentors. I was unceremoniously rolled over onto my back, all eyes on my uncovered prick. Of course, with four young nubile naked girls rubbing against me, I had gained an erection. This too was a subject for much laughter.

'What shall we do with this silly Englishman?' said one. Then they burst into rapid Danish, with me not understanding a word. One bent and gripped my prick, holding it upright in her hand and saying something to the others. From their eager replies it was obvious they were agreeing with what she'd said. Next moment she bent her head and nibbled at the knob of my cock with her teeth.

It wasn't so much painful as ticklish and I howled in

protest. To silence me, one of them lowered her haunches over my face, pressing her bared cunt over my nose and mouth. Her pubic hair rubbed my lips, meanwhile my cock was being sucked. I feared I would suffocate as the girl squatting over me rubbed her cunt against my nose and chin. I gulped in air, then her cunt was mashed down again, rotating on my lips, tasting of her sex. At the other end, the mouth was withdrawn from my cock and one of the girls threw a leg across me and directed my prick to her cunt, bearing down to push it up her. She began jiggling about over me, fucking herself on my stalk. Of course, by now I was terribly aroused and jerked my hips up to meet her downward thrusts.

My reaction was noticed and I heard more screams and squeals of delight from the girls. Another one exchanged places with the girl who had squatted over my face – this after her rapid movements indicated she had come off.

'Lick me,' ordered the girl, grinding her bottom into me. I didn't know who was on the other end by then, but someone was bouncing herself wildly on my prick. Then, naturally, I was thrusting back and shouting as best I could with a juiced-up cunt over my mouth, coming my load.

'Dirty, dirty boy,' the girls had the brass neck to call me as they sat around me while I lay panting on the sand. OK, I had come and you can't do that unless you are excited. All the same, what I'd been through wasn't far off rape – even if I *was* hoping for a repeat performance.

But the next day they were busy viewing some ruins and the following day they returned home. Coming down for breakfast, I saw them standing at the reception desk with their suitcases beside them. When they saw me, one gave a little wave of her fingers, another stuck her tongue out at me. To console myself, I took another trip to the nudist beach, seeing plenty of bared tits, cunts and arses. But history did not repeat itself – worse luck!

Maurice, Slough

Object of Adoration

I couldn't help looking at her everyday in the office and thinking of that shapely woman getting into bed with her husband. The lucky bastard would fondle those big heavy breasts and suck on those prominent nipples that I so lusted after. Then, so I imagined, he would stroke between her thighs, feeling the lush triangle of hair on her cunt mound. No doubt a finger would slip into the crack, finding it warm and moist, then be withdrawn to be replaced by a rampant prick. She would give a little moan of satisfaction, lifting her bum as he thrust. How I wanted to fuck her myself! I was obsessed by the cool and voluptuous Marguerite.

She had interviewed me when I applied for the post of trainee accountant. Sitting behind her desk, the sight of her smiling face and full breasts made me fall for her right away. At the time I thought I'd blown it, but I got the job. Later, when she brought work to my desk, the sweet scent of her body was enough to give me a raging erection. Unable to stop thinking of her, one dark evening I went to her house, a bungalow set apart from others by a large garden. Cowering among the bushes, I saw a light go on in a bedroom and my adored one started to undress without drawing the curtains. Hating myself for being there, I saw her husband enter and unbutton his shirt, ignoring the woman near him who was taking off her bra. Oh, such glorious tits! And he didn't seem to notice.

At other times I went armed with binoculars and waited

patiently for my reward. They'd watch television or entertain friends; sometimes he would work late at a desk in another room and she would go to bed herself. Always, before she reached under the pillow for her nightdress, I'd get a good look at her completely naked. Seeing her in the office the next day, so band-box neat in a jacket, blouse and skirt, I would mentally undress her, seeing once more her high-tilted tits and rounded thighs with the lush bush of hair between. I was soon to discover she was well aware of my interest.

One afternoon she phoned me from home and asked me to take a client's folder to her house. I found Marguerite in her garden when I arrived, cutting flowers. We chatted about the file I'd brought and she congratulated me on my work. Flattered, I told her it was a pleasure to do work for her. With flowers in her hand, she went to the bushes where I used to conceal myself on my furtive spying expeditions.

'I'm sure we have a prowler,' she said, looking me straight in the eye. My face turned bright red and my stomach churned with fright. 'Look at all the footmarks around these bushes. I think a Peeping Tom comes here at night.'

As ever, her voice was calm and controlled, her gaze level. Oh God, I thought, I'm sure she suspects me. 'Have you told the police?' I asked, deciding my midnight expeditions were over forever. My voice sounded high-pitched and I trembled. To my amazement, she shook her head, regarding me like a naughty child and smiling at my discomfort.

'It's you, isn't it, Ronnie?' she said kindly. 'For some time I've felt that I was being watched. Then I found the footprints and I was certain. I didn't tell my husband because I suspected you, well aware how you look at me at the office. When I saw dirt on your shoes one morning, that was it—'

What could I do but hang my head in misery, completely ashamed of myself? 'What can I say?' I said, utterly humiliated. 'I've never done this kind of thing before. I just couldn't help myself. You have such an effect upon me. I love you. I wanted to see you—'

'How sweet,' she smiled, 'but it's very naughty of you. You deserve punishment for being so wicked. Don't you agree?'

'I'll resign from the firm today,' I said unhappily. 'Thank you for not reporting any of this, Mrs C. I'd die of shame if it were known. Thank you for that—'

'I don't want you to resign,' she replied. 'I had another kind of punishment in mind. Would you say that a good warming of your bottom with a strap would be just retribution for spying on me?'

The very idea of it made my balls tighten and cock twitch. I *wanted* this object of my adoration to beat me and nodded my agreement eagerly. I was led into the bungalow and through to the very bedroom where I'd witnessed her disrobing. I began to wonder why, if she suspected I was eyeballing her nightly, she had continued to stand naked in front of the window.

'How do you want me?' I asked timidly. 'Shall I undress?'

'You've seen all of me, so – yes,' she said, a gleam in her eye that told me she was enjoying the charade. 'Strip and bend over that chair, and grip the arms for support. Have you been beaten before, Ronnie?'

'At school sometimes,' I admitted. 'A senior boy liked to do it—'

'And did you enjoy it? I've heard what goes on in those schools—' She added slyly, 'Did it arouse you?'

'I didn't mind,' I said, taking off my suit with trembling hands. I guessed she wanted me to admit to lewd feelings. 'I couldn't help liking what it did.' What it did was evident as I stepped out of my pants, revealing a stiff erection.

'Then you were a naughty boy then,' Marguerite said triumphantly. 'What if I stripped off myself, would you like that?' Without waiting for a reply, she began to undress revealing all her lush naked flesh. 'Over the chair,' she ordered. 'Remember what we are here for.'

She took a belt from her husband's wardrobe and whacked it down across my upraised bum until I howled out in protest – as I was sure she wanted me to do. Glancing back as she struck me, I loved the way her big bare tits bounced and wobbled. Then she tossed the strap aside, regarding me with a satisfied look.

'I've always wanted to do that,' she said. 'I've suggested it to my husband, but he won't hear of it, the old stick-in-the-mud. Every time I hint that we do something a little kinky he holds up his hands in horror. What a good sport you are, Ronnie. You didn't mind me trying it out on you, did you?'

'Anytime,' I assured her, facing her with the biggest hard-on I could remember. 'Look what you've done, you've made me so stiff. Much more and I'd have come off—'

'All over the chair and we couldn't have that,' she said mischievously. 'I can think of a better place to put that naughty thing. Lie on the bed, Ronnie. Another thing I've always wanted to do is to get on top of a man. Shall we try it?'

She came into my arms and I kissed her madly. I felt for her cunt as her fingers curled around my rampant tool. 'Did you think I was like this?' she asked, mounting me and enveloping my shaft to the hilt. 'Don't you know I've thought about you fucking me when I've caught you looking at my breasts? Do control yourself, Ronnie, don't you dare come until I say so. Oh, this is heaven, darling. Let me fuck you—'

228

Fuck me she did, squirming and grinding down on my cock, her tits bouncing as I strove to contain the urge to let go into her. Finally, she screamed that she was coming, so I thrust up at her and emptied my balls in helpless spurts up her grasping cunt. And not for the last time!

Ron T., Birmingham

4. I CONFESS

Putty in his Hands
Respectable Wives
Daniel in the Lioness's Den
Briefs Encounter
A Helping Hand
Bare-Faced Cheek
Dishing it Out
Plastic Fantastic Lover
In the Potting Shed
In Her Little Snapshot Album
Three Times a Lady
The Last to Know
Who Wears the Panties?
The Second Time Around
A Spanking Good Time
The Sexy Stand-In
Caught With Her Knickers Down

Putty in His Hands

I know it's wrong but I'm having a torrid affair with my nineteen-year-old daughter's boyfriend. I love it when he fucks me. It must be because of the poor sex life I have with my husband, but I can't refuse the lad anything. He only has to touch me and I'm his to do with as he likes – things I've never done before. I know I should put a stop to it but I can't resist him.

It began when my daughter first brought him home to meet us. I fancied then that he gave me the eye. He made a fuss of me and, though I should have known better, I became infatuated with him – despite the difference in our ages. He's only twenty and I'm forty-three. Soon after, he came to the house when I was at home alone. I let him in, butterflies in my stomach, and feeling like a teenage girl with her first boyfriend. He had a lovely bunch of flowers with him from his father's garden. When I said how thoughtful it was for him to bring flowers for Sylvia, he said they were for me.

'You've made me so welcome here, I had to repay your kindness,' he said, standing close to me as I fought to control my feelings. 'I could kiss you for being so nice. I mean for being so nice when I call here. I could kiss you for that.' I was sure the young devil was chancing his luck and his wiles worked.

'Kiss me if you want to,' I heard myself say. Then he had me in his arms, kissing me as he did my daughter, no doubt, with his mouth open and his tongue sliding into my mouth. He knew at once from my response that he had me. 'I've always wanted to kiss you like this,' he whispered into my face. 'Ever since I first came here I've fancied you like mad, Mrs K—'

'No, Simon, it's wrong,' I kept saying weakly, while kissing him in return, our bodies pressing together so that my breasts flattened against his chest and his stiff prick dug into my lower stomach. 'You're my daughter's boyfriend and I'm a married woman – it's not right—' But his rubbing against me with his hardness, up and down, right against the fork of my thighs directly on my cunt mound, made me lose all control and I jerked my hips to meet his thrusts. We were both fully clothed and clinging together tightly, our mouths and tongues joined, his hands clutching my bottom cheeks to pull me closer when I cried out 'Go on, go on!' and couldn't stop having a powerful orgasm.

When the spasms lessened, leaving me breathless and shaken, I held him at arm's length, repeating that it was wrong, he was my Sylvia's boy and we must never ever do what we'd done again. He looked at me and said, 'You didn't stop me, Joyce, and we both liked it. I could tell you had an orgasm. Think what it could be like in bed together. Both of us naked. That's how I've pictured seeing your lovely body—'

I felt so guilty that I ordered him out of the house. But after he'd gone I couldn't stop thinking about his kisses. I was amazed that he had brought me to a shattering come while in his arms.

He had not long left when he phoned me. 'I won't apologise for what happened,' he said. 'I've always thought you were lovely, and I found that was even more true when we were kissing and cuddling. Don't you feel the same way – that making love together would be marvellous?' I wanted to shout back 'Yes!' Just hearing his voice had my stomach turning to jelly. I had been infatuated, now I feared I was in love with him. Worst of all, I know my daughter was crazy about the good-looking lad. She had told me once, in a mum-and-daughter talk, that Simon was a fantastic good lover, that she had slept with him on holiday and made love with him in his car and even in our house when we'd been out.

'I'm coming back to see you,' he said, replacing the phone before I had the chance to shout 'NO!' I guessed he was at the phone box along our street and I knew that if I let him in I'd be unable to stop him doing as he wished with me. That I would *want* him to do as he wished.

I tried to refuse him entry when I answered the door, but he pushed his way in, taking me in his arms again and kissing me even as he led me into the living room.

'We shouldn't, we mustn't—' I repeated hopelessly as he undressed me, flattering me with talk about my body. He stripped me naked, kissed my nipples, felt between my thighs and lowered me to the couch. He threw off his clothes and stood before me, his stout prick rearing from his belly. Then he went on his knees to bury his face between my breasts and slid his mouth down my heaving belly to my cunt. When his tongue entered me I was lost to everything but the pleasure of it, begging him to do it to me.

My head jerked as he licked me, my eyes catching sight of us in the large mirror that hung over the fireplace. If it had been positioned for that purpose it could not have been better placed. It showed me lolling back among the cushions on the couch, breasts heaving as I arched my back and tilted my cunt to his mouth, my hands holding his head tightly.

'You'll make me come!' I hissed between my teeth as he performed on me – as if that were not the whole object of the delightful exercise! My excitement was such that I pulled his head between my thighs in my eagerness to have more, wanting his tongue far up me. I gabbled out orders, completely wanton in my delirium. I had a powerful orgasm on his tongue then told him to fuck me. Simon lifted my legs over his shoulders and pressed forward into my crotch. Like a guided missile homing in on its target, his prick pierced my outer lips and, well lubricated as I was, penetrated deeply first go. I gasped out my joy at the sensation of a young man's stiff prick embedded so solidly up my cunt.

Simon fucked me with urgent strokes, bringing me to a second come almost immediately. My heaving and jerking continued apace as I sought further climaxes. He muttered that I had a delicious cunt and that he'd be back for more now that he'd been there. The reflection in the mirror fascinated me, seeing Simon's buttocks clenching and thrusting as he fucked me, my feet over his shoulders, our bodies positively clashing in the heat of the moment. It struck me that my daughter too had taken his prick on the same couch. She'd told me so.

'Did you like fucking Sylvia as much on this settee?' I found myself saying wickedly, really it was an inexusable thing to bring up, but my lewdness and excitement was beyond normal bounds.

'Like mother, like daughter,' he threw back in my face, 'I'd love the pair of you together, you both love my prick so much.'

He came in long shuddering jerks, filling me with his hot love juice. When he left I bathed and prepared the evening meal for my husband and daughter. I could hardly look at them, feeling terribly wicked and unfaithful to both, yet glowing inside from the afternoon's fucking.

Simon pops in whenever he can during weekdays now

and, of course, I can refuse him nothing. He's quite a stud, evidently having Sylvia as often as he's having her mum, and although I feel eternally damned by my behaviour I am helpless to stop his visits. These are always preceded by a phone call to let me know he's on his way, and what calls they are! He really is a lecherous young man.

'Are you sitting comfortably?' he always begins when he phones. He then tells me to loosen my dress, unhook my bra and stroke my breasts, making me describe what I'm doing. 'Feel your cunt, make it nice and juicy for me, play with it—' Of course I get hot and randy, ready for his arrival. I wonder what it will be like when he marries my daughter, as they've planned. No different from now, I suspect. I hope not!

Joyce, Swindon.

Respectable Wives

It's a lunchtime party for expatriates living in Africa. Barbecued ribs, steak, sausages, plus all you can drink. Male and female gather in separate groups. The men discuss their jobs. The women talk tennis, golf, servants and children – the latter being conveniently home in England at boarding school. Do they ever compare love affairs? Discuss who is fucking whom? Perhaps not, as they are all superior people and ultra-respectable – on the surface.

Yet plenty of extramarital nookie goes on, I'm aware. With servants around, wives have little to do and financial worries don't arise. So the devil finds work for idle hands – and pricks and cunts. My wife, Ann, and I have had a liquid lunch, tall glasses of iced gin and ginger beer. The sky is purple with heat and we leave the garden to go inside our host's house. Several couples dance to slow smoochy music, no one is with their regular partner. Jumbo MacPherson asks Ann to dance. The big bastard shuffles around as close to her as he can get, his sweaty belly hard against her light cotton dress. She returns to me giddy with the dance and drink, grinning a tiddly grin. 'He got a hard-on and kept pressing it into me,' she says. 'A real brute too. Take me home and fuck me.' The drink and Jumbo's dong against her crotch had made her randy.

I'm in the car preparing to pull out of the driveway when MacPherson draws up alongside in his Mercedes. 'Come back with me for a drink,' he suggests. I know he has a strong letch for my wife and I can't blame him. I've seen the way he ogles her at the club. She's dark and voluptuous, well-fleshed at tit and buttock. I consider that Jumbo can afford to ply us with drink, it's a fair way to spend a Saturday afternoon, but he won't get a sniff of Ann. I'm saving her for later.

All the same, she's nodding and smiling at the bugger through the car's open window. She's half-pissed and horny. We enter his lounge to find his wife at a typewriter, wearing a silk wrap-around robe. I'm glad she's home, more often than not she's off researching one of her travel books. She's American, she met and married Jumbo when he was stationed in Washington with the Foreign Office. Dolores is dark like my wife, her light brown skin tanned by the sun. Jumbo pours drinks all round then wheedles Ann out to the balcony to admire the view of the lake. I'm left with his woman and a most attractive piece she is, too. It's a fair exchange.

Her robe is partly open and there's nothing underneath but smooth skin. I glimpse pointy tits almost to the nipples.

'How was the party?' she asks. 'I couldn't stand any more of those boring snobs. One at home is enough.' As she turns in her chair the robe parts. She doesn't seem to care that I am eyeballing her tits. I agree with her. We hear Jumbo's coarse laughter from the verandah and my wife's giggles. 'You know of course, Derek, that Jumbo wants to fuck Ann,' she says matter-of-factly. 'The big letcher has told me he fancies her rotten – all that soft arse flesh and big tits appeals to him.'

'You don't mind?' I say, drink in hand, staring at her left breast which is now completely uncovered.

'Not if you don't and your wife wants to try that big

239

prick he's blessed with,' she says slyly. 'You don't seem the type to be shocked—'

'She's had men before,' I say conversationally. 'And I've had women. We like changing partners occasionally.'

'Good for you,' she says. 'If your wife lets Jumbo get his end away, you can fuck me. If you want to—'

'Don't I just,' I enthuse. 'I've always wanted to give you one. Why do we have to wait for them—?' My hand cups one silken tit, thumb flicking a hardening nipple.

'It's better that way,' Dolores advises. 'I've seen wives turn nasty when hubby starts on me. Let's see what happens with those two.'

She's a cool customer right enough, I decide, but lithe and choice. I've seen her in her bikini at the pool and admired those pointed pear-shaped tits and flat stomach. We go to the verandah and Jumbo and Ann jump apart. I can see from her red mouth that they've been kissing and the top buttons of her dress are undone, revealing her swollen cleavage. Jumbo's khaki shorts bulge at his crotch alarmingly.

'We're going down the garden,' Dolores announces. She takes me to the hut facing the lake where she writes. Her arms go around my neck, her lips wet and open, her tongue pushing into my mouth. 'They won't come here,' she says dropping her robe to the floor and standing naked, a black muff of hair between her legs. 'Let's fuck, Derek. Take off your clothes.'

One doesn't overdress in Africa. In seconds I shed shirt, shorts and kick off my flip-flops. We kiss again, her body damp with the sweat of the hot day. I suck her long nipples, stiff like little fingertips. Her hand clasps my prick, stroking it teasingly. She falls back across her desk, legs spread and knees raised. I stoop to kiss her cunt. A veritable forest of black hair covers the split bulge and crawls thickly between the cleft of her tight arse. My lips to the crack, I suck and tongue her avidly, intending to get her well worked up. She moves sensuously, sighing, taking my hands and pulling them up to her breasts. Her hips writhe and jerk.

'Later,' she says urgently. 'Do that after, lick me out when you've fucked me. I like it better when I've come. Fuck me now—'

'My pleasure,' says I, my cock straining upright in her grasp as she draws it between her thighs.

With my balls bouncing between her bum cheeks, I screw her as if sex is going out of fashion. Dolores can certainly fuck. She loves a stiff cock up her, grinding her cunt and heaving to match my thrusts. The back of her ankles hooks on my shoulders, her arse and back rise off the desk. Her strong cunt muscles grip my shaft, squeezing like a suction pump, milking the juice from my balls.

'Thrust, damn you,' she orders. 'Thrust harder, get it all up. Don't you dare come yet till I've finished with you!' Her breath comes in guttural grunts as the surge and heat in my balls coincide with her quickening pace. Timing, that's what it is – she shudders to her climax as I shoot my load. 'Now,' she says languidly as I look down upon her sprawled across the desk, legs dangling over the edge. 'Now you can lick me out, Derek. Lick me clean—'

She comes again on my tongue, then sits up. 'I wonder how Jumbo and your wife are doing?' she says sweetly. 'Shall we go and see?'

We dress and stroll back to the house. Dolores pours me a drink and, holding a finger to her lips, leads the way up a passageway to the bedroom. We hear grunts and moans, the pounding of a bed. Looking in, Ann is mounted over Jumbo's belly, riding him like the fury. 'Let's leave them to it and use the bedroom next door,' I

241

am told by Dolores. 'Anything they can do, we can do better.'

'Of course we can,' I agree, as I am led away.

Derek, Surrey

Daniel in the Lioness's Den

At the age of thirty-six and recently divorced for the second time, I felt I'd had my fill of men. My husbands just didn't do what I wanted them to, either in bed or around the house. I was the one holding down the exacting executive job, earning more than either of them. So why should I have to return home to clean and cook? Both of them claimed I was too bossy, so we split up. Being a healthy attractive woman, the one thing I did miss about being single again was sex. Of course, I could have had men, but I'd decided the next male to share my bed would be one who agreed to do exactly what I wanted.

Most available guys around my age were set in their ways, brought up by their mothers to expect wifey to wash, iron and cook. Then Daniel came into my life. He was nineteen and a boyish-looking office trainee whom I barely noticed at first. But I soon got to like the way he jumped at my command, slavishly obeying my orders. I sent him for coffee and sandwiches, to the bank and the dry-cleaners. I even had him change a tyre on my car while it was raining as I sat in my office waiting to drive home. All these things he did with grateful appreciation, as if I were doing him a favour. At times I caught him looking at me with worship in his eyes as if I was a goddess. It struck me that the youth was completely under my spell.

I liked that, and used him mercilessly. When he came to my office I found myself arching my back as if stretching, thus making my breasts bulge in my white blouse, the nipples starkly impressed through the silk. And I'd pretend to straighten my stockings, which entailed lifting my skirt to show off my legs. Glancing at the boy, I'd see him hypnotised, shy but unable to look away.

One night in bed, while relieving myself with the vibrator, the fantasy that came to me in the final throes was of me naked in front of Daniel in my office. The climax that resulted was so intense that I decided I must satisfy my letch for the boy.

The next day in the office I could hardly keep my eyes off him, I daydreamed about him, drenching my panties as I imagined seducing him. I hoped he was a virgin – what a delight it would be to instruct him sexually! The idea came to obsess me. When masturbating, sometimes on my couch after work or in the bath, I pictured Daniel tied down to my bed while I rode his prick, and kneeling to lick my cunt. I wanted it for real, so I invited him to my flat on the pretext that I wanted to move some furniture.

Of course, he was delighted to be of help. When he arrived I was in a loose kimono, the neck of the garment open to show the swell of my breasts. He manhandled my music centre and a sideboard as instructed, then stood back awaiting my next command. The lad couldn't have had any idea what that would be!

'You look so hot from your exertions, Daniel,' I told him. 'Why don't you have a shower to freshen up?' He actually gulped. I gave him a little time alone in the shower cubicle then went into the bathroom with a large fluffy towel. I opened the glass door and found him rubbing a good-sized stiff prick.

Of course, he was embarrassed to death, cowering and stuttering his apologies. 'What are you doing?' I asked calmly. 'Is this something you get up to frequently? Tell me, I want the truth, Daniel.'

He stood before me a figure of shame and misery. 'It was being here with you, Ms Spencer,' he whined. 'Thinking of you using this shower, I couldn't help myself – it just happened.' Then he actually began to cry!

'Stop that blubbering,' I said, berating him as an angry mother might and enjoying it immensely. 'I'm well aware young men do that to themselves, but I thought you'd be above such a disgusting habit. Tell me, have you never been with a woman?'

He looked at me with brimming eyes and shook his head. I knew he was too shocked to be other than honest.

'Dry yourself and come with me,' I told him sharply. 'Don't dress yourself. I think it's high time you learned the facts of life, don't you? Really, Daniel, you're such a baby I shall have to treat you as one.' I was loving every moment of his agony.

Naked and vulnerable, Daniel obediently followed me into my bedroom. I sat on the bed and told him to stand in front of me. His head hung and his hands were clasped in front of his still-erect penis. I ordered him to straighten himself up and not slouch.

'That's better,' I snapped. 'Goodness knows what kind of upbringing you've had.' I was relishing the thought of the gullible clay that was mine to fashion to my liking. I stood up, face to face with him, my breasts to his chest. He was so giddy I had to steady him. 'Has no girl ever seen you like this before, Daniel?' I aked. Again he shook his head, overwhelmed by the situation. 'You have nothing to be ashamed of, you silly boy. You're a handsome and well-endowed young man. Since you are naked, wouldn't you like to see my body too? That would only be fair, wouldn't it?'

He was going to see me nude whether he liked it or not, such was my desire to display myself to him. The garment I wore was sliding to the floor even as he whispered, 'Yes, please, Ms Spencer.' I stood naked before him, my big breasts swollen by my wanton arousal, the nipples elongated. I saw him take a swift glance down to the well-furred mound at the fork of my thighs.

'There,' I said, 'you can see I'm not ashamed of *my* body. Do you like me? Tell me what you think of my breasts. I insist that you do, Daniel. Look at them, don't turn your eyes away,' I demanded sharply. 'If you want to become any kind of man, do as I order you!'

'You're so lovely,' he managed to croak out, after several attempts. 'Your breasts – breasts – are so *beautiful*. I've only seen pictures before—'

'Yes,' I said sternly, 'I've no doubt, and in grubby magazines that you keep hidden from your mother. And you masturbate over them, don't you, Daniel?'

He gave me a look of abject humiliation, but I observed too that his prick stood mightily erect. It was so stiff it must have been painful. As for myself, the seduction scene I was conducting had my juices seeping out from my hungry cunt, running down my inner thighs. I fought a desire I would fulfil later, wanting to make him taste my pussy. This was too good to hurry.

'I see you like my breasts,' I said. 'You may touch them, kiss them if you wish and suck my nipples. This is all for your own good, Daniel. I'm showing you what you should be experiencing at your age. It's better than abusing yourself like some dirty little schoolboy.'

His hands grasped my breasts tentatively. 'Squeeze them – they won't break,' I told him fiercely. 'Have a good feel. Now suck on them. Damn you, boy! You're acting like a baby. So, be like one – take a nipple in your mouth and suck me! Do I have to teach you to do that?' His lips fastened over my left nipple and he sighed as if in a state of complete contentment. I fed him the other nipple and his excitement was such that he pulled the breast into his over-eager mouth, sucking so hard that I cried out in pain. I pulled on his shoulders, falling back across the bed with him on top of me. Positioned as he was, his prick pushed against my cunt lips and slipped inside me. Suddenly he was fucking me.

In his excitement he went at me like a battering ram, despite my protests. I had intended to be the instigator but, even as I was attempting to get him to slow down, he lost control. Impaled up my cunt, thrusting madly, it was all too much for him and he came with an anguished cry. I pushed him from me angrily.

'That,' I told him, 'was how *not* to make love. You went at it as if your own gratification was all that mattered. Now I've been left unsatisfied. What do you intend to do about that?'

'Whatever you want,' Daniel muttered, flinching under my glare. 'Do tell me, I want more than anything to please you. Anything, only don't send me away—'

I had no intention of doing that. 'We'll put that down to experience, then,' I conceded. 'In future, you will let me do the leading and you follow. Now, kiss me, feel between my legs and play with my tits. I'll massage your prick. I'm sure a young man like you will soon be aroused enough to fuck me as I like, slowly and to my entire satisfaction.'

Our lips fused, our hands wandered. His erection came back nobly and it was with an impatient 'Yes!' that I got on top of Daniel in the squatting position and embedded his prick inside me. I ordered him to lie still while I pleasured myself on the upright shaft, grinding down, my tits bobbing over his face and going from climax to climax without pause.

'*I'm* fucking *you* now,' I told him. 'From now on you are mine alone, young man, mine alone!' When his hips began to work against me in upward thrusts, I slapped him hard and told him to lie still. Only when I knew from his moans and shudders that he had come did I fall forward over him, sated and triumphant.

Daniel's visits to my flat continued until he was no longer the little boy lost. I made a man of him and he went his way a changed guy, experienced in all the permutations of torrid sex that I could dream up. In time he became something of an office romeo, taking out several of the young girls from the typing pool. Obviously I'd taught him too well.

Never mind, now there's a new office junior falling over himself to please me. I can't wait to show him how to really get into my good books!

Julia, London

Briefs Encounter

When shooting the breeze about past sexual adventures it is noticeable that nobody ever mentions marvellous honeymoons or even great sex with their spouses. All agree that the most memorable encounters come by chance. Like the following.

I was out on my rounds as a rep and stopped in a village in the Midlands to have lunch. It was just after noon when I made a purchase in a chemist's. I was leaving the shop when a woman I'd noticed because of her full figure and handsome face followed me out. I held the door open for her and she smiled and thanked me. 'A pleasure,' I said on a whim. 'I always hold open doors for good-looking women.'

To my surprise she stopped on the pavement and looked at me with some interest. I'm in my middle twenties, smart, clean and reasonably handsome. 'Do you consider me a good-looking woman?' she asked, an amused smile on her lips. 'Did I catch you giving me the once-over in the shop?'

I was a little flustered at the response to my bit of flattery, but recovered somewhat to say I was sorry if she thought me forward and that I was certainly not insincere. She was indeed a very pretty woman. 'In that case,' she said, 'come and have a coffee with me, or would you prefer a drink?'

As I was driving I said I'd prefer coffee, thinking of taking her to a nearby café. I had no idea of her motive in being so friendly. I guessed she was well-heeled, being beautifully made-up and expensively dressed. She did not look the sort that needed to seek company. She said we would have coffee at her home and I followed her new BMW out of the village for a mile or two until we pulled up before a splendid house at the end of a gravelled driveway.

She made coffee and we sat making small talk in her lounge. With her coat off, her blouse positively bulged with ample tit and the seat of her tweed skirt was moulded to a fine buxom arse. I wondered if I dared make an approach, thinking it would be great to see her naked. To find out if those voluminous breasts, so thrusting and shapely in their captive bra, sagged pendulously when freed. To see how well thatched with hair and how plump her cunt might be. As if reading my thoughts, she said carefully, choosing her words, 'I've been a widow now for six months. There are no end of friends who insist on consoling me, but what I miss most of all is sex. Would you consider making love to me?'

'Consider!' I cried. 'I've been sitting here thinking of nothing else. Do you want it right here?'

She laughed at my eagerness. 'I think the bedroom, don't you?' she said, leading the way upstairs. 'Am I keeping your from business—? How long can you stay?'

'There's nothing urgent,' I assured her, resisting the impulse to add: 'just the way I feel about screwing you.' Keep your head, I warned myself, following her up to an airy bedroom with a canopied double bed, the lady wants satisfying and won't be pleased if you go off at half-cock. 'Why me?' I asked as we faced each other.

'Because I've often thought of having someone here to do the necessary,' she said honestly. 'You saying what you did today made you the ideal candidate. Shall we begin? Please don't hold back or be shy. I'd prefer it if you say what you like and do what you want to. That's what we're here for, isn't it?'

'Anything I like to say or do?' I insisted, intending to fulfil a few favourite fantasies if the lady was so obliging. She nodded assent, so I sat in a chair, and said, 'Undress before me then. Strip right off and let me see your big tits and hairy cunt. I'll sit and watch—' It felt great to be so masterful with a woman. My dong was already stiff with anticipation, poking a hole in my pants.

She stood a few feet from me, her lovely face amused at my forthright request and began to unbutton the front of her blouse. She revealed an overflowing lace bra, her creamy tits swelling out from her tight cleavage. 'I hope you won't be disappointed with what you see, Gordon,' she said. 'Big tits, yes, but no hairy cunt. I've always shaved my pubic hair—'

'All the better to eat you with,' I assured her, ogling with a mixture of lust and admiration as she discarded her bra. Indeed her tits were two beauties, full and perfectly matched globes surmounted with round brown nipples, not a droop in them either as they stood out proud from her chest. I resisted reaching to grab them with difficulty. She ran her hands over them, holding them out to me and pinching the nipples, enjoying every moment of flaunting her goodies.

'Do you like them?' she asked. 'Shall I continue?' I swallowed hard and nodded, watching the skirt drop to her ankles with a push of her hands and wiggle of her bottom. She kicked it away and stood, a splendid figure of a full-bodied woman with flaring hips and smoothly rounded thighs, clad only in flimsy briefs and a matching suspender belt and stockings. These were taken off almost casually before me, her eyes watching my reaction, until she was finally naked. She posed with her hands clasped behind her head, tits raised, legs slightly apart to show off a clean-shaven cunt mound with surprisingly small outer

251

lips. 'Will I do?' she teased me. 'Now you must do the same for me – get down to your skin.'

To say I threw off my clothes was no exaggeration. My prick stood up thick and menacing as I advanced on her, pressing against her soft belly as I pulled her close and sought her mouth with mine. As my hand clasped a heavy tit, hers went down to encircle my shaft and give it a loving squeeze.

'I can't wait,' she said urgently. 'Fuck me now – I want it up me. Do it to me, Gordon!'

I had intended to run through my warm-up repertoire before mounting her: fondling and sucking her magnificent boobs, lapping at her shaven haven, working her into a frenzy, but she was already dragging me down on the bed. Her grip on my prick tightened as she drew it to her cunt and I found myself going into a warm wet channel, her own thrusts ensuring my cock was buried inside her at first go. It was like being raped, the woman under me was so desperate. Her arms and legs clamped me to her in an unbreakable hold and she worked her cunt up at me like a piston.

'Lie still and let me do it!' she said sternly. 'Don't move!' Thus she heaved and thrust until she let out a loud shuddering groan and came in helpless jerks. When her motions had slowed I was still up her, containing my own climax by sheer willpower. She jiggled her cunt on the hard bar of flesh as if savouring the feeling. 'I had to do that,' she explained gratefully. 'It has been so long. God, it was good. Now fuck me again.'

It was my turn. I told her to roll over and raise her arse, in those words, and she complied, giving me a sweet smile as she turned. Her beautiful twin-mooned bottom, uplifted so enticingly for me, made it impossible for me not to kiss each cheek reverently and part the halves, delving with my tongue to pay her homage. She gave a little squeak and a giggle as I sucked at the juicy fig-like quim, muttering 'Oh, yes, do!' and gyrating her bottom against my mouth. When I curled over her back, reaching under to grasp her hanging tits, my eager prick slid into her crevice until my balls bounced against her thighs. Her hands came back to part her cheeks wider and I let go, thrusting and releasing a volley up her receptive cunt. I continued without uncunting, delighted to bring on further spasms that had the lady crying out in ecstasy. It was morning before I left her house.

Gordon, Cheshire

A Helping Hand

Our marrige was breaking up because I couldn't please my husband in bed. I often refused his advances because I knew I was hopeless at sex – not that Phil was all that experienced, for we were both virgins when we married.

In three years together I never achieved an orgasm and it made him mad with himself, although I thought it was my fault. Another thing was, I couldn't make love to him with me on top. I felt I was doing it wrong and he was doing all the work. No matter how I tried I couldn't get the movements right and didn't find any of it enjoyable. I was shy, too, and soon our sex life became almost non-existent. I was sure Phil was looking for a more suitable woman.

Then I became friendly with a woman at work. She was about twice my age, which was twenty. We took our lunch break together and I used to tell her about my marital problems. Sheila was a brassy dyed-blonde, big-bosomed and cheerful.

'Gawd,' she said, 'at your age, you and your hubby should be at it every night. It's the best thing since sliced bread and you don't know what you're missing, Pam. My Tom and I go at it like mad, even after all these years. Don't you *want* to enjoy a good fuck?'

I said of course I wanted to be like other wives who please their husbands and enjoy sex. 'I've read all the books,' I said, 'I think I must be frigid.'

254

Later that week my husband was away for the night, assembling a new machine in a factory up north. Sheila invited me out and I went with her and Tom to a pub where I drank more than usual. I soon became quite light-headed and merry. Tom went off to play darts and Sheila told me that he had said I was a little cracker. It gave me a glow in my tummy to think he found me attractive. I said Tom was all man, big and handsome. It was the drink talking.

They walked me back home and came in for coffee. In front of me on the couch, Tom and Sheila began to get amorous, their arms around each other and him groping her big breasts. She didn't mind, in fact she turned her face to him and they kissed. Sheila herself unbuttoned her dress and he delved his hand in to fondle her bosom. Watching them I was both embarrassed and aroused.

'Pam's blushing,' Sheila said. 'Let's give her something to blush about. I feel like a good fuck. She can watch a couple of experts at it – she might learn something.' The pair took off all their clothes there and then; Sheila with her big hanging breasts and Tom with a stiff erection rearing up his stomach. I expected him to get on her right away, which was more or less the routine Phil and I had, but the randy pair began to make a real meal of it.

To my astonishment, he spent a long time kissing and sucking her nipples while his hand played with her pussy. She meantime was stroking his fat penis, rubbing it up and down and even lowering her head to suck it! Their hands roamed lovingly over each other's bare bodies and then Sheila pushed Tom back on the couch and straddled him, directing his cock to the lips of her pussy. She thrust down and it disappeared right up her and she began a see-sawing motion. Tom lay back grinning while she pleasured herself on top of him. Watching them at it gave me a thrill such as I had never known.

'Fancy taking my place, Pam?' Sheila said suddenly. 'Tom can go on for hours and there's plenty there for both of us—'

She got off him and Tom lay back with his thing sticking up, red and glistening from his wife's juices. Disregarding my protests, Pam undressed me, saying she was sure I wanted a bit of fun. Naked, she pushed me into her husband's arms. My nipples were sucked and my pussy felt, then his head was between my legs, licking and sucking at my very core. My excitement was tremendous, I wanted his big cock in me and pushed him onto his back to mount him as Sheila had done.

'That's right,' she urged. 'Hold it upright and just lower yourself down, Pam. Do what comes naturally.'

The stiff shaft filled me right up and it was lovely to feel it inside me. 'Oh, what am I doing?' I moaned, but began to squirm down to get more of that lovely feeling. Tom put up his hands to clasp my breasts, moulding them in his big palms like a baker kneading dough. 'You're going to make me come!' I squealed, bucking faster on top of him, my pussy pulsing with unstoppable tremors that shook my whole body. Then Sheila was hugging and congratulating me, saying she knew I had it in me. If she was referring to her husband's hard stalk, she was right!

I visited them regularly for some time and became quite at ease in taking off my clothes and sharing Tom's virile cock turn and turn-about with my friend Sheila. We did everything, I think, humanly possible between a man and woman. Tom was a wonderful teacher, with his wife suggesting many thrilling variations. My shyness and inhibitions soon vanished and little by little, I introduced my husband to the finer points of sex. Needless to say he was delighted with my newfound sexuality. I don't

know what he would say if he ever discovered that my
friend Sheila had given me a helping hand!

Pamela, East London

Bare-Faced Cheek

On the night before I was due to marry Ernie's lively daughter, when both of us were pretty pissed, he warned me that I was taking on a handful. I knew that, of course, Pippa being a hot-tempered girl but lovely with it. Despite our frequent arguments, I knew that she was the girl for me. Besides, we'd been fucking and sucking over the past months and a hornier piece I'd never met. 'I can handle her,' I bragged. But during the evening Ernie handed me a parcel and said I was to open it later. Next morning, getting ready for the ceremony, I did so and found a short strap about eighteen inches long and two inches wide.

Pippa was late, of course, and when she finally took her place beside me in front of the vicar, she lifted her veil and poked her tongue out at me. At the reception, having a drink with my new father-in-law, I said, 'What is the strap for?'

'You'll find out when you're living with that minx of mine. You whack her bottom to keep her in line. I used to do that until she got too grown-up for the belt, but I reckon she still needs it—'

I laughed, but I liked the idea, and he was right. I took the strap with me on our honeymoon. I had no complaints about the first night – the randy little piece wore me out by the middle of the night. At a dinner dance at our hotel the next night she flirted outrageously with a swarthy young Spanish guy, who danced with her and asked for a date. In our room later she teased me that she'd felt his cock up hard against her while they were dancing and she fancied a go with him. Joking or not, I was not amused. As she was naked and ready for bed, waggling her tits at me in defiance, I hauled her across my lap. I didn't waste time going for the strap but, with her wriggling bum upwards over my knee, I applied the palm of my hand to her bottom in a fury of smacks, reddening her cheeks and making her scream more in humiliation than pain. Afterwards, she cuddled up to me like a good little girl.

A few weeks later she came home very late after a night out with the girls. Again she teased me about the lads who had chatted her up at the social club. I felt it was a deliberate ploy to get me riled. This time I brought out the strap.

'I remember that,' she giggled. 'Where did you get it?' I told her I had been warned she'd need it and grabbed her as she tried to evade me, pulling her over my lap. This time I raised her skirt and lowered her tiny knickers. She howled and protested, but I warmed her lovely bare bottom with the length of soft leather. It gave me a tremendous hard-on, which she taunted me about as she got up and rubbed her smarting backside. It had aroused her too, for when I lowered her onto the couch, she was all for it. She fucked like a whore.

Since then I have had many occasions to spank her. I even believe the minx sets me up to get a walloping, knowing that a strenuous fucking is bound to follow. Her sister came to tea once and told me that Pippa deserved spanking and was glad to hear from her that I kept the belt handy. She said my wife would only respect a husband who was firm with her. I knew there was more to it than that – she positively enjoys the mild smackings and strappings. I'll bet there are countless husbands who'd like to spank their wives – and wives like mine who would enjoy it, too. One other thing, after I've thrashed her

bottom and we've made up, I always kiss it better for her –
which is all part of the fun.

S. M., Doncaster

Dishing It Out

I kicked my husband where it hurts most when I discovered he'd been dallying with a young girl from his office. I was so furious I threw punches at him and blacked his eye until he cowered in a corner, sobbing like a frightened kid and begging me not to hurt him. It felt so good I realised I thoroughly enjoyed punishing him. Having him beg and plead gave me a great feeling of power. He came to my arms crying, saying he was just being kind to the girl in her first job and that only a few innocent kisses had been exchanged. He wouldn't do it again, he promised like a wimp. It was just that he'd felt ignored by me for some time and sought comfort with another.

'I'll give you comfort,' I threatened, making him cry real tears. But he was right. At that stage in life, we had been married some twenty years and our partnership was stale. I had had two lovers at that time and spent many evenings out with them. So my husband had been ignored and our sex life was infrequent. I only let him when my boyfriends weren't available for both were oil-rig men – on separate rigs of course. Looking at my dejected husband, cowering like a whipped pup before me, it struck me that in a curious way he was enjoying his humiliation as much as I enjoyed dishing it out.

'You can get your own dinner,' I told him. 'I'm going out, so expect me back when you see me. What's sauce for the goose is sauce for the gander. I could easily find a bit on the side like you!'

I left him with his head hung in abject misery and went off to take a bath and make myself up in my war-paint to meet Terry, one of the boys I was having it off with. At twenty-three he was eighteen years my junior and great fun to be with. For once it felt good to be going out without having to make an excuse and say that I was visiting my mother or my sister.

When I came downstairs, John was peeling potatoes. 'I'll do anything, Mary—' he began, but I just went out and slammed the door behind me.

Terry took me to a club where we danced and dined, and then fucked me in the back seat of his car. Being so young, of course he was terribly horny, wanting me naked. His hands and mouth were all over my body as he shagged me with his iron-hard prick. I let him go on longer than usual because I just didn't care what my husband would think, feeling I had him where I wanted.

It was almost three in the morning before Terry dropped me at my door. As a light was shining in the bedroom above us, I was certain that Fred was watching and I gave Terry a long kiss.

My husband was sitting up in bed. 'I hope you had a nice evening dear,' he said, eager to appease me.

Nice evening! It was three in the morning, his wife had just come home with a flash young stud and the weak creature felt it necessary to toady to me. How could you treat him like a man?

'I had a great time,' I informed him, taking off my clothes and standing naked. My breasts were still swollen from Terry's fondling and mouthing and my cunt was soaked and stretched from being poked so vigorously. I wanted Fred to notice. 'Don't you think my nipples look big? You'd

262

think someone had been sucking them, wouldn't you?'

'Are you still angry with me?' he asked. 'I'll never look at another woman, honestly. You were right to hit me—' His voice sound so anxious and timid that I laughed outright.

'It'll be the worse for you if I do,' I said, getting into bed naked just to inflame him. He cuddled up to me, whimpering, his face nuzzling my tits, his mouth finding my nipples and sucking contentedly.

'What's this?' I demanded. 'You big baby! Does baby want to suck his mammy's titties then? Didn't she smack you today for being naughty? I think you love this, Fred—'

'I don't mind what you do, as long as you don't leave me,' he whined against my breast. 'I don't mind if you have other men. You can tell me about them if you like, dear—'

'You Peeping Tom,' I said. 'You were looking out the window, weren't you? Well, I was with a real man tonight and he fucked me properly. What do you say to that?' He didn't say anything, sliding down in the bed to push his face between my thighs, licking at my cunt as if it were a honeypot. He was, in effect, doing what I considered the basest act a husband could do after his wife had been unfaithful, licking me out. His eagerness to do so, the probing tongue searching every corner, made excitement grip me.

'Yes, lick me clean,' I told him, pushing my crotch to his mouth and gripping his hair. 'I bet that little bitch at work wouldn't let you do this – and she'd better not!'

As if by unspoken agreement his passiveness and my dominance over him became the normal way of things. He loved it, and indeed our marriage became much more interesting and happy for us both. Coming home late after a meeting with one or other of my lovers, I'd give away nothing of what had gone on until Fred actually got down on his knees and begged me to tell him how I'd been fucked. And if he displeased me over some little thing, he'd bring me the strap and go upstairs to await my pleasure, bent over a chair to get his bum warmed. He'd be disappointed if I didn't whack his bottom hard, always getting a terrific hard-on after the beating which I couldn't resist letting him fuck me with. It makes me think of all the wasted and dull years of our marriage when we didn't know what really suited us. Now, I wouldn't change him. Mind you, I make sure he behaves!

Mary, Great Yarmouth

Plastic Fantastic Lover

I hadn't made love to my wife for almost a year, and Madge is a full-blooded sexy female who loves regular nookie. In better days she would nudge me in the night, whispering, 'Fuck me, love, put it in,' while reaching for my prick. Sometimes I've been roused in the small hours with her sucking my dick. At other times I'd wake up with Madge pressing her cunt into my hip as I slept, masturbating and telling me to lie still when I offered to roll over and shag her, enjoying some fantasy that was turning her on. So we used to have a good sex life together.

Then I started my own business. After a few years of successful growth, employing some thirty blokes, I got into debt trying to make my firm larger. Then came the recession. I had to lay men off, I worked every hour I could and soon became a nervous wreck. In a word, I was impotent. I couldn't get it up. Sure, Madge did her best to help with fancy bra and knicker sets, suspenders, hand jobs, mouth jobs and a whole lot more. But none of it made the reluctant chopper rise as of yore. Nor did medical advice, creams, pills or yoga. Imagine not able to get a hard-on with your luscious wife cuddling her naked body up to you, desperate to be fucked! The shame of it! I gave up making excuses. We stopped trying.

Madge was sympathetic at first, but as months went by with no success she got angry and sarcastic. It showed in her growing depression and I was accused of not being a real man. In the row that followed, I moved into the spare bedroom. From then on, Madge perked up considerably and I wondered if she had a lover. Meals were ready when I came home from work, she was cheery again and we got on not so much as husband and wife but as man and housekeeper. I was scared to approach her sexually again in case of more embarrassing failures, so I left it at that.

Don't think I didn't have salvaging my marriage in mind as well as my business. To me Madge was the perfect woman – handsome, with milk-heavy tits, strapping thighs and a plump cunt with ridges like soft fingers on each side of her split. That comfortable quim was perfect to rub my pubic bone against while my prick was embedded deep inside her hot and slippery love-nest. A forest of thick growth surrounded her grotto and spread between her pillowy arse cheeks – a lush bush that a family of field mice could have happily nested in.

So I was bereft, as you may imagine, having all that to suck, fuck and generally make a meal of. Madge used to be loving. Even after years of marriage she'd want it at all hours – if I popped in for coffee during work or when I was watching the television. By the ploy of simply getting naked and standing directly in front of the set she knew she could divert my attention at any time. Sadly none of that happened any more.

I was at home one afternoon with my wife's sister, Joan, who worked as the accountant for my business. Things, it seemed, had much improved between Madge and I, which cheered me. We drank coffee and talked. Joan was a shrewd woman and very different from Madge. I mentioned her sister was in town at the hairdressers.

'She'll be with that woman Helen Gray who I don't like,' Joan said. 'If you and Madge got on better, she wouldn't need a friend like that.'

Joan gave a short sarcastic laugh when I said Helen Gray seemed a nice enough woman. 'You've been too occupied with work,' she said. 'Come with me and I'll show you something that'll wake you up.'

I followed her upstairs into the bedroom my wife had to herself since I'd moved into the spare. There Joan pulled out the bottom drawer of Madge's dressing table, carefully lifting aside some silk underwear, until she exposed a rolled-up towel.

'You shouldn't be doing that,' I said. 'I never look in there myself. What is it you think I should see—?'

I suspected she was searching for letters from a lover, but was more surprised as the towel she had in her hands was unrolled for my inspection. She laid it on the bed and I saw a large rubber dildo in the shape of a cock with a plum-sized crown, a thick shaft and a big pair of balls on the base. There were other plastic vibrators of varying sizes and a jar of lubricant.

'You can guess what she does with these,' my sister-in-law said grimly. 'I think, Bob, you had better take your duties as a husband more seriously. Madge is too bloody fond of sex and always has been.'

What could I say? That I was impotent? 'You shouldn't be prying into her private life,' I said. 'Sisters you may be, but it's none of your business.'

'No, but it's yours,' Joan snapped back, 'and you'd better find out what's going on. It's all to do with Helen Gray, I know. She gives parties where sexy underwear and these disgusting objects are for sale. I went to one with Madge and walked out. Helen Gray's a bad influence—'

She left, leaving me feeling strangely amused at the thought of my wife using sex-toys. The notion of her masturbating with dummy pricks proved a great turn-on. For the first time in ages I felt my balls tighten and my tool gave a twitch. I was getting a hard-on! Sitting on the bed and imagining Madge fuck herself with a lubricated vibrator, I heard voices from below. Quickly replacing her goodies, I went quietly out to the landing. Below, I caught a glimpse of my wife and friend going into the lounge. 'We'll have one more drink for luck, Helen,' I heard Madge say, sounding giggly. Obviously they'd had a liquid lunch.

I crept into my bedroom, wondering whether to announce myself. Then they were coming upstairs and going into the bedroom opposite my door, leaving it wide open, confident I was at work. With my door ajar, I had a perfect view of the bedroom on the other side of the passageway. To my intense excitement I saw the two women kissing passionately, clasped in each other's arms like a man and woman. They undressed down to their panties, bare tits almost touching as they stood face to face. My wife's were heavy and rounded, her partner's more pendulous, the long hanging kind. I had my prick in hand as I watched, a dong as hard as it had ever been. Madge was quite a big woman but Helen was taller and broader. She had a strong curved back and a wide curvaceous bottom. The wispy briefs she wore, from her home sales' collection I guessed, barely covered the deep cleft of her arse. She had a splendid big cheeky bum just made for spanking. What a turn-on!

The two women stood nipple to nipple and kissed deeply again, pressing their bodies against each other. Helen then lowered Madge onto the bed, leaning over to lick her breasts and belly, pulling Madge's panties down over her feet and casting them aside. My horny wife knew what to expect, for she parted her legs at once and raised her knees. I caught a flash of hairy muff before Helen went down and began to lick Madge out. I had a fine view of my wife's bent legs and Helen's big arse as they pleasured each other lewdly. I distinctly heard Helen's gobbles and loud slurping noises as she feasted on my wife's juicy quim, making Madge moan and gasp, her hands drawing her partner's head tight to her crotch.

'The dirty lesbian whores,' I chuckled to myself in delight at the sight. 'The horny cows.' It was the best sex show I'd ever seen. Madge was bucking her arse, legs trembling as she came. Helen stood up and caught her breath as my wife lay sprawled out beneath her. 'That's not all, my darling,' I heard Helen say. 'I know what you want now. Shall I get him?'

Madge, recovering from her first climax, leaned up on an elbow, tits lolling, and grinned impishly at her companion.

'Fuck me then,' she giggled. 'Strap Roger on and screw me silly. Is that what you want me to say? You're going to do it anyway—'

Roger! They even had a name for the plastic brute! Helen walked out of my sight, returning moments later with the thing strapped on, standing sideways to me so that it reared up at an angle. It looked huge! It was the most grotesque sight to see a woman with heavy-hung pendulous teats, plump female buttocks and a lifelike cock and balls. My wife did not find the sight so absurd, however, reaching out her arms for her lesbian lover to join her on the bed.

'God, yes, Helen, I want *that*,' I heard Madge tell the woman who was now lowering herself between her parted thighs. 'All of it, my love. Fuck me with it now—'

And fuck her Helen did, driving the stout shaft in to the balls, her buttocks flexing and clenching as she aped the motions of a man fucking a woman beneath him. I heard my wife cry out as Helen cupped an ample bum cheek in each hand and thrust. I ventured into the passageway to get a better look at the big dildo pistoning in and out of

Madge's gaping minge. Both became very vocal, their bodies humping and clashing, their sweaty bare bellies smacking, their tits flattening against each other. This was an exhibition to be long remembered, the pair lost to everything but their lust. My prick was in agony, such was its engorged state. It demanded relief.

'Nothing so base as a hand-job for you, pal,' I told my prick. Not with two horny women at hand. I felt I had nothing to lose and a hell of a lot to gain. There in the passage I threw off my clothes and walked boldly into the bedroom bollock naked, a massive erection before me. Over Helen's shoulder, Madge saw me approach.

'Bob!' she shrieked in mid-fuck.

'Carry on, girls,' I ordered the startled pair. 'Don't stop on my account. I've got the biggest bone-on watching you two horny cows.' My wife made as if to move from under Helen but I pushed her flat. 'I said, carry on. I want to join in—'

'He's got a huge hard-on,' Helen observed, looking over her shoulder. 'I thought you said he couldn't—'

'I can now,' I retorted. 'And I'll fuck you for starters, Helen, while you shaft my missis. Fair's fair, I think.'

'Bob, don't you dare!' screamed Madge from under Helen.

'You're in no position to tell me what to do,' I said, fiercely assertive. 'What d'you think you're doing – dancing? You do your thing and I'll do mine!'

Madge fell silent and Helen didn't seem to object to my intentions as I positioned myself behind her upturned buttocks. Maybe she was in shock, both were still, the dildo half-embedded up my wife's cunt. I fingered Helen and found her erect clitty. She moaned and shifted her arse as if to allow me access. I pushed my fingers up her and found a real hot-box of a drenched cunt. Adjusting the direction

270

of my knob, I placed it to her pussy lips and thrust.

The effect of my insertion was to make her resume prodding Madge. I grasped her arse cheeks, working my hips as I fucked her vigorously. Her bum rotated and waggled as I attained full depth.

'Go it, girls!' I called out in triumph, for good measure smacking the beefy buttocks that buffeted back at me as Helen became excited. 'He's fucking me!' Helen cried out. 'Your man is fucking me, Madge. What would my husband say—?'

As I plunged in harder, I laughed aloud. 'And what would he say if he knew you were fucking my wife?' Helen just moaned and jerked back at me, my thrusts into her sending the dildo deep into Madge.

'Stick your arse out more,' I ordered, as the come surged up my shaft.

I would have loved some video buff to have captured the scene, with me heartily fucking Helen, her arse going like a piston and Madge now jerking in ecstasy under the pair of us, mouthing unintelligible words in the throes of being dildoed. It was indeed a rare triple romp.

'I'm coming over and over – it's killing me!' I heard Madge scream out. Helen was reduced to hoarse gasps as I fucked the air from her body. At last we collapsed in a heap, all three of us fucked to a frazzle.

That, I am happy to write, was only the beginning of our private circle which is still in being today. Two's company, but three is a cock-happy crowd – so we've discovered. Need I add I no longer have any trouble getting it up?

Bob, Madge and Helen, Lancs

In the Potting Shed

This tale is strange but true. My sister and I lived with our parents in a house with a large garden, well over an acre, and our gardener, George, used part of it as an allotment. George was about forty and always wore overalls and didn't shave. I was seventeen and thought nothing about him. My sister Agnes was nineteen and a plain girl with no boyfriend.

One day I went down the garden to fetch Agnes for dinner. Not seeing her at first, I looked through the window of George's shed where I knew she sometimes went. Bulbs and tools hung from the rafters and there was an old table where he potted his cuttings. The window was always dusty and cobwebby inside and out, but I cleared a space with my hand and peered in. What I saw astonished me. I'd never had a boy, I'd only ever masturbated, but I knew what I was seeing, all right. Agnes was leaning back with her bottom against the table, with her dress open and her plump tits out of her bra. George was handling them, moving them about in circular movements, his thumbs pushing at her nipples. Agnes just lolled back and let him, her head reclining on her neck, looking up at the roof as if lost in pleasure.

The wicked bitch, I thought excitedly, fancy letting George play with her bare titties, and him an old man. Of course, I had played with my own breasts at times and had often wondered what it would be like to let a boy do it. Agnes was evidently loving it. George stood before her quite calmly, I thought, fondling her titties and then he suddenly leaned forward and began to suck on her nipples like a baby! As I watched, my cunt grew moist and pulsed like a heartbeat. More was to follow. George stopped sucking her nipples and raised her dress up. Agnes dutifully held it above her waist while George pulled her knickers down to reveal her split bulge with its wispy hairs between her thighs.

My excitement was intense and I rubbed myself furiously. They were obviously unaware of me spying as they pleasured each other. George's hand went to my sister's cunt, palm up and middle finger crooked, entering her tight entrance. I saw her body shake and her head roll about as she wriggled on the titillating finger. Her hips shook violently, then slowly subsided, making me aware that George had brought her off by hand. She buttoned up her dress and straightened her skirt, not saying anything as George turned away to pick up his pipe.

I ducked down smartly, creeping away and circling round to meet Agnes walking up the path to the house.

'Where have you been?' I asked. 'It's time for dinner.' She just shrugged and walked past me, no doubt still feeling the glow of her orgasm.

That night I was dying to tell her I'd seen what George did to her. But I didn't because I thought that would give the game away and she might stop going there through shame. I wanted to spy on them again and watch while George fondled her tits and played stink-finger with her cunt until she had a come. I did just that on several occasions. Once, to my great delight, I saw George get a big upright cock out of his overall and let Agnes rub it in her hand until he spurted come all over her fingers. Oh, how I wanted to hold that big thing and let him play with *my* tits and cunt. I masturbated many nights imagining the scene.

One day that summer my parents went off shopping in town and Agnes went with them. I saw George arrive on his bike. Picturing what he did with my sister made me all het-up. I thought about playing with myself but decided to go one better. So I took a mug of tea to the potting shed and called George in from his vegetable patch. While he drank it, I deliberately leaned pack against the rough table as Agnes did and asked if he had a girlfriend. He put down the mug and regarded me suspiciously. Like my sister, my breasts were full and firm. By leaning back I thrust them right out before him, almost in invitation.

George may have been a country bumpkin but he was shrewd enough to recognise what was on offer. 'What are these then?' he said roughly, big hands reaching out to encompass both my titties and squeeze them. 'You young girls do like 'em played with, right enough. That why you came here, miss?'

Though I blushed at his words I had no intention of stopping him, eager to know the feel of a man's hands on my young breasts. 'Take them out, George,' I said, starting to unbutton the front of my cotton dress for him. Opened down to the belt at my waist, my bra was revealed, the cups swollen with two creamy mounds. He slid the straps down over my shoulders until my tits thrust up bare, the nipples sticking out. He stared at them hungrily and I wanted to hurry him along.

'Suck them, George,' I heard myself say, and his rough hands gripped them again, tilting the nipples and taking one to his mouth. 'Oh, yes,' I sighed as he sucked, my lower belly in a turmoil. Reaching for the front of his overall, I felt a long and very hard stem and clutched at it.

'So you want to see this, do you?' he said gruffly, his

mouth nuzzling my tits. He pulled it out and for the first time I held a prick. It was warm and stiff and I rubbed the silky flesh eagerly.

'Not so blooming hard or fast, young miss,' he complained of my inexpert stroking. 'Easy does it, nice and gentle like.' And so I received my first advice on the art of wanking a cock.

We never quite know our hidden desires and I was surprised to find that I had an uncontrollable craving to hear crude words while we pleasured each other. Brought up as proper young ladies, 'dirty talk' was to me the very height of lewdness. 'It's a lovely stiff cock, George,' I told him. 'I do like playing with it. I love you sucking my titties but don't you want to feel my hairy thing—?' Quite naive for a first attempt, I know, but I rapidly improved. As it was, my words stopped George in his tracks.

'You horny little baggage,' he said. 'I can tell you're all for it. And the word's cunt, didn't you know that? Cunt! And that's a prick you're holding there, my love. Made to go up young things like you, only it would make a baby unless I had a Frenchie. Here, I'll bring you off on me hand—'

I rushed to pull my knickers down for him. As he fingered me, he remarked that I was 'well juiced up in there' and I squirmed to his groping. Then he balled his fist, pressing it to my crotch and stuck his long hard gardener's thumb into my cleft. The feeling was indescribable. I muttered and groaned, bearing down on it, working my hips, coming off and starting to feel the urge returning even in my throes.

'Oh, George,' I whimpered, 'it's heaven, heaven!' In my hand the prick I held had gone limp and my fingers and wrist were sticky with goo. When he stepped back I was still all of a shudder, thinking what a delightful thing it was to be brought off by a man.

'I've got work to do now,' he said. 'You get on your way and never a word about this, miss. Enough's enough for the moment.'

But it wasn't enough for me, still glowing and feeling wicked from our session. As I pulled up my knickers I had to ask him, 'Have you fucked Agnes, George? Have you used a Frenchie on my sister? I know she likes to come here—'

'Why do you want to know that?' he said. 'I bet you want the same? But not here, it's too risky. Come to my cottage—'

So I did, many a time, giving my unwanted virginity to our gardener. Once in the privacy of his own home George was no slouch. He it was who first saw me naked. I got quite expert at rolling the rubber sheath over his erect dick and did everything it is possible for a girl to do with a lecherous male. My visits were always timed so as not to clash with sister Agnes for he was busy with us both.

Years later George was a guest at both of our weddings, looking out of place in a stiff collar and blue suit. I wondered what he thought, seeing us in our white bridal gowns, having had his fill of us over several years. Well, it didn't do our husbands any harm, for neither Agnes nor I had any inhibitions after George had finished with us. In fact, I had to show my bridegroom some of the finer points of sex on our honeymoon – which delighted him no end. I firmly believe young girls are all the better for training with an older man. Though if I catch my Brian dishing out lessons to any wide-eyed innocents I'll take the secateurs to him. As you can tell, I've always been a keen gardener!

Barbara, Kent

In Her Little Snapshot Album

My wife was a good mother and brilliant homemaker, perfect in every respect except that she thought sex was a duty. She never made the first approach and was even shy of me ogling her as she undressed for bed. She would not hear of my suggestions for more adventurous sex, such as the oral kind, and daytime screwing was out – she would only do it in bed with the light off. Yet, for all that, when we fucked she could get highly aroused and come in torrents, her body writhing, lost to everything but the pleasure of a stiff prick up her juicy cunt.

So she was obviously highly sexed even if that part of her nature was repressed. Of course I wanted more than I was getting. That it came about, I owe to the unlikeliest source, her maiden aunt, Gertrude. The old lady lived by herself and when she died Linda was the sole beneficiary of her will. It was left to us to clear the old girl's rented cottage.

Among a collection of mementos we found a faded cardboard folder tied with string in a locked drawer of a roll-top desk. I'd gone to make a cup of tea and returned from the kitchen to find my wife with the opened folder on her lap, looking hot, bothered and embarrassed. I joined her on the overstuffed couch and took from her hand a sheaf of black-and-white postcard-sized photographs.

I had to suppress a chuckle at the first one. It was patently Aunt Gertrude but the naughty girl smiling wickedly at the camera was about twenty. It must have been taken some sixty years ago. She stood on a grassy knoll surrounded by trees, impudently thrusting out a fine pair of rounded tits; between her plump thighs was a veritable thatch of cunt hair.

That the lass so pictured was enjoying revealing her charms was obvious from the impish look on her face. She was curvaceous in the extreme, rounded hips swelling out from a narrow waist into strapping thighs and long shapely legs. In the next photo her long hair was down her back and she looked over one shoulder with the sauciest smirk, doing to the photographer what's now called 'mooning', and what a firm rounded bum she presented. Hands reaching behind, she held both spheres wide apart showing the hang of her cunt and tangle of hair in the delightful cleave of her cheeky arse.

'Naughty Gert,' I chuckled, 'she must have been a right one in her day. What a splendid specimen too. Your old auntie had hidden talents, Linda. Absolutely perfect tits and bum on her. I wonder who the lucky photographer was?'

The next pic was of Gertie in close-up, head and shoulders, leaning forward so that her large breasts became elongated and hung down sexily. I could imagine that she and the fortunate camera-wielder flattened some grass after that with a great fuck. 'Somebody found a good model for his snaps,' I had to add. 'He took a bloody good picture too—'

Linda still looked uncomfortable and ill at ease sitting beside me with the opened folder and dozens of the old photos in her lap. 'I suppose it must have been the chap Aunt Gertie was engaged to,' she said quietly, as if still bemused. 'She told me he was a keen photographer. He had his own darkroom and stuff—'

'I don't blame him for being keen,' I said, eyeing one more shot of Gertie on her back, legs apart to show off a fine hairy minge. 'I would have thought he'd have married her after this lot and made an honest woman of her.'

'He was killed in the war,' Linda said. She was blushing deeply as she made to put the pictures back into the folder. 'I don't think you should look at any more, John. They're not very – nice—' Needless to say I took them from her.

'It depends what you call nice,' I said. I thought they were great! Beside me Linda moved her bottom on the old couch as if in some agitation while I more or less made her share the viewing with me. There was Gertie in close-up, with a man's belly in the picture and her holding a goodly length of erect chopper, the knob of it being sucked between her sweet lips. Her fiancé must have had some kind of timing device, I reckoned, for in others he was getting across Gertie and fucking her. This was shown in a variety of positions, with the girl on hands and knees getting shafted dog-fashion and, in others, mounted on top of him. There were lots of pictures, some taken in a bedroom with Gertie playing with herself across the bed, and a few penetrating herself with what looked like a home-made dildo. 'It just shows,' I said, 'that they were at in those days. Good for them—'

I thought I heard my wife gulp and murmur something that might have been approval. It suddenly struck me that her unease was because she had been turned on by the explicit photos. I slipped an arm around her, cupping a luscious tit, hefting it in my hand and feeling the nipple harden. I squeezed her closer and kissed her neck, delighted she did not attempt to remove my hand from her breast. She sighed and I suspected she was grinding her upper thighs together as she squirmed on the couch. Encouraged, I slipped my hand inside a bra cup and fondled bare breast, flicking at the stretched nipple.

'I can see where you got your lovely big tits from, Linda,' I whispered. 'They're just like your aunt's. The pictures have got you all worked up, haven't they? Me too, love. Cop a feel of this,' I invited, drawing her hand to my unzipped fly. Her fingers clasped my hard shaft and held it fast.

'You're a dirty beast, John,' she complained, but not without a little giggle in her voice. The folder and photos fell to the carpet as I kissed her, my tongue deep in her mouth. She responded as she had not done for years. I pulled up her dress, dragging it over her head in haste, fumbling at her bra. She even helped me as I disrobed her completely. I laid her back along the couch, parting her legs. I was determined to go the whole bit while she was so amenable. I licked and kissed her tits, gave little bites and sucks to her nipples, then went down to cover her cunt with my mouth.

'Oh, that, that—' she groaned. 'Do it if you must then. Oh, oh, what are we doing? You dirty thing, John – oooh—'

By now I had my tongue deep in her cunt passage, rolling it against the moist folds, flicking at the taut little nub of her clitoris. Her response was to twist and grind her quim against my face, her hands gripping my ears, making unintelligible throaty noises of ecstatic pleasure. I really had her going as I tongue-fucked her and she was loving the new experience.

Then the doorbell rang making me lift my head and curse the interruption. Linda sat up, gathering her clothes in a bundle. 'Send them away,' she said urgently. Then, with a flash of her bare arse, she dashed off to hide in the kitchen. The lady doesn't want to stop, I thought happily, straightening my clothes and answering the door.

It was one of our teenage daughters, calling with her latest boyfriend to say they were going out for the evening.

When they left, Linda returned, still naked, and got back on the couch. 'Goodness knows what's up with me today,' she said. 'It's those damned photos. I've never felt like this before—'

Good old Aunt Gertrude, I thought, looking down on Linda with tits splayed and legs apart. To do justice to the occasion I threw off my clothes and then went down on her again. My tongue slid into a juiced-up cleft and Linda sighed, glad to continue the treatment. 'I do like this,' she moaned as if in an agony of pleasure. 'Oh, you are making me come. Fuck me now – I want it so badly! Fuck me, dear—'

It was the first time I'd heard her use the F word and it delighted me. 'You bet I'll fuck you,' I cried. 'I'll fuck the arse off you, Linda. Front, back and bloody sideways before I'm finished and about time too!'

'Yes, yes,' she agreed eagerly as I thrust my rigid tool up her to the hilt, my balls slapping into the soft divide of her tilted arse. 'Do what you like with me – shove it all up – make me come!'

I did, several times in fact as the evening light faded and the room darkened. In between bouts we inspected Gertie's photos again, discussing the positions and actions, trying them out with Linda kneeling for me and also riding over my cock with her big boobs bouncing as she fucked away. Fondling my prick to get me erect again, she shyly suggested putting it between her tits as depicted by Gertie in the snaps. Then, on her own accord, my semi-erect dong under her chin, she sucked tentatively at the knob. Finding it to her liking, she gave it a full mouth blow-job, telling me later how much she'd loved it growing between her tongue and the roof of her mouth. I had a confirmed cocksucker of a wife after that.

We returned home that evening with the folder of naughty photos and, since then, others have been added, including many explicit ones of Linda and me. It's strange to think how the sexy goings-on between two young people some sixty years ago have so improved our marital relations. Linda is always quick to be excited by visual aids, so you can guess how she reacted to the first porno video I obtained! I'm sure the ghost of Aunt Gertie must look down on us with pride.

John W, Swiss Cottage.

Three Times a Lady

My husband John is a trucker who does a regular run to the continent. One night when he was away I went out with some other women from my work. I got off with two lads at a night club and, when the taxi dropped me at home, I found they'd followed in their car. I asked them in for coffee and one thing led to another. I ended up having sex with both of them, sleeping between them naked and loving what they did to me throughout the night. I had come after come as they kissed, licked, fondled and fucked me, in turn and together. When they left at dawn I was sore but satisfied by the torrid session. It had been so much better than with just one man pleasuring me.

If I thought it was going to be a one-off, I was mistaken. I thought about it a lot, feeling aroused every time. Then one of the boys – he was also called John – phoned me, asking if he and his mate Jacko could drop by. I should have said no but the temptation was too strong. Both my children are safely out of the way at boarding school, that's why I work to pay the fees although my husband earns good money. What I mean is, I was alone and lonely and had gained a taste for having two men in my bed. So the pair of young men arrived with a carrier bag of drink and we partied. With two lads kissing me and feeling me up, it was not long before they had me stripped off. They both fucked me on the couch before we all went off to bed.

The second time was every bit as good. They had me in

every possible position, insisted I suck their cocks and made me play with my tits and cunt. They made me want sex like never before and I became a wanton whore in my behaviour. In the morning I was left stretched out in bed fucked to exhaustion, but feeling a complete woman as I had satisfied two randy lovers. My husband returned and, as he always was after a week or so away, was ready for a good night of sex. When he was fucking me I was fantasising about the two boys, even calling out 'Oh, John, yes!' as I was coming. It was the other John I meant, though my husband was delighted I'd been so responsive. The strong climax I'd had was as much the result of my fantasy as my hubby's prick. I realised then I was hooked on threesome sex, wanting it to be a regular thing. When my husband drove off on his next trip, it was I who phoned the lads at their flat, suggesting I visited them, being worried in case the neighbours began to notice my night callers.

Of course the usual threesome followed. I found it terrifically exciting to be naked and fucked while the other boy watched closely. I loved being entered from the rear position while on my elbows and knees and sucking one of them off at the same time. In their flat I went about naked, enjoying flaunting my tits, cunt and bottom, getting all three felt up continuously. I was a different woman, a sexual creature.

My hubby takes two popular girlie magazines on his trips and, for the first time I began to read them and enjoy the readers' letters. I asked him if he would like to see me with another man. He said, 'Never on your life,' so that was that.

I think he doesn't know what he is missing. Anyway, with him away so much, the other John and Jacko are more than delighted to accommodate my desires. They both have girlfriends, but at least once a week when my John is away

I call on them and we let our hair down. Twice is nice, but three is for me! Try it, girls.

Joanna, Cleveland

The Last To Know

There I was, in front of the telly, glad that my wife was out with her sister so she couldn't moan about the football on the box, when my doorbell rang. I cursed and got up to see who it was. At my door stood a blonde woman of about my age, a well-developed one, too, I couldn't help noticing. She was in a rage, her face blazing with anger. 'You want to keep your bloody wife under control,' she shouted right away. 'Keep her away from my son. She ought to be ashamed of herself, twice his age and leading him on—'

I thought every neighbour would hear, so I hastily asked her in and led her to the living room where she stood shaking with fury. I turned off the television and poured her a whisky. She drank it in one go, then handed me the glass. 'I think you're a decent enough man,' she said, 'but I can't say the same for your slut of a wife. She's out in your car, I suppose?'

'Out with her sister,' I said, about to ask what the hell this was all about.

She gave a bitter laugh. 'Out screwing my son,' she said, 'and not for the first time by a long shot either. Haven't you any idea what's going on?'

'Frankly, no,' I said, 'but you are about to tell me, I suppose.'

'Don't think I'm making this up,' she said. 'I caught them at it. I came home to find that trollop naked and doing it with him on my fireside rug, the shameless cow.

On top of him too, she was, tits flying—.'

'Jesus,' I said, imagining the scene. As for my wife having it off with a young bloke, well, that was her business as we were at the point of parting, having agreed to go our separate ways. 'What did you do?' I asked her, intrigued. 'I bet you put a stop to that—'

'I went for the bitch,' she said grimly. 'I pulled her off him and gave her a good hiding.' That I would have loved to have seen. 'But it evidently hasn't stopped them. I know they're together tonight—'

'How old is your lad?' I asked.

'Twenty-two.'

I shrugged. 'He's old enough to know what he wants,' I told her. 'As my wife and I are separating, what she does is her own business.' All the same, I thought, what a horny cow. Fancy having it off with a toy boy and telling me she was out with her sister!

I walked the woman to her house, stopping on the way to take her into a pub. With a drink or two inside her she calmed down and became quite friendly. She was separated herself, she informed me, having slung her husband out years before. At our corner table her leg rubbed against mine. At her door, I promised I'd have a talk to my wife, which I didn't intend to do but it pleased her. She stood in the dark porch right up against me, so I took a chance and kissed her.

'Why did you do that?' she asked, but not angrily. I assured her it was because I found her attractive, very much so.

'I haven't been with a man since my husband left,' she said.

Taking that as a hint, I kissed her again.

'You'd better come in,' she offered when our lips parted. 'We shouldn't be doing this – it must be the drink I've had.'

287

Inside her living room I saw the fireside rug where she'd caught my wife and her son fucking. She did not object when I started to kiss her again, feeling her breasts, telling her this was one way to get her own back on my wife. To my delight she responded and let me put my hand up under her blouse to feel the heavy tits in the cups of her bra.

Before I left that night I'd had the pleasure of screwing her on the self-same rug where my wife had shagged her son. Naked, her body was the creamiest white I'd ever known, even the blonde hair on her cunt was a mere wisp. Against my black body hers was a stunning comparison.

'You're the first coloured man I've been with,' she said, using the old term. 'What they say about you fellows is true, isn't it?' I said I was no expert on other men's cocks. But she evidently enjoyed mine – and still does!

Calvin, Birmingham

Who Wears the Panties?

For some years now, since my divorce, I've enjoyed
dressing in female attire. I especially enjoy wearing ladies'
underwear against my skin. My sex life as a husband
was the cause of much complaint by my ex-wife. I wasn't
really interested and, sexually dissatisfied, she left me.
After she went, I was lonely. I felt the need for someone
else to share my pleasure with, yet I didn't really fancy
sex with another man – and I'd had a woman and failed
her.

Then it was my good fortune to meet Gemma, and a
real gem she has proved. She prefers male attire and has
had female lovers. She's the dominant kind while I'm happy
to be submissive. At first we were just friends, meeting at
the local history society. Then I asked her out for dinner.
She warned me that if I had any sexual inclinations towards
her I should forget them. She told me bluntly that she had
no desire for sex with men so I confessed how it was for
me.

In time, finding mutual interests, she came to live with
me. We sleep together but I've never had sex with her. The
nearest we've been to full intercourse is that sometimes
I'm allowed to tongue her cunt and give her an orgasm.
She also allows me to suck her nipples, especially when I
sob and cuddle into her after a ritual spanking or caning of
my bottom.

Our intimacy has progressed to bondage. I am tied up

to a chair or our bed if I displease her (which I do deliberately at times). Then I am spanked or 'queened' by her broad buttocks.

One day she produced an anal dildo and insisted I try it. The thought excited me terribly. She greased it thoroughly and I bent over for her. I found the experience highly enjoyable. She applied this to me in the rear over several weeks, sometimes with me naked and at other times dressed as a woman. One night she produced a strap-on double dildo, like two plastic pricks joined together almost in a boomerang shape. I watched, fascinated, seeing her insert one end in her cunt and strapping the belt around her waist – which left the other end sticking up exactly like a male with an erection.

She told me to lie on the bed, face down and bottom raised, and came behind me with the oiled dildo, easing the head of it into my anus. She inched it all up inside my back passage. It gave me sensations such as I'd never experienced before, especially when she curled over me with her breasts heavy on my back and began thrusting the dummy cock in and out. I loved it, telling her to work it faster into me, pushing my bottom back against hers. It made me feel very amorous and loving and more feminine than when I was dressed as a woman. I was her 'wife' and told her so in my throes. It was so exciting that it made me ejaculate all over the bedcover. When she saw that, I was thrashed soundly and made to go to bed. Then she joined me and I begged her forgiveness and she allowed me to suckle on her nipples.

I must say that our living together and sexual preferences have made me happier than ever before. To make more certain of keeping her I have even offered her marriage though, of course, I would be the wife. She doesn't want to tie herself to anyone, she says, but I know she is fond of me and does just what she likes with me. I would not have it any other way.

Anthony, Cambridge

The Second Time Around

I lived with my wife for eight years and, though we had been divorced for two years, I still wanted her. If I saw her in the street she'd wave and walk on, leaving me to admire her lovely arse moving under her tight skirt. In fact, since leaving me, I noted she wore younger clothes and didn't look her age of thirty-seven. I blamed myself for not being a better husband to her and was quite tortured to think that such an attractive and shapely woman would now be going with other men. I hated the thought but was really turned on thinking of her sleeping with a new bloke – him playing with her luscious tits and imagining her begging him to fuck her harder and make her come.

One night I saw her in a club with a young chap who looked half her age. I positioned myself at a table where I could watch them and, although I was with a woman myself, I could concentrate on nothing else. They drank and laughed together, then she allowed him to kiss her openly. How I hated it, yet I got a raging erection seeing them at it. He groped her tits and her hand was under the table, gripping his cock, I was certain. She saw me, gave me a little wave and a cheeky smile, then returned to kissing her boyfriend again. When they left I was sure they were going off to fuck. I went home alone and wanked.

Though I was not normally a frequenter of that club, I returned several times and saw her with other men.

Evidently she was making the most of her freedom and was very popular.

I still lived in the house where we'd spent our married life and, one Sunday, I answered the door to find Elaine standing there.

'Are you following me about and spying on me?' she asked. I hotly denied it, but was embarrassed at being caught out. 'You're such a fool, Dennis,' she said. 'If you want to take me out, all you've got to do is ask. Aren't you going to invite me in?'

She entered and looked around, complimenting me on the house being tidy. I made coffee and she sat on the settee. 'This is like old times,' she laughed. 'I miss this place.'

'I thought you were enjoying life,' I said bitterly. 'You aren't short of men to go out with. I suppose you sleep with them all?'

'That's none of your business,' she said, eyeing me shrewdly. 'I'm beginning to think it excites you. Of course I sleep with men, I'm not past it. The trouble with you was I thought *you* were past it. You were a real couch potato, asleep in front of the telly half the time. You used to be good fun to be with and a really good fuck in the old days.'

'Give me the chance again,' I said, going to sit beside her. 'Come back and I'll show you who's a couch potato.' She did not stop me kissing her, taking my tongue in her mouth, allowing my hands to cup her breasts. 'I could fuck you here and now. I don't care if other men screw you, I still want you.' Then we were kissing and pulling off our clothes, she falling back naked and raising her knees. In our haste I went straight in, hard up her cunt and thrusting stenuously. It was what she wanted and she held fast to me, lifting her cunt to my urgent shafting. 'How I've longed to screw you like this again!' I shouted.

'Oh yes, screw me rotten, Den,' Elaine yelled. 'I can

really feel it up my cunt. This is more like the old you! Fuck it all up me. Go on, give me more—'

Such hectic coupling could not last and, sated, I lay beside her on the settee. 'That was what you'd call a quickie,' I laughed. 'Give me a little time and I'll make it one of those long easy fucks we were so fond of.'

'A Sunday morning special,' agreed Elaine.

I toyed with her tits while her hand held my flaccid dick and gently massaged it – just like a married couple. 'You came off beautifully,' I said. 'Did those young lads I saw you with fuck you so well?'

'They tried,' my ex-wife laughed, 'but there's no substitute for experience. They were so *eager* that I suppose I was flattered. They'd leave my tits blue with love-bites, even my thighs. I hardly ever had a come with them. That was the best fuck I've had for ages and I'm looking forward to the next,' she added saucily.

I made sure it was worth it, kissing every inch of her body until she was begging for me to take her. Having already come, I screwed her until she had repeated orgasms before the sperm in my balls erupted. Like we used to do in earlier days we took a bath together then went off for lunch before returning to the marital bed.

Some months later she stood in front of the wardrobe mirror naked, regarding her swollen stomach. 'We'll have to get married again now,' she announced. 'I'm not going to be a single mum at my age.'

Dennis and Elaine, Bradford

A Spanking Good Time

My father walked out on my mother after twenty-two years of marriage, leaving her devastated. I was working away from home as a nurse and on the weekends I came back it was hard to console her. She lost weight and all she did was stay in and smoke and drink. Her friends made her take a job with them at the supermarket and in time she perked up, going out with the other women for an evening drink. I was delighted at her recovery. She dressed younger, made herself up heavily, and even went to discos with some of her younger friends. At forty-one, I thought she should be more circumspect. I even found a half-empty box of condoms in a drawer in the living room and assumed she'd entertained some man. She certainly had changed.

One Saturday evening I came home to find her out, as usual. I went to bed and was awakened later by voices. My watch told me it had gone one o'clock. There was ribald laughter from below and it sounded as if several people were with her. I went to the bathroom and, before returning to bed, descended a few stairs, crouching down in the gloom to see what all the noise was about. I saw a youth in the hallway, carrying an armful of beer cans, going into the living room. He looked about my age – twenty – and I thought, surely not a toy boy? Anyway, from the whoops and shouts, he was not the only one there. There was music too.

I went downstairs, switching off the light in the hall and

peering cautiously around the living-room door which was slightly ajar. To my great surprise there were four of them, all about the same age, in jeans and tee-shirts, lolling over the couch and armchairs. In front of them, stark naked, her clothes lying in a heap on the floor, my mother swayed to the music, her breasts bouncing, showing all she had between her legs. They who watched shouted bawdy remarks to encourage her.

She was obviously drunk, or at least very tipsy, as she wobbled her big breasts at her admirers and waggled her buttocks. I could, of course, have stormed in and demanded the boys leave, but I wasn't sure they wouldn't turn nasty. And would my mum, who seemed to be enjoying herself so blatantly thank me for interrupting the lewd display? What's more, I had to admit, the thought of what she was doing was strangely thrilling. Most girls, I suppose, have fantasised about titillating several men with their naked bodies. I also wondered if this was not a regular occurrence. She was a good-looking woman and she certainly knew how to please her audience.

Then one lad reached out and pulled her over him as he sat in the armchair. He grabbed her breasts, pressing his mouth to hers and they clung together in a long kiss, she every bit as keen as he. I saw his hand go between her legs but she pulled away and got to her feet, teasing the boy by shaking her full breasts in his face. She crossed to the next chair and sat across the boy's lap, pressing her naked body to him, kissing him lewdly, looking back at the lad she had just left. He got up – he was bigger than the others – and pulled her back across his lap, she giggling and squealing in mock protest. She was face down now, her breasts pointing to the floor and her large bottom upwards.

'She's asked for it,' I heard the guy say. 'Shall I give it to her?' There was a chorus of approval as he brought his

296

hand down smartly across my mother's cheeks. She howled and tried to twist her bottom away from him only to be held down firmly and given a good spanking. Whap, whap! went the palm of his hand as he smacked her bum. She protested but, from the giggle in her voice, she was evidently enjoying the whole scene. When she fell to the carpet on her hands and knees, she crawled across the room to those on the couch as if seeking help, showing off everything she had – a big reddened bottom, curly hair and a winking bumhole. As she passed the other chair, the boy there gave her two or three good smacks on the arse in passing.

She stopped before a lad on the couch. He unzipped and pulled out an erect penis and presented it to her face. With a moan, as if of gratitude, she clasped it and kissed the head lovingly, licking her tongue up the shaft and then sucking it into her mouth. I couldn't believe my eyes, but I defy anyone witnessing those boys and my mother's wanton behaviour not to have been erotically affected. She sucked as if loving every inch she had in her mouth, the boy before her squirming in his seat. Then the tall young man who had spanked her got up and pulled off his clothes. He had a penis that reared mightily – long and thick and menacing. He was obviously the leader of the gang, the one the others followed. I gulped at the size of his erection.

He got down on his knees behind mother, placing an arm around her waist and cupping one breast. She continued sucking the boy on the couch, making whimpering sounds, and I saw the lad behind her direct his knob to her vagina. Next moment every inch of it slid up between her buttock cheeks, forcing a passage into her. She dipped her back and tilted her bottom to make it easy for him. That was the start of the serious fucking.

Sucking avidly on the penis in her mouth, my mother jerked and thrust her rear back to the boy who was penetrating her. I saw her get wilder in her undulations, her bottom clenching and working furiously as her climax approached. She came with a shout and dropped to the carpet, leaking spunk from both ends. One of the other boys now stripped and lay down on the floor beside her. She turned to him and at once reached for his penis. Kneeling beside her, one of the others was playing with her breasts.

They were too engrossed to see that I was watching. The orgy continued with mother more than willing to accommodate them all. Eventually I went back to bed and masturbated till I was exhausted.

In the morning I took mother tea in bed and she looked as bright as a button. She does not pine for my father any more, that's certain!

S. R. N., Doncaster

The Sexy Stand-In

After eight years of marriage to Robert there were never any signs of me getting pregnant. My three sisters all had children, so I didn't think there could be anything wrong with my reproductive system. Although my husband longed to be a father, he refused to have a sperm count even after trying for a child for so long. He said we'd manage it someday, but I gave up on him after getting him to have sex with me every night with no result.

By now I was determined to have a baby come what may. It had become an obsession. Next door to us lived a man who had lost his wife the year before and with whom we were good friends. Gerald was a nice-looking man who was very good with his grandchildren. When they visited, they played in the garden and I often joined them. I loved being with the little ones, wishing one special little girl was my own. They had just departed with their mums one day when Gerald had me in for a coffee.

'You're so good with kids, Steph,' he said, 'I wonder you haven't a couple of your own by now.'

Of course it struck home and I began to cry, admitting through my sobs that we'd tried and tried. 'I know I can have children,' I blubbered. Gerald put his arms around my shoulders and I buried my face in his shoulder.

'What's up with your Bob,' he said, 'doesn't he want kids?' I sobbed against him even more unhappily, saying we had tried and tried, but I was sure my husband wasn't fertile. When I lifted my face to him, he dabbed my eyes with his handkerchief, then said he'd always thought what a lovely girl I was. Then he was kissing me and I kissed him back.

It just happened, I suppose, being close at the time. I needed someone to be sympathetic and for a long moment we clung to each other, our mouths fused passionately. He pushed his tongue into my mouth and cupped my breasts, saying between the kisses how much he wanted me.

Now we were standing upright and hugging each other tightly, my breasts to his chest, the bulge of his cock pressed against the fork of my thighs. We were even beginning to move our hips when we both leapt apart, realising things were getting out of hand.

Gerald apologised, as if it had been all his fault. I went home shaken, well aware my cunt was moist and throbbing. Surely not Gerald, I thought! He must be as old as my father! It left me uneasy for the rest of the day.

'I bet he'd like to give me a baby,' I thought, musing on the passion he'd shown while kissing and cuddling me. Such was the germ of my idea. Gerald was dark like my Robert and about the same size and shape. No, I thought, it was impossible – but I did so desperately want a child. What if I seduced our older neighbour and got pregnant by him? Robert would think it was his doing and we'd all be happy.

Now it was on my mind I even fantasised about having sex with Gerald, which got me more aroused. I'd never been with another man and the kissing and cuddling in the kitchen with Gerald made me feel very horny and wicked. I went up to the bedroom later to get a suit of my husband's I was to take for cleaning and, standing at an upstairs window next door, I saw Gerald. He gave me an embarrassed wave, as if unsure of our friendship after kissing and fondling me. I turned away as if I hadn't seen him.

I didn't turn away because I was angry at him, but because a naughty urge had came over me in a flash. Flash is the right word, for I began to remove my dress, standing as if unobserved as I drew it over my head. My excitement was tremendous and a glance showed Gerald watching me avidly. I unhooked my bra and tossed it aside, shaking my breasts as if enjoying the freedom of releasing them from the tight cups. Sure that he had got a good eyeful, I walked from the window but the desire to display my body was too strong. I stepped out of my panties and tights, then sauntered back in front of the window several times. Finally I stopped in his full view, my breasts, pubic hair and all of me open to his gaze. My agitated state of arousal was such that I withdrew to the bed and played with myself, my fingers delving into my sopping cunt, bringing me to a furious climax.

He couldn't see me, but I imagined he could and it made me all the more excited. The next day it was all I could think of and, after resisting the urge several times, I picked up the phone and invited Gerald over for coffee. When he came in we were both on guard and embarrassed. I was thinking of him seeing me naked, and I wanted him to again. I hoped he had the same thought.

'Stephanie,' he said at last. 'I'll have to go. I don't want coffee, I want you. If I stay I'll make a fool of myself like I did yesterday—'

We were both trembling as I went up to him, falling into his strong arms, our mouths searching. Again I felt the iron-hard bar of his penis against me and I pulled him down across the kitchen table, eager to fuck him right away.

'No,' he said against my mouth, breathing heavily. 'We must do it properly. I want your body naked, to see your

301

lovely tits, your hairy cunt and that round pretty arse. Let's go to your bedroom—' His words excited me even more, for my husband never used crude terms when we made love.

Oblivious to everything but my urgent desire, I guided Gerald to the bed I shared with Robert and where we had tried so often to make a baby. Gerald pulled off my dress, unclipped my bra and stripped off my panties even as I fumbled at his belt. Then we were both naked and he was kissing and sucking my nipples, running his big hands over my thighs and bottom, muttering his delight.

Gerald too had a body to admire with not an ounce of fat on a muscled frame. Best of all, I saw a magnificent cock sticking out from his belly, so much thicker in girth and length than my husband's. I cradled it lovingly between my breasts, pressing kisses to its crest.

'It's lovely, such a big hard one,' I told him shamelessly. 'I want to suck it. I want it in my mouth, Gerald. Would you mind?'

He allowed me to take it between my lips and suck hungrily for a moment. 'There'll be time for that later and I'll return the favour by licking out your pussy,' he said, laying me across the bed, his tongue lapping at my labia, the tip gaining entrance. I groaned my pleasure and clutched at his head. I was about to give in to the unstoppable surge of a come when I remembered what I wanted most – his sperm filling me.

'Fuck me, Gerald,' I begged him. 'Fuck me, darling, go on, go on! Put your fat cock up my cunt—' I could have added 'and give me a baby', but refrained.

He raised himself over me, my thighs spreading as his rigid cock entered me easily. I was penetrated to the hilt, feeling the hard cylinder of his tool in my tunnel, its knob pressed to my cervix and its girth filling me wall to wall. I heard him groan. 'Oh, what a lovely tight cunt!' and my own voice encouraging him, 'Yes, yes, fuck me harder, give me it all!'

The plum-shaped knob of his prick pistoned into me gloriously, so deep up my cunt I felt it was touching my stomach. I thrashed about under him, coming once and then coming again. Still I raised my bottom and tilted my cunt for more of the same, urging him on, my hands pulling at his arse cheeks, thrusting against him wildly.

'I'm coming, coming!' I heard him cry out. 'Let me off, Steph, I shall come inside you—' But I had no intention of letting him withdraw. 'No!' I screamed, gripping him with my arms and legs. 'Keep fucking me! Give me a baby – it's what I want—'

With me encouraging him in the lewdest terms, he cupped the rounds of my bum cheeks, thrusting out of control. Then he gasped and shot spurt after spurt of hot come into me. When at last he rolled off me he said, 'Do you realise what we might have done?' I nodded and kissed him gratefully.

Just to make sure, I arranged for repeat performances the next couple of months until my doctor confirmed I was pregnant. My husband was delighted and Gerald swore he'd never disclose our secret. In time I got the beautiful little daughter I had longed for. She is two now, and I think it's about time she had a baby brother. Time, I think, to tell Gerald he can stop using those condoms!

Stephanie, Liverpool

Caught With Her Knickers Down

I thought it couldn't happen to me but it did – I caught my wife with another man. I had no clue anything was going on as Jo seemed her normal self in our day-to-day life. I was out of the workshop lunching a client and the meal lasted so long that by mid-afternoon I decided to call it a day and go home early for once. I parked and went indoors, finding the downstairs deserted. But on the lounge carpet I saw a pair of men's shoes. They were not mine and, puzzled and already suspicious, I went upstairs quietly.

Even on the landing I could hear the noise of a strenuous fuck coming from the bedroom. I advanced to the door, finding it wide open. The first thing I saw was the curve of my wife's bare back flaring out at her waist to her rolling bum cheeks; two rounded spheres that worked agitatedly as she plunged down on a stiff length of prick. My immediate feeling was of resentment that she had not fucked me with such evident fervour for years!

The obvious thing to do was rush in and demand what the hell was going on. Instead I was rooted to the spot, my prick hard and bulging my fly. Jo had both knees planted firmly on either side of her lover's waist and, as she thrust her cunt down on his thick penis, I could plainly see the darkened skin of the divide of her cushiony arse. It was all there – the puckered arsehole, the fleshy bulge of her cunt and the outer lips of her pussy gripping the bulbous knob of her fucker's prick before she impaled herself on its full

304

length. His shaft, glistening with her juices, disappeared into her as she bore down. I watched until their motions became frenzied, their cries and utterances growing louder, my wife's bottom gyrating furiously, her tits swinging out under her arms. When her head fell forward and his hip movements ceased it was quite obvious both had shot their bolt.

It was then that I walked in, giving them a slow handclap. 'Bloody great,' I said as they sat up, startled. 'How long has this little lot been going on?'

I knew the man slightly, a married bloke that lived in the same street. He was on his feet collecting his clothes in panic. 'You'd better get the fuck out of here,' I told him, 'and don't come back. I'm sure your wife would like to hear of this little session. Get lost before I beat the hell out of you.' He went out of the room on the double.

Jo stood by the bed stark naked, making no attempt to cover herself.

'What are you going to do?' she asked nervously. 'I wouldn't blame you for telling me to go—'

'Nothing so drastic as that,' I said, deciding to take full advantage of the situation. 'First I'm going to paddle your hot little arse, then I'm going to fuck you. I think I've been neglecting you. We'll start making up for it right now—'

I could see she didn't know what to make of me as I folded my clothes over a chair. I did it slowly to show I was the master of the situation, but the erection that jutted out as I peeled off my underpants gave the game away.

She giggled and said, 'Yes, fuck me now, love. I can see you want to,' and she stood close to me with her tits jiggling.

'You don't escape that way,' I said, determined to fulfil a desire I'd long had. 'Bend over my knee,' I ordered, sitting on the edge of the bed. 'Don't you agree you damn well deserve punishing?'

In our years of being together I'd never hinted that I'd enjoy giving her a bottom smacking. Jo made a face and shrugged, but draped herself obediently across my knees, no doubt considering she'd better play along after being caught so blatantly with another man. Looking down upon her raised bum, I said to myself, 'It's an ill wind.' In my time as her husband I'd had an affair or two myself. Statistics showed that a large percentage of wives were unfaithful at some time, so why should I expect mine to remain true?

'Let this be a lesson to you,' I said. 'Any time I think you need it, you'll get your bare arse warmed.'

I gave her at least a dozen good smacks with the palm of my hand, reddening her cheeks and making her squirm. She arose from me rubbing her posterior, noticing too the engorged prick I sported.

'You enjoyed that,' she accused me, but I noticed an admiring glance in my direction as she said it. 'It fairly warms a bottom up.' Then she sniggered, 'Some of the nuns used to do that, smack the bare bums of us girls when I was at convent school. We quite enjoyed it.'

My, my, I thought, I've a soul mate here and didn't know it. 'Come and sit on this now, Jo,' I instructed her. 'Ride me like you did with that other guy.' I fell back on the bed, cock in air and she squatted over me, her gaping cunt hot and moist from her previous bout.

I was so hard that she let out an 'Ooh, aah,' as she bore down and my full length penetrated her first go. 'Ride me, you horny bitch!' I ordered her sharply as I lolled back, determined for once to enjoy being masterful with my wife – determined too to contain my own climax until she had ridden me to exhaustion. 'Ride me hard,' I repeated sternly. 'Grind that cunt down on me, get those tits swinging! Fuck me like you did with that bastard

306

just now. Show me what a horny cow you really are—'

Her squirming and jerking on the prick embedded up her cunt was no act. Her tits swung over my face like bells and her hips jerked wildly as her frenzy grew. 'Yes, sod you, yes!' she groaned in her excitement. 'I am a horny bitch. Do you think I'd have let him fuck me if you'd wanted me like this more often? This is what I need – fuck me good, fuck me often. Smack my arse, do what you like, only show me that you want me—'

'I love you!' I shouted back, unable to resist thrusting up into her, feeling the spunk rise from my balls and spurt into her in strong jets.

'Fantastic,' she muttered, falling across me as her own spasms weakened. We kissed and stayed together on the bed until I was ready for another bout, a long slow fuck on top of her that brought her to a shuddering climax once again.

It took an affair to awaken me to my wife's true nature. Then I discovered that she was a demanding and highly sexed woman, the kind I'd always wanted yet had been too stupid to notice right by my side all the time.

Gavin, Manchester.

More Erotic Fiction from Headline Delta

Lust and Lady Saxon

LESLEY ASQUITH

Pretty Diana Saxon is devoted to her student husband, Harry, and she'd do anything to make their impoverished life in Oxford a little easier. Her sumptuously curved figure and shameless nature make her an ideal nude model for the local camera club – where she soon learns there's more than one way to make a bit on the side . . .

Elegant Lady Saxon is the most sought-after diplomat's wife in Rome and Bangkok. Success has followed Harry since his student days – not least because of the very special support lent by his wife. And now the glamorous Diana is a prized guest at the wealthiest tables – and in the most bedrooms afterwards . . .

From poverty to nobility, sex siren Diana Saxon never fails to make the most of her abundant talent for sensual pleasure!

FICTION / EROTICA 0 7472 4762 5

Bonjour Amour

EROTIC DREAMS OF PARIS IN THE 1950s

Marie-Claire Villefranche

Odette Charron is twenty-three years old
with enchanting green eyes, few
inhibitions and a determination to make it
as a big-time fashion model. At present
she is distinctly small-time. So a meeting
with important fashion-illustrator Laurent
Breville represents an opportunity not to
be missed.

Unfortunately, Laurent has a fiancée to
whom he is tediously faithful. But Odette
has the kind of face and figure which can
chase such mundane commitments from
his mind. For her, Laurent is the first step
on the ladder of success and she intends to
walk all over him. What's more, he's
going to love it . . .

FICTION / EROTICA 0 7472 4803 6

MASQUE OF FLESH

A SENSUAL SAGA OF VAMPIRE LUST

Valentina Cilescu

Trapped within the insatiable but alien frame of
luscious sex-slut Anastasia Dubois, white witch
Mara Fleming is forced to bow to the commands
of an evil sorcerer hell-bent on world
domination – the Master. But now, inexplicably,
the Master's plans are being thwarted. His sex-
hungry vampire followers are failing in their
duty to corrupt – and his once-sharp psychic
vision is clouded by an unfathomable force.

With the world poised on the brink of disaster,
the Master sends Mara and Andreas on a make-
or-break quest to restore his powers. Compelled
to obey, the lovers begin their search for the
magical Eye of Baloch, unaware that their
profoundly sensual natures are about to face the
ultimate test . . .

FICTION / EROTICA 0 7472 4864 8

HARD SELL

There's no holding back when it's time for the HARD SELL

Felice Ash

In the advertising game it pays to use all your assets. And Sue and Gemma certainly know how to make the most of what they've got.

Sue – she's the one with the creative ideas, both in and out of bed. Not so much an accident waiting to happen, more a sex bomb ready to explode . . .

Gemma – she likes to get down to business, using whatever it takes to get what she wants. And sometimes she wants to handle more than the client's account . . .

The bottom line is that they're both under threat from vindictive rivals, blackmailing gunmen and countless males on the make, all keen to offer their own brand of – HARD SELL

FICTION / EROTICA 0 7472 4804 4